Wizard Quest and the Temple of Grace

Part B

Bill G. Butler © 2022

Before We Begin

Each character name appears above their text when they are talking.

Narration runs from the left of the page and speech the middle.

When a character's speech is <u>underlined</u>, they are thinking the words rather than saying them.

Bethany, Boden, Henna and Navek, excited about the journey ahead but sad to leave Sunlin behind, travel forth.

On the outside, Sunlin's wall is short and long and made of grey brick. They travel to the edge of the clearing around it and into the paths of the Sityan Forest.

Henna

So many natural paths.

Boden

Yeah, let's not bother creating a path.

The Wizards take the path that feels most comfortable. The path itself shines green in the morning sun from a carpet of moss that grows over the trees and ground, leaving a beautiful deep green fissure through the forest. The bits of bark that do show are light brown or greyish white and the tops of the trees are bluey green firs. The ground is soft and squishy underfoot and as the Wizards walk through, the trees' wet leaves softly whip against their faces. As they travel, the sun rises and the greens start to glow, with bright yellow rays breaking through the leaves, leaving golden beams of light shining down into their path. They breathe deep, smelling the fresh air. They take their time, admiring the path in front of them. They travel for a long while, not saying anything, just a silent march through the moss-covered forest. By mid-day, they come to a clearing. The side they came from is made up of fir trees, the other side is made up of tall, thin trees with stacked ring like trunks, all connected at the top by a raggedy grown, bright green canopy, made up of triangular leaves. The canopy is thick and there appears to be a squarish hole in it, lined with branches.

Henna

Ahh, look.

Bethany

You reckon that is?

Henna

Sure looks like it is.

Navek

What are you talking about?

4

Henna

It's a Puzzle Tree.

Navek

Like a Monkey Puzzle?

Henna

Yeah, it's a type of Monkey Puzzle.

Navek

What's so great about it?

Henna

It's a maze.

Navek

A maze?

Henna

A naturally occurring maze.

Navek

Wow, Zingy!

Boden

So, what's the plan?

Henna

I say we set up camp here, and then a pair of us can go through, while the other pair keep camp.

Navek

Yeah, ok, sounds fun.

Bethany

I'll stick back in camp.

Boden

Yeah, me too.

Navek

Ok, so what do we do?

Henna

Well, see that dark area there, with a kind of square hole lined with branches?

Navek

Yeah.

Henna

That's the entrance.

They go over and Navek and Henna climb the tree and peer down from the square hole.

Henna

See you guys later.

Bethany

Bye.

Bethany turns to Boden.

Bethany

Have you ever been in a Monkey Puzzle before?

Boden

No.

Bethany

Yeah, I thought so. It should be fun.

Boden

Has Henna?

Bethany

I don't think so. It was in a book me and Henna read, that's how we know about them.

Boden

Anywho, let's start getting lunch ready.

Meanwhile, in the trees, Henna and Navek walk down a corridor made entirely from leaves.

Navek

Wow, this is thick.

Navek puts his hand against the leafy wall and presses hard.

Navek

These leaves are so thick that I can't even put my hand through them.

The Wizards walk on down the green corridor and reach a path open to the sky. The sky itself is a beautiful blue in colour.

Henna

Ok, so there are paths that are sort of like indoors, that cut off the Sky Worlds, and there are paths that aren't, like these we are on.

Navek

It's a nice view of the sky.

Henna

Yeah, the tree views are the best. In Monkey Puzzle Mazes there are also paths that are climbing paths, and paths that are like these corridors. Look up ahead, we are coming to a junction.

The Wizards walk into a round area with several entrances. They pick an entrance and go down its tall thin lane, with the path sloping down towards the center.

Henna

Monkey Puzzle trees work like a maze, except they get energy from the people lost in them. As people try to find their way out or explore them, they create an energy that provides sustenance for the tree. In return for the energy, the trees make it like a little adventure.

Navek

Snazzy.

Henna

My mum said so. Anyway, she's been through several. You can even create paths and directions. Most wizards use spells to do it.

Henna

Remember, any path created in a Monkey Puzzle Maze is not like other paths. It is hard to make out where you are going, or to navigate them and you can get lost in them.

Navek

Can you go down paths others have created?

Henna

Yes, sometimes, but they are even worse for getting lost in.

Navek

So, how do we get out?

Henna

Well, we should be able to find our way out. If worse comes to worst, the tree can make out when somebody is in distress, and it will let them out.

Navek

That's very nice of it.

Henna

That's why Monkey Puzzles Mazes are great.

As they go down another leafy corridor, they come to a junction.

Henna

Ok, here goes.

The room is hazy and it's hard to make out which direction to go. They begin looking around. Instead of a path being created, the room becomes less and less hazy, till they are able to make out several paths. They pick a route and head down it and find it covered completely from the sky. They are forced to crawl through the long low passage until they eventually hit another junction. Henna stops and looks at a spot in its wall.

Henna

Here, let me have a go.

Henna lets out a streamer and it touches the leaf wall. As it does, the junction opens up into another path to their side.

Henna

Oh, zingy, we found a secret path.

The path that opens out has tons of branches inside.

Navek

Wow, looks very hard to get through.

Henna

It's a climbing path.

Henna goes up and crawls into the branches, followed by Navek. They climb up through the thin and thick branches for a while, until they squeeze out the top. There they find a small round entrance, with a lot of wind flowing through it at high speed, causing a whirring sound.

Navek

What the hell is that?

Henna

It's a Plunge.

Navek

A Plunge?!

Henna

Yeah, if you go into it, you get thrown down the path to the next clearing.

Navek

You sure?

Henna

Yeah, remember to go feet first.

Henna sits in front of the entrance and puts her legs in, as she does, she gets sucked in, out of sight from Navek. She whizzes past the tunnel of leaves.

Navek

Wait for me.

Navek runs up and throws his feet in and gets sucked in. Henna screams and laughs as she and Navek get thrown through a big, long path, travelling faster and faster through odd angles and down the weird shaped tunnels.

Navek

This is scary.

Navek shouts.

Henna

Yeah!

The leaves fly past at breakneck speed, until the Wizards come sliding out into the next junction.

Henna

Wow, zingy.

Navek

Yeah!

Back at camp, Boden and Bethany sit on their blanket, in front of their tents, preparing food from their Jars. From where they are sitting, they can hear Henna's and Navek's screams and laughter.

Bethany

Sounds like they are having fun.

Boden

Yeah.

Bethany

Normal mazes are fun, but they are no Monkey Puzzles.

Back in the maze, Henna chooses a path and when they go in, they see that it's full of water.

Henna

Oh, interesting.

Navek

What's this?

As Henna steps forward, a big round leaf emerges from the water, then another and another.

Henna

We have to jump across the leaves to get to the next junction. Don't fall in, or you will have to wade back to here.

Navek

Ok.

Navek runs and jumps on the first leaf, which takes his weight sturdily, then the next, and going really fast, he jumps from leaf to leaf, until he has to wait for the next to come from the water. Henna, not far behind, waits for him to leave the leaf before jumping to it. Navek goes to jump as a leaf quickly pulls out of the water. It slows down suddenly, and Navek lands on the leaf, ankle deep in the water. He curses himself.

Navek

Grack!

Henna

Ha, you should have had patience.

The leaf raises slowly under his weight.

Henna

Least you don't have to go back through the water.

Eventually, they get to the last leaf and jump out to the next junction.

Navek

Ok, I think we should try and get out now.

Henna

Are your legs cold?

Navek

Not really, but I'd like to dry off.

Henna

Ok then, well, it's about looking hard.

Henna concentrates and starts to look around in the next junction. The next corridor contains leafy floors moving up and down in an odd pattern. Navek nearly trips several times as his wet clothes cause him to slip.

Navek

The water makes it so slippery.

Eventually, together, they manage to stumble across it. They get to the next junction, where Henna looks around again and they find an exit tunnel.

Henna

Ok, here we are.

They emerge out of a hole, up in the tree and as they climb down, they see that they are not far from camp. They walk back up to greet Boden and Bethany.

Navek

Hey.

Bethany

Oooh, you got wet.

Navek

Yeah.

Navek goes into his tent and changes.

Navek

You guys didn't light a fire?

Bethany

Yeah, it's so warm, there's no point really.

Navek

Hhh.

Navek takes out his clothes and uses his wand to start blasting them with hot air.

Henna

So, you guys gonna have a go?

Boden

Yeah, there are some meals here. We used your jars of jam for dessert.

Boden hands them forks and plates full of food.

Navek

Oh good. That'll cheer me up.

Next, Bethany and Boden get up and climb the tree. Inside, their first corridor leads immediately into a junction.

Boden

Do you reckon we could go down the same path as them?

Bethany

We could try, but our entrance is probably different and the tree changes.

They go into their first junction and choose an exit using a streamer to clear the fuzziness. As they walk down the wide path made of leaves, the distance stretches out far in front of them.

Boden

Do you think we should have used streamers?

Bethany

No, we'll leave them in the next junction, maybe create a path.

The corridor they walk down goes on for a quite a bit, forcing the Wizards to jog on to the next junction.

Boden

Ok then, you can do the honours.

Bethany begins looking around, and a path forms in front of them.

Bethany

Ouh, lucky! I think I hit a natural seam through the trees.

They walk out into the path and look ahead of them. They have trouble discerning what way to walk, so they stand there looking around for a bit. No way presents itself, so they just start walking. After a while, they find an entrance and head to it. They go through and before them is a slide made of leaves, dipping off the side of the lane that ends ahead of them. The slide is as wide as a house and disappears beyond view.

Bethany

Wow, this thing is huge.

Boden

This looks like fun.

Bethany

I wonder do the trees get some sort of energy from us sliding. Like how they get energy from people trying to find their way out.

Bethany says, with a big smile.

Boden

Maybe, great if they did.

Bethany and Boden sit in front of the slide, with their legs laying over the edge. They push out and slide, lying on their backs as they go. The wind rushes past them as they travel, getting faster and faster. Boden and Bethany look at each other and then look down. The slide recedes far into the distance ahead of them.

Bethany, Boden

Ha, ha, ha, **WAHOOOOO**.

They slide so fast now, the wind shoves itself against their faces as they look down. Eventually the slide comes out into a large flat area, which they sail out into and come to a stop on a soft ground of leaves.

Boden

Wow, that was nice.

Bethany

Hey, there's a vine that leads back up along the side wall.

Bethany points to the edge of the slide. Together they climb back up and have more goes before adventuring on. Inside the next junction, there are a lot of paths. Boden selects an interesting looking route, and it turns out to be a climbing path. At the top of the branches, there's an opening that they stick their heads out from and look out over the maze.

Bethany

Wow, this Monkey Puzzle is incredible.

The maze's top slopes down in front of them and appears to go on far into the distance. Around them are different paths and obstacles that shimmer in and out of view. They climb back down a bit and go over to another opening and into the next junction. The next room they visit is wider than the slide and the floor looks like frozen smoke.

Bethany

This must be some sort of magic room.

As they move across the floor, their feet start to slip from under them, causing both Wizards to almost fall over.

Bethany

Ha, it's like ice.

Boden

Zany.

Boden and Bethany lay down a magic streamer each and use it to pull themselves around the room, their feet sliding like ice skates.

Bethany

Ha, ha, this is so much fun.

They skid and slide and then grab each other and spin around.

Bethany

This is the best.

They let go and shoot off helter-skelter around the room. Eventually, they skate down the hall and hit the next room.

Bethany

Ok, another junction.

Bethany lets out a streamer and it opens out in front of them.

Bethany

Ok, it's an exit.

The Wizards look out over another slide-like surface that goes down above the ground. They slide down it together, and as they near the end, the leaves and branches start to bend and sweep downwards, leaving the Wizards sitting on the forest floor. This time, they are a bit further from camp than Henna and Navek, and they have to trek back a bit before they return.

Navek

Have fun?

Bethany

Yeah, we found a skating room and a slide.

Henna

Wow, snazzy! Yeah, we found a Plunge.

The Wizards sit down on their blanket and eat the food they prepared, topped off with Navek's bright green, lovely Jam sandwiches. The day grows long, and the Wizards lay down in the heat and doze silently. Night falls and the sky is blanketed in stars.

Bethany

Gosh, it's too warm to sleep in the tents.

Boden

Back home, around now, there would be the Solstice Festival.

Bethany

The longest days.

Henna

Mum would have made smoothies.

Navek

Banana Milkshakes.

Boden

What about now? We could always Sky Circle.

Bethany

Sky Circle?

Boden

Yeah, I just came up with it.

Bethany

Ok, what's the invention?

Boden

Well, we all lie down in a circle, with our heads in the center, gazing up at the sky.

Navek

Sounds good.

The Wizards all orienteer themselves so they are in a circle, with their heads in the middle and their legs lying outwards.

Bethany

We could hold hands.

Bethany grabs Navek's and Boden's hands and Henna does the same. They look into the sky scape. Across the star blanket there are thin, bright, grainy, milky-white streaks, blue and red swirls of galaxy and wispy nebula that paint the sky in a twinkling shimmer.

Henna

I wonder where the sun goes at night.

Bethany

Yeah, and where the stars go in the day.

Navek

The sky's a funny old world.

Henna

When I was a kid, my mum used to say, "If you wished upon a special star, someday it would come true". That star there was my special star.

Henna points to a small little star in the sky.

Boden

Why that star?

Henna

It didn't seem to shine too bright. It was quiet.

Bethany

What did you wish for when you were a kid?

Henna

To have great friends.... I guess it really did come true.

Henna goes quiet and contemplative.

Henna

It's funny.

Boden

What is?

Henna

When I first met you guys, I didn't think my life would change this much.

Bethany

Really?

Henna

Yeah, my life was so... how should I put it...... unfulfilled.

Boden

We can't have had that much of a change.

Henna

Well, my early childhood was amazing, but yeah, after that, it got to be very bad.

Bethany

It was that crowd you hung around with.

Henna

Yeah, it got really horrible when they started trying to pick on people, and it wasn't just that, all they could talk about was "He said this", "And she said that", and "Oh! we're not happy with her", "And doesn't she look stupid". The amount of things people said behind each others' backs. Everybody was afraid to be themselves.

The carpet of stars twinkles over them.

Henna

Then that day, it was like being woken up.

Boden

The day you saved that kid from torment.

Henna

The day I met you.

Henna looks at Boden.

Henna

Do you remember what you said to me?

Boden

Be yourself Henna, you're an amazing person, your bravery is who you are.

Tears start to well in the corners of her eyes.

Henna

I love you guys so much.

Bethany

Oh Henna!

Bethany lets go of the boys' hands and grabs Henna by the hand.

Bethany

We love you so much too.

Navek

Yeah Henna, we don't know what we'd do without you.

Boden

You're our Henna.

A giant shooting star streaks across the sky, leaving a sparkling trail.

Henna

<u>I'll make a wish for them on it.</u>

As they lay there, a moment branches away, a small side era of them watching the sky.

Henna

Ever think a shooting star could land?

Henna says, choking back tears.

Boden

Maybe over the rainbow.

Henna

Yeah.

The Wizards lie in silence, watching the sky.

Navek

Ha, it's funny, nothing has ever fallen out of the sky in history.

Bethany

Except birds and dragons and the occasional bat.

Henna

Do you ever wonder where the birds and dragons go to?

Boden

All the time.

Bethany

It'd be nice if they lived in the clouds.

Henna

Yeah.

The celestial sky sparkles up above them.

Navek

So, tomorrow we head for the caves.

Bethany

Yeah, well we can treat that as our Solstice Adventure.

Boden

What do you reckon is gonna happen about the Damned Wizards?

Navek

We'll probably find them and just force them to take the Oath or lock them away.

Henna

What about that creature?

Bethany

And are there other Legendary Abominations?

Boden

Yeah, what are they and why are they important?

Navek

They are some interesting questions. I hope the guard are able to capture the damn thing.

Henna

Yeah, it's awful to think of such a creature on the loose.

Bethany

I can't believe he told us to keep the wand.

Navek

Yeah, I thought Pops would never have done that.

Boden

Or maybe he thought we needed it.

Henna

Ha, yeah, I hope we won't run into that much trouble again.

Boden

Well, when we reach Trader Kingdom, we might get a few interesting jobs.

Henna

Probably nothing that dangerous.

Boden

I suppose.

Navek

Anybody want to keep watch?

Bethany

I guess I'll take first shift.

The Wizards get up and get their beds out of their tents. They sleep around the camp, while Bethany takes watch. In the morning, the air is still and warm, and the Wizards wearily get up and eat breakfast. Henna takes out the map the King gave them, and they sit around looking at it.

Henna

I'd say we'll get up there by night, if we head out early.

Bethany

Yeah, ok then.

The Wizards finish up their breakfast and start to pack.

Boden

Everybody ready?

Henna

Yep.

The Adventurers head out from the clearing in front of the Monkey Puzzle tree.

They walk together in silence, the sun beating down a heavy heat on them and on the path as they walk. The ground underfoot between the long grasses changes from moss to baked hard mud. They come out from under the trees and to a wide area of land, which is mostly made up of hip-high bushes and shrubs. They can see the path cut into the bushes quite clearly, and it goes on beyond eyesight. They walk on this path most of the day, stopping only to drink water or take a small snack. As they go, their skin starts to get slightly redder and redder. Eventually, they come to the base of a hill that climbs up gradually. At its top they can see out further than before. Henna takes out her map and they can see the landmarks around them. From there, they are able to see far off in the distance are the mountains that the King and Queen of Sunlin had found.

Henna

Ok, so we need to travel towards that mountain.

Henna says, pointing.

Navek

I think we should set lunch here.

The Wizards take out their blanket and some jars of food.

Navek

So, how far is it to Trader City from us?

Henna looks over the map.

Henna

Maybe a few days.

As they sit there, enjoying their lunch, birds fly around the bushes, playing and tweeting, and a herd of deer passes by in the distance. The Adventurers get up and put their things away and start travelling towards the mountain. The bushes around them transition to becoming knee-high and full of long, sharp leaves. They walk on for a while through these bushes till they come to a short similar knee-high rise in the ground, it stretches in a straight line out the sides of the path to beyond eyeshot. The small, steep sloping ridge is bare of bushes and made of rocky dirt. At the top of this small rise, there are more knee-high bushes that are black, or a very dark green and are full of tiny blue and purple flowers and orange berries. They walk among these bushes for the rest of the day, until they eventually hit the mountain's base, walking out onto the short grass near sunset and starting to climb.

Boden

Does it become a mountain scape?

Boden asks, as they start to climb up the rocky base.

Henna

No, I don't think so.

Henna replies, half unfolding the map to get a look at the area. They climb in a zig-zag fashion, rocks becoming bigger as they travel up. As they ascend, they see massive boulders and the light starts to get darker.

Navek

Are we nearly there yet?

Henna

Yeah, just a bit more.

Eventually, the Wizards make their way to the heights of the summit. From there, they can see fireflies in the distance over the land.

Henna

This is it. The cave the King and Queen recommended.

Henna says, pointing at the cave at the top of the mountain. The Wizards go in and the cave is completely empty.

Navek

How far back does it go?

Henna

Not very far.

Navek

It's a bit of a let-down.

Bethany

Yeah, I was expecting something amazing.

The cave is no bigger than the bedroom of a house.

Bethany

Ok, I guess we can camp out here till morning.

The Wizards use the cave as a makeshift tent. They get out their sleeping bags, pile rocks around the entrance and leave a small gap for air. They place their Glaze Hiding Staff at the base of the cave. Tired from their treck, the Adventurers go straight to sleep without saying much. In the morning, something amazing happens when the Adventurers open their eyes. As they look up, they see lots of wonderful colours.

Bethany

Wow!

Henna

What is this?

All of the cave they are sitting in is covered in gems of flowing colours, looking like stained glass. The sun from outside shines through the gems, causing the floor of the cave to be carpeted with a patchwork quilt of light. The Wizards get up and look around in amazement. They take down the rocks, and outside the cave the ground is powdered with tiny gems, giving it a rainbow colour.

Henna

This place is spectacular.

Boden

Yeah.

The Wizards look around the area, enjoying the colours and the scenery from where they are. They eat breakfast in the cave together, looking out through the crystals as they shimmer in the sunlight.

Bethany

Ow.

Henna

You ok?

Bethany

It's just the damn sunburn that's sore.

The Wizards look over each other. Their faces, legs and arms are all covered in a light red burn.

Henna

This is going to get worse.

Bethany

Yeah, we should of brought some Herbal Block.

The Wizards pass around a satchel of water and wet their skin.

Navek

Let's have a look at the map.

Henna takes it out and unfolds it on the floor between them.

Henna

Ok, so if we follow this river, we should come out near the walls to Trader City.

Boden

Seems simple enough.

After breakfast, they rest up. Boden writes to his journal. Bethany gets some of her knitting done. Henna mixes up some more food for their jars and Navek writes some lyrics. They try some of Henna's food before she packs it away.

Navek

Mmm, this is delicious.

Henna

Thanks.

The Wizards pack up their beds and belongings and head out into the sun.

Henna

Ok, so that peak over there is where we have to get to.

The Wizards walk down the crest connecting the mountain tops. Below them rages a giant river, gushing out from the mountains behind them and flowing through the valley between the foothills.

Henna

Ok, so we follow this river until it reaches the walls to Trader City.

The Wizards walk on down the side of the mountain, following the river's side as they go. When they reach the bottom, the river widens out and slows. Either side of the river, the land is flat and made from a dark wet silt, edged with hedges. The Wizards walk along until the late morning. They set up camp by the river. The sunburn on their bodies having taken on a darker red.

Boden

God, this is awful.

Bethany

Yeah, pity we don't have any Aloe herb.

Boden

We'll buy some in the next town.

Navek

Well, I don't know bout you, but I think I'll stick my feet in the river.

Navek takes a log he finds sitting in the grasses and puts it in front of the river as a seat, he sits down and takes off his shoes and dips his feet in the river. Boden, Henna and Bethany come up and sit beside him on the log, putting their shoes on it and sitting their feet in the travelling water.

Henna

Another day should do it.

Bethany

That's good.

Henna

Yeah, I reckon we will be there the following morning.

Boden

Ohhh good.

Henna

We might meet my brother there, he goes to Trader City a lot.

Boden

Yeah, that's right, your brother and his company.

Henna

They have seaports and docks in the city, so they are a lot easier to trade with than other places. At the moment, he is selling clothes and food between the ports.

Navek

Chandrin's quite an interesting guy.

Henna

Yeah, well he was always business orientated.

Bethany

Well, you weren't too bad at business.

Henna

Ha, my school shop was a bit of fun.

Bethany

Yeah, remember what a hit your sweets were.

Henna

I think my brother said it best.

Boden

What did he say?

Henna

It's always special when people endeavour.

Boden

He said that?

Henna

Yeah.

Boden

I like that.

The sun gets higher in the sky and Boden goes and takes out his tent and shoots a spark into it. The sides pull up like a stage curtain, folding up in round curves till they are in the top. Without the sides, it looks like a giant umbrella. He sticks it beside their log.

Boden

There, that should provide us with some relief.

He says, as he props it up to create a shadow for them. The Wizards sit on the log for the rest of the day and sleep during the night. In the morning they get up and head out for another day's journey. They follow the river for the rest of the day, which gets wider and shallower. Most of the walk is spent in silence as the sun beats down on them. Sweat builds up and they take dinner early, setting up the tent umbrella. The birds fly in and out of their camp, chirping and enjoying the warmth.

Boden

Here, let me look at the map.

Boden takes the map and looks at where they are and where they are going.

Boden

Ok, yeah, so tomorrow morning we should be there.

Bethany

Phew! First thing we are going to do is hit the herbalists and get some Aloe vera for all of us all.

Henna

Yeah, straight away, my burn is horrible.

Boden

It's gotten incredibly uncomfortable.

They eat cold food from their jars and use a small filter to fill their bottles full of water from the stream. After a while, they set out again. By the time it hits nightfall, they can see the castle in the distance. At night, the outside walls are lit with giant fire torches. The wall is long and stretches out of sight. In the morning, the Wizards head on down. The wall is a dark sandy colour and torches blaze along it. The top of the wall is flat, without battlements and there is a square, raised ridge running along near the top. The stream beside them takes a turn down into a new direction and leaves the Wizards walking into a sparse, flat grassland between them and the castle walls. As they reach the castle, they see lots and lots of carts and carriages around the entrance, all carrying goods through the walls. They go to the dried dirt site around the gate and are forced to join the line of carts going into the castle. When they reach the portal tunnel, they travel through the high arch entrance. On the inside in the city is a massive junction, full of castle walls with entrances. The junction itself is a giant circle, with long, dusty yellow stones cut to the shape of the circle for the ground. The carriages there, are all parked on the outside, with the inside full of tent stalls and traders. The junction is massive.

Henna

Wow!

Boden

Yeah.

Bethany

Ok, first stop Aloe vera.

Navek

Do you think any of the traders might have some?

Bethany

I don't know.

They walk on down through the stalls as they are being set up. At a large castle wall entrance, they can see a herbalist's sign and they head for that. Inside the shop is walls full of different herbs and tinctures. As the Wizards look around, Bethany finds a large jar of Aloe vera and takes it towards the counter. As she does, several other people walk up in front of her and behind her and form a queue. The Shop Assistant breezes through each of the customers before her. Then Bethany goes up to the till.

Bethany

Am, I just need enough for me and my friends here, we have sunburn and would like to treat it.

Shop Keeper

Ok, so those Wizards then?

As they talk, the crowd behind Bethany grows impatient.

Bethany

Yeah.

Shop Keeper

Ok, so this should be enough.

She says, taking out the long, green tentacle like leaves.

Shop Keeper

Is this alright?

Man In Queue

Come on, get a move on.

Shop Keeper

It's ok sir, we'll be finished in a moment. Ok, here you go, Hun.

Bethany taps her coin on the tray and the gold pours off and turns to little flowers that boil to liquid and flow into the center. She walks over to the rest of them, as she does, the cashier breezes through the rest of the customers before the Wizards get to the door.

Bethany

Gosh, this place is fast.

Outside, on the street, people walk up and down at a frantic pace, bumping past each other in large crowds like a sea of chaotic fish.

Bethany

Everybody seems to be in a rush.

Navek

Come on, let's get some breakfast.

The Wizards walk up the street and get bumped by several high-speed walkers. They go into a long, thin, brown lunchrooms on the corner at the end of the street. Inside, they buy cooked zorza, a type of noodle like wheat pasta, boiled then fried, with a clear white broth and crunchy vegetables stirred in. They take a seat at the back of the lunchroom in the window and watch as the people walk up and down the street at such a fast pace.

Henna

It's frantic here.

A man walks by the window and looks in at the woman sitting near the entrance. He walks off and waits at the street corner, looking over his shoulder at her.

Henna

So, what now?

Boden

I guess we find a place to stay.

The man at the corner starts to pace back and forth and then comes back to the window and looks at the woman again.

Navek

Ok, I think we should ask in here, I don't think we are going to get help out on the street.

Henna

Yeah, if we stopped somebody around here, they'd probably punch us.

As they sit there, the man on the corner walks into the shop and up to the lady, grabs her by her upper arms and lifts her out of her seat.

Man

Why are you staring at me?

He shouts at her.

Her expression remains calm and confused. He gets a shock at the realization that she was just staring off into the distance.

Man

Oh.

He lets go of her. She goes back to sitting at the table as if nothing had happened and the man goes back to the corner.

Navek

Wow, what happened there?

Henna

I don't know.

Navek

The pace of this place is too much.

The Wizards go up to the counter and ask where there might be a place to stay. The woman at the counter says to ask somewhere else, as she's busy serving customers. In a huff, the Wizards walk out into the street.

Boden

I guess we just wander around till we find somewhere.

They head on, trying not to get in anybody's way. As they walk, they get bumped and knocked into by speedy passers-by.

Henna

Gosh, this place is ridiculous.

They walk around random junctions and get an odd feeling to follow a certain path. With it, they find an inn called the Round Duke.

Henna

I wonder if it has anything to do with the Round King.

The Round Duke is very big, running the length of the street, it is made of light grey stone. The middle of the building is rounded out into the street. Along the walls run small pillars, with large pillars around the middle part. It gives off a secure feeling from being nestled into the street around it. Inside, the entrance is the same grey stone, with dark brown wooden doors around the room. From the center back wall, there is a semi-circular mahogany counter with a marble top, that has several employees in black stationed behind it. The employees talk to people from a big queue in front of the desk. The Wizards queue up and catch conversations of the people around them.

Black Haired Man

Gosh, yeah, I'll be trading with John all day.

Sandy Haired Man

John?

Black Haired Man

Yeah, we hang out in the lunchrooms.

Sandy Haired Man

Then what's the problem?

Black Haired Man

I never get any work done when he's around. We just end up talking.

Well Dressed Man

Do you see this jacket?

Stout Man

Yeah.

Well Dressed Man

I traded it for a meal.

Stout Man

A meal?

Well Dressed Man

Yeah, the guy didn't want to pay in coin, so he gave me this jacket. Pretty snazzy.

Stout Man

Pretty weird.

The Wizards finally get to the desk and talk to the Assistant.

Assistant

So, how can I help you?

Bethany

We would like a room with separate beds.

Assistant

Ok, give me a moment.

The Assistant takes out a set of small keys and hands them to them.

Assistant

Just sign the register.

The Wizards sign in and pay, their gold turns to a little bed with its linen being folded, that drifts to the center of the tray and is absorbed by it. They then leave through a door beside the counter and head up a hallway. The corridors have dark wooden floors with dark green carpets down their centers, that are framed near their edges with brass strips. The walls' bases are all wooden panels, with bright wallpaper above them and a plain white ceiling. The halls have a dry smell to them. They walk up a marble stepped flight of stairs and hit the next floor. On this floor, they hit a corner, then find their door and use their keys to get in. They unpack and head out onto the balcony of their room that overlooks the street. Bethany takes out the leaves of Aloe vera and hands them around.

Navek

What am I supposed to do with this?

Bethany

You squeeze it and then rub the gel on your burns.

The Wizards squeeze the leaves and cover all their burns with the gel. There is a wonderful soothing feeling, and the pain of the burns goes away completely. The Wizards enjoy the warm breeze as they sit out over the street. Down below them, people and horse-drawn carriages travel the street. The street they are on is wider than a house. Down the opposite side of the street there are cycle lanes, where wooden cycles go by, ridden by fast paced delivery people.

Navek

It's amazing, this place.

Henna

Yeah, I've never been somewhere this busy.

Navek

You said your brother might meet us here.

Henna

Yeah, I said I would send him a letter, see if he was in town.

As they look out over the streets, the pace of traffic doesn't die down. The Wizards sit in their comfy chairs and watch as different goods carriages and people go by.

Henna

So, the Card Tournament is coming up.

Navek

Zingy.

Bethany

Remember the battles in the schoolyard.

Boden

Gosh yeah, those were the days.

Henna

Yeah, Boden and Jared.

Bethany

Oh my gosh, that match went on for so long.

Navek

Yeah, the teachers, ha, they had to stop it.

Henna

Yeah, I remember being angry at you.

Boden

Hhhh, yeah.

Henna

You were the reason they banned Spirit Cards. Well, you and Jared.

Boden

I really wish I never played that match.

Navek

Jared was a good competitor, I wish I had battled him.

Henna

Thought you weren't the biggest fan of Spirit Cards, that you were a bigger fan of Castle Crashers.

Henna says, jovially.

Navek

Well yeah, that requires you to use your own magic to fight rather than the card's magic, but yeah, the Cards wouldn't be far off Figurines.

Henna

I remember your strategies, they were always very strong.

Bethany

Yeah, that's what got you your nickname.

Navek

"The Hammer", ha, it's a weird one.

Henna

Really? Hammer's zingy.

Bethany

It's a pity I never played.

Boden

You're just too sweet to play.

Bethany

Henna "The Mystery".

Henna

Oh yeah, well I got quite good at them.

Bethany

And Boden "The Survivor".

Boden

Well, it's no "Hammer".

Henna

You were so difficult with your grand strategy.

Boden

Yeah, very few people liked the nitty-gritty of the game.

Henna

Gosh yeah, those are a fun few eras.

Bethany

I loved watching you lot play. Do you think you guys will enter the tournament?

Henna

Probably.

Navek

Oh, definitely.

As Navek says this, they look at each other and smile.

Henna

We never played each other, have we?

Bethany

Yeah, in the tournament, you guys might end up against each other.

Boden

That would be interesting.

Navek

Hmm, I never liked the idea of playing you guys in the schoolyard.

Henna

Yeah.

Bethany

Well, I am sure it will be fun either way, you're all pretty good.

Navek, Boden and Henna look at each other with slightly awkward expressions.

Bethany

I was thinking, while you guys play your games, I could do some study on my Healing Magic. See if I can get any better for us.

Boden

That would be great.

Bethany

Thanks.

They smile at each other.

Navek

I wonder who else will be at the tournament?

Henna

Well, they are getting carriages of players sent in.

Navek

Really?

Henna

Yeah, my brother said they will be sending top players from Olreon.

Navek

Wow.

Henna

Yeah.

Boden

Interesting, this will be a big tournament then.

The Wizards go down for dinner. They go around the other side of the entrance counter and through a pair of large double doors and into the inn's dining hall. The inside is loud and full of the sound of talking. The large room is full of rows and rows of long tables, jam-packed with people. The floor, walls and ceilings are made of rounded, grey cobble stones and there are large, thick, wooden beams running across overhead. At the top end of the tables is a large counter, full of Waiters and Waitresses. The other end of the room has a pathway across it and some private room entrances in the wall. The path leads to a stairs in the far wall, which has a blue carpet running down its wide middle, with its steps leading out of sight. A Waitress greets them from a plinth by the door.

Waitress

Is it just yourselves?

Henna

Yeah.

The Waitress looks around the room.

Waitress

You don't mind being seated with somebody?

They look at each other and smile.

Navek

No, not at all.

She hands them menus and they follow her.

Waitress

Anywhere around here.

She points, and they seat themselves opposite a pair of people in a deep conversation.

Bethany

So, this is interesting.

Henna

Yeah.

The Wizards look through the menu, and the pair of the people in front of them stop talking and turn and start staring at them.

Henna

Ah, hi.

Staring Man

Hi…. So, you guys are Wizards?

Henna

Yes, that we are.

Staring Man

What are you doing in town?

Henna

We are Adventure Wizards.

Other Staring Man

Adventure Wizards, really?

Henna

Yep.

The other people around them continue talking to the larger groups of people either side.

Staring Man

Hi, I'm Tarver.

Tarver has a big wide chin and is slightly grey haired, he looks like his skin is tired.

Other Staring Man

And I'm Hector

Says the other man. Hector is just as old, with a wide face and has curly brown hair. He smiles at them.

Staring Man : Tarver

We're carriage builders.

Boden

Oh, interesting.

Other Staring Man : Hector

We're introducing our new Horse Cycle Carriages to the market.

Bethany

Oh, fascinating. You make those types of carriages?

Tarver

Yeah, they are expensive, but ultimately it allows a lot more speed and control over where you are going.

Hector

It also allows the horse to sit inside the carriage and not have to brave the elements.

Tarver

So, how do you Wizards earn gold to keep your adventure going?

Bethany

We do odd jobs from the town work guilds.

Tarver

Odd jobs, hmm, we might have a job for you, if you are interested.

Henna

What is it?

Tarver

Well, on our way here, we passed a gem cave.

Hector

It's got to be the biggest we've ever seen.

Tarver

You do know how gem caves work?

Henna

Yep, there was a small gem cave in our last town.

Tarver

Well, when we are leaving, we are thinking of clearing it out.

Hector

We'll have a lot of free carriage space on the way back.

Tarver

If you'd like to help us?

Bethany

How would you like us to help?

Tarver

Well, we need to make sure it's safe. Could you do some spell work and keep us from danger.

The Wizards look at each other.

Bethany

We could give it a look. What do you reckon?

Navek

Yeah, sounds easy enough.

Tarver

Brilliant. When we leave, we'll send you a letter and we can meet up.

Hector

Well, that's handy. We were headed to the work shop to put the job up. Guess we won't need to do that.

Boden

So, tell us about the horse carriages you make?

Tarver

Well, our carriages are for the horse's comfort and driver's security.

Hector

And the horses we use are specially trained, so they are very powerful.

Tarver

If you want to take a look, there's a carriage show coming up. That's why we are in town.

They hand them pamphlets for the carriage show. The Waitress comes up in the background and asks them what they'd like to eat. The Wizards quickly look down through the menu.

Navek

I'll have potato shards and stuffing.

Boden

I'll have a vegetable aspic and some shards too.

Henna

I'll have the kale mash, potato shards and beans.

Bethany

I'll have the fried basket of food and shards as well.

Waitress

What about drinks?

Boden

Well, if there's hot chocolate?

Waitress

If you're all having it, I can give you a big pitcher.

The Wizards nod in agreement.

Boden

Yeah, sounds good.

The Waitress takes their menus.

Tarver

We have to go, but we'll leave the letter in the inn when we're going.

Boden

Thanks, we're in the Ashen Suite.

The Carriage Builders leave. The Wizards look around at the other tables. The food is served in such generous portions that they smile at each other. The Waitress returns with Henna's and Bethany's food, then she goes off and comes back with Boden's and Navek's. She then brings the giant pitcher of hot chocolate, which is so huge, that it has a handle on either side and is all that she can carry. She returns another time with a bunch of roundy cups for the chocolate. The Wizards eat away at their food. The aspic tasting like a beautiful vegetable soup, shaped into an ingot by vegetable gel. Boden slices it up and eats it with a spoon and fork. The potato shards are long, thin, pointy potato bits, fried deep in oil. The Wizards season the crispy, crunchy, chewy shards with vinegar and salt. Navek's order turns out basically to be a large mound of green stuffing, that is beautifully seasoned with parsley and thyme, with a slightly soft chew and salty crunch to it. Henna's kale mash is hearty in flavour, and it mixes well with the beans and their tomato sauce. Bethany's potato basket is made from thin, flat string like potato, fried over a bowl shape and stacked inside each other. She breaks off bits of the bowls and uses them as edible spoons for the fried earthy garden of leaves and vegetables. Great flavours percolate as they wash down the salty greasy buttery food with the hot chocolaty drink.

Boden

I was thinking we try find somewhere to train today.

Henna

Yeah, it's been too long since our last training session.

Navek

I want to try the techniques Pops gave me.

Henna

Snazzy, did he give you a new regime?

Navek

Yeah, it's basically what all the wall guards do to keep themselves powerful.
Also, some exercises he does too.

Boden

Brilliant, I also have a new technique I want to try out.

Navek

Yeah?

Boden

Well, I've been working on it for a while, but I think I have it down now.

Henna

What is it?

Boden

It's a new invention of mine. I'll show you when we go.

Navek

What about you lot?

Navek says to Henna and Bethany.

Bethany

Well, I've been training in healing a lot before we went. I could give you guys a few pointers and some self-healing stuff.

Henna

Yeah, and I have a new spell, if you guys would like to try it out.

Navek

It's not a family spell, is it?

Henna

No, you can learn it, ha, I am sorry about the other spell. Gosh I am never going to live that down.

Bethany

It was funny.

Henna

It felt like inheritance magic when my dad showed me, but my brother told me
it wasn't. He was trying to see if I would teach it to you guys.

Navek

Playing a prank on us?

Henna

Yeah, I should get him back. Gosh that was funny though.

Navek

No it wasn't.

Henna

The expressions on your faces when you tried to do the magic.

Henna laughs away to herself.

Navek

What expressions?

Henna

Well, you were trying so hard, and your faces were red and scrunched up in
concentration.

Bethany

Yeah, and we had to keep making that stupid noise.

"Hhhhhuuuuuyyyyaaaaa"

Henna

Yeah, oh stop, that was the funniest part.

Bethany

Heh, heh, yeah, us standing there like idiots as you perform the spell perfectly.

Henna

I thought I was really good at magic that day.

Navek

So, you're sure now, we can learn this magic?

Henna

Yeah, definitely. I created it, so I know.

Boden

Man, this is good food.

Navek

Yeah, we should eat here every day.

Henna

Yeah, if we want to gain huge weight.

Bethany

Hmm, I'd rather not.

Navek

You girls shouldn't worry about that.

Bethany

We don't, but these meals are a bit too far.

Boden takes another swig of hot chocolate and Navek eats hungrily at his meal.

Navek

Well, don't starve yourselves, training is going to be intense.

Bethany

I suppose.

Navek

So, this Card Tournament.

Navek says, with a wicked smile.

Henna

Yeah!

Navek

I am not going to go easy on you guys.

Henna

We wouldn't expect it from you, Mister Hammer.

Navek

I wonder who will be the first to kill any of Boden's cards?

Bethany

Nobody, that would be harder than beating Boden.

Henna

Ha, that's why they call him "The Survivor".

Bethany

What's funny is, that you haven't killed a single card in your victories.

Boden

Hey, you gotta know how to win.

Henna

As for you Hammer, do you think you can win against an opponent as strong as that Alvay?

Navek

I'll see. I thought she would have beaten me. I think I got very lucky.

Boden

You beat her very cleverly, I wouldn't put yourself down.

Navek

Yeah, but I wasn't better than her.

Henna

Well, you are unbeaten.

Navek

So is Boden and so are you. I've lost at other things. Winning isn't important, what's important is the effort.

Bethany

I wonder who else will be at the tournament?

Henna

Yeah, there was a lot of good players at our school and I heard there were in the other schools around Olreon.

Bethany

There were a few unbeaten players like you guys. I'd say they will all be there.

The Wizards finish their meal and pass their plates to the middle.

Bethany

I think we should look around before we train.

Boden

Yeah, wait for our food to digest, we don't want to get a stitch.

They look up and down the long scrubbed wooden table. All sorts of people line it. There are a few Wizards, a group of Knights in armour at the end of the table, to the side of them are some plump men and women, eating heavily from a giant fried basket that is full of stuffing and small aspic bars.

Boden

What do you reckon, we order that next time round?

The man beside them smiles.

Navek

Yeah, that and potato cakes.

The Waitress comes over and she gives them the pay note. They head up to the counter at the top and tap their coin, their gold turning to the shape of food on the pay tray and getting eaten into the tray by a golden set of teeth.

Navek

Ok, I guess we have a look around.

The Wizards walk out onto the steps in front of the inn, around them the crowds walk at breakneck pace. They head down the steps and precariously make their way into the crowd and head up the street. All the roads are made of small, square, yellowish stones, well-worn from the treading of high-speed walkers. As they travel, the buildings either side of them are all higgledy-piggledy, none of them matching up at all, each with different heights and different roof shapes. The walls have different stonework and are also different colours. Some buildings are squashed down low, others are tall. Some have a green painted finish, others white or rust red, different colours here and there. There are flat rooves made from green slate, others made with a thick thatching, some fronts having pillars or wooden signs jutting out at odd angles. The buildings continue on like this into the next street and most of the others, none of them fitting in well between their neighbours. Each looking like it's squeezing into the buildings next to it or being pushed out by the buildings beside it. The whole place looks like the buildings are trying to muscle each other out of where they are sitting. It all looks very jumbled.

Bethany

This place is very odd.

Boden

Very!

Henna

My brother says it's because it doesn't have a central power.

Bethany

Oh really?

Henna

The governing body is made up of the trader councils, which are essentially powerful trading groups and officials from several towns, including Olreon. With no central power, it's quite an unusual place.

Navek

Do they have guards?

Henna

Yeah, but it's a merchant guard, paid for by the councils.

They walk up several streets, over a massive, dusty stone bridge, that has ships going under it in a flooded valley below.

Henna

The town has several seaports.

As they walk up a particularly wide street, they see a giant castle keep in the distance at the end.

Navek

What's that?

Henna

Oh that, it contains trading halls. The councils also meet in them.

Navek

It's huge.

Boden

Yeah, much bigger than any of the buildings in Olreon.

Henna

Well, there are several places all over town, laid out specially for trading.

They take a turn onto a smaller street and walk towards the end where it narrows and forms a small backward D shape area for turning carriages around. At its end, the street leads to giant park, that is held behind tall dark hedges and large black railings. On the corner of the street is the entrance, which has a Guard tending a booth for people to go in.

Bethany

Ooh, a park, let's go in here.

Navek

Good idea, we can do our training in there.

They go up to the man in the booth.

Henna

How much is it in?

The man points to the sign on top.

Henna

Not much.

Bethany

And can we come back today?

Man

Well, every time you go in, it costs.

Bethany

Ok then.

Henna

I guess we can come back later.

Navek

Yeah, and we can get our training gear.

The Wizards walk back to the inn and go to their room. They change into their training gear, which in Summer form consists of robes that contain short sleeves and short ends and are specially enchanted to get rid of sweat and smell fresh. Bethany also gets some extra stuff for her training. They head back up to the park and pay in. Inside, it is huge. They walk around it for a while. There are several gazebos with ornate carvings, small arch bridges over small streams and several sports lawns. They decide on warming up first. They do stretches and then take a jog around the park. They stop in a long narrow field with a gazebo in it and finish their warm-up by doing several magical exercises, such as projecting streamers, containing themselves in an aura and shooting sparks that don't do anything.

Boden

Ok, so who wants to go first?

Navek

I'd like to try my exercise, if that is alright?

Boden

Yeah, sure.

They all agree.

Navek

So, my first exercise is a fireball and iceball regime.

Navek limbers up and shoots out a thick ball that's blue and white and cold, and chills the air as it goes, creating dusty cloud trails of white. Then he shoots a fireball that scorches out and hits the iceball, exploding them in mid-air.

Navek

The idea is to exercise different Hot and Cold Magics. Get a balance for control.

Boden

Ok, I think we can do that.

The Wizards send out iceballs and then hit them with fireballs. Each exploding in the air, not with a violent sound, more like a thud as the balls erupt into a blue grey cloud. They continue to do it until they are ready to move on.

Navek

Ok, rest up and I'll teach you the next exercise.

They stand around for a while, letting themselves rest.

Navek

Ok, this is a Shield Magic exercise, some of the most important forms of Guard Magic.

Boden

Sounds good.

Navek lets out a yellow streamer from his hand, and the end forms into a translucent disk-shaped shield with yellow sparkling in it. Then, using his other hand, he lets out another streamer and its tip forms into a blue disk shield.

Navek

Ok, the idea is to use the streamers to slam the shields together. The shields should try and destroy each other.

Navek draws the shields apart, then starts to slam them into each other. As they collide in the air, they give off loud, exploding expanding nebulas of colour. Boden, Bethany and Henna join in, their shields showering in sparkling dusts. Together they do this for a while, then stop.

Navek

Ok, try and keep the shields up as long as you can.

Boden, Bethany and Henna hold it for quite a long while, but then stop when their shields fail. Navek continues long after each of the others have stopped, eventually stopping himself to allow the others to rest.

Navek

When you get good, you can do it for an age.

Boden

<u>Always trying to save our blushes, you have barely done it more than we have.</u>

Boden thinks, with a smile.

The others rest in silence as Navek connects his hands with a streamer and sends little sparks through it for fun.

Navek

Ok, I think that is enough of my exercises for today. I'll teach you the rest later.

Bethany

Great, I'd like to show you guys my healing technique.

Bethany takes out some sewing needles and hands them around.

Bethany

Ok, if you are up for it, I want you guys to magic your fingers so you can prick them with the needles. Take this clove oil and rub it onto your pointer finger.

They each rub some clove oil into their fingers, causing them to go numb. Then they send magic to their fingertips to weaken their skin and then prick themselves with their needles.

Bethany

Ok, I am going to teach you the magic you need to do first.

Bethany sends out a streamer with a golden spiral around the outside and connects to them via it. She sends down a green energy across the streamer and the others concentrate on it, absorbing and learning the magic. After a while of this, they manage to create their own green healing energy.

Bethany

Ok, you all got that?

Boden, Henna, Navek

Yeah.

Bethany

Ok, use the magic like this.

Bethany creates the green magic around her finger.

Bethany

You need to focus on the damaged spot with the Healing Magic and imagine it healing, creating the imagining in the magic.

Bethany's finger glows bright green and stops bleeding. Next it forms a scab, then the scab drops off, leaving a little red piece of skin which turns the colour of the skin around it, leaving no blemish from the pinprick. Boden, Henna and Navek have a go. They manage to stop the bleeding but are not able to get it to scab.

Bethany

Very good. I'll show you some more of the magic.

58

Bethany connects them up with streamers again and sends more of the green magic down the connection. Henna, Boden and Navek continue to concentrate on the magic, learning from it, forming new ideas with it and honing their Healing Magic by it. After a while, they stop and try the pinprick test again. On this go, they are able to get to the scab stage.

Bethany

Very good, very good. You guys learn so quickly. Soon you'll be able to heal cuts and wounds.

Bethany goes over and fully heals all the pinprick wounds with her magic.

Bethany

Ok, that's all for now. You did very well!

Navek

Thanks.

Boden

Ok, so you guys get to see my new exercise. I call it "Full Body Exercise". Basically, what this exercise is, is an amalgamation movement.

Bethany

Like when you use several muscles together?

Boden

Exactly, except you use every muscle in your body with this exercise.

Bethany

Oh, yikes!

Boden

Yeah, it's kinda like a dance.

Boden shows them the intricate movement, which he created. As he says, it looks like a dance movement, a bit like running on the spot. Boden shows the movement again and again and they all try it, creating their own style of the exercise until Boden is happy that they have it down.

Boden

Ok, there is several ways to do this.

Boden readies himself.

Boden

There's the endurance way, which is like jogging.

Boden does the exercise, and it looks like a methodical running dance.

Boden

There's the sprinting way, which is like this.

Boden does the exercise with a really fast movement.

Boden

And then there's the muscle-building way.

Boden does it with a slow and strong movement.

Boden

What you have to do, is to do it heavily, then when you fatigue, you do it in the fatigue stage. That's what builds your muscle fast. The only thing about this way is, you can damage yourself if you don't do it right.

Boden stops and smiles.

Boden

I also created this steamer resistant thing.

Boden creates long, red and yellow translucent streamers over his arms, legs and body.

Navek

What's that do?

Boden

Well, it creates different types of resistance to the exercise.

Navek

Wow, that's clever.

They decide to do the exercises together. Navek tries the muscle building technique, Boden does the sprinting, and the girls do the endurance technique. After a while they stop and sit on the grass to catch their breath.

Navek

So, Henna, what's your spell do?

Henna

Ok, have a look.

Henna holds up her hand and concentrates. As she does, a shadow shines from a spherical spark grown in the palm her hand.

Navek

Wow, what's that?

Henna

It's a shadow light.

Navek

A shadow light?

Henna

Yeah, if you shine it in somebody's eyes, you can keep them from seeing.

Navek

Ooh, clever.

Bethany

That's really zingy.

Boden

It was that magic that helped me create my Glink Staff.

As she shines it around, a patch of darkness shows up wherever she points her hand.

Henna

Here, let me teach you.

Henna lets out a streamer and dark wispy threads flow down it.

Henna

The spell signature is Evishio Olavon. You can say the words in your mind.

They each have a go and are able to shine a shadow. Theirs aren't as dark as Henna's, but they are still good. They spend the rest of their training session shining shadows around the park. After they finish, they sit on a bench, opposite a stream and watch the ducks go by.

Henna

Darn, I wish I had some bread.

Bethany

Yeah, pity.

Henna

So, can we go to the museum tomorrow?

Boden

Sounds good to me.

In the background, as they sit, people juggle, and others lay out with picnic baskets and blankets.

Navek

This is a nice park.

Bethany

Yeah.

Henna

I wonder what this gem cave that the Carriage Builders came across is like.

Bethany

It sounds big.

Boden

What's great, is we don't need to do it.

Navek

Yeah, we have enough gold that we don't have to do any job.

Henna

I suppose. I still like the idea of doing some work in this town before we move off.

Bethany

Yeah, me too.

The Wizards get up and wearily walk back to the inn. They wash off and rest into the evening in their night clothes. They sleep through the night, and the cockerel calls in the morning and the Wizards rise early.

Henna

Yay, museum day.

Bethany

I've been looking forward to this.

The Wizards change into their day clothes.

Henna

Do you think they will be open now?

Boden

Well, we can go down and ask at reception.

At the reception desk, they see a pamphlet that tells them the museum is open. They take it with them and head out to the streets. The city in the morning sun is just as busy as any other time from the days before.

Navek

Wow, the hustle and bustle this early.

It's crazy, this city never sleeps.

The Wizards walk out into the early morning traffic and head to the road containing the museum. The walk is long, but the Wizards don't mind as they look around at the higgledy-piggledy streets they haven't visited yet. Eventually, they end up on the street the museum is on, which is a dark cobblelock street. The outside of the museum is tall, without windows, made from thick, white stone. The bottom and top of the walls have giant stone lintels sticking out. There are pillars in front of the walls, running from on top of the lintels on the ground to the bottom of the lintels at the top. The entire building's pure white draws the eye. There is a circular floor in the center of the front, surrounded by pillars. It leads up to an indented round wall entrance. The center of the stone floor has an elegant curving pattern in it. The roof over the entrance is a large dome. There are long stretches of black hedge in front of the museum that are behind black, iron railings. The entrance has a deep curved arch over it, full of detailed white flowers on its surface. The Wizards go up to the open marble doors and enter. Inside the main entrance is a large room with a giant glass dome high above them in the rooms center, giving the room a very bright appearance. The place has a museum sound to it, a sort of quiet and echoey feel. The floor is light brown wood and the walls white. The center of the room is a ring-shaped marble desk, with Staff in the middle. The room smells of fresh paint. As the Adventurers approach, they are greeted by a green robed, friendly-faced woman.

Museum Stewardess

Hello, and welcome to the Museum of Colours.

Henna

Hi, we were wondering if we could take the tour.

Museum Stewardess

Oh yes, brilliant. I'll get some tickets for you now. When you're finished the tour, there's a dining hall over there and gift shop over there.

She says, pointing to the windowed rooms.

Museum Stewardess

Ok, there is a special class today, I presume you also came to see that?

Boden

A class, no, we just came for the tour.

Henna

What's the class?

Museum Stewardess

Well, it's being held today after lunch, if you would like to attend. They are a very special guest. A Wizard who creates her own colours and uses them in her magic.

Henna

Sounds brilliant!

Museum Stewardess

Yeah, the class will teach you about colours, originality and at the end you can purchase her book, which will guide you through advanced colour making.

Henna

Wow, can we buy tickets to the class as well?

Museum Stewardess

Yeah, sure, let me get them for you.

The woman gets them the tickets for the museum, as well as the tickets for the class.

Museum Stewardess

Also take this.

She hands them pencils and pieces of paper.

Museum Stewardess

We also make pigments of the colours in the museum. If you take down the names of the colours you like, you can buy them after the tour.

Henna

Thank you.

Bethany

Thanks.

The Adventurers walk up to a giant set of dark wooden doors and hand their tickets to a man standing behind a small wooden plinth. He pulls a leaver on the wall and the large doors open in front of them, leading to a long, tall room with white walls and a round, glass tunnel roof high above them. Inside the room are giant picture frames. Each frame, instead of containing a picture, contains just a canvas painted in an individual colour.

Boden, Bethany, Henna, Navek

Wow!

These colours have never been seen by the Wizards before and look nothing like any other colour they know of. Stunned, the Wizards walk up to the large picture of the first colour and stare at it. They smile, as new and wonderous feelings wash over them. This first colour is warm, bright and glows deep, it feels like a fantasy colour that has a lot of energy in it. They look at each other and smile as they feel energy course through them from the colour on the canvas. Outside the frame is the name of the artist and the name of the colour. "Sanguine Storm" by Lisa J. The next colour is also by Lisa J. It is a nice dull shade and soothing on the Wizards' eyes. The colour looks matt and as if it would belong as specks or veins running through a rock. A cool relaxing feeling flows from this picture. The next colour is soft and fluffy, it's called "Light Home" and it's by M. Burlington. It looks soft and cute and gives the Wizards a feeling of cosy warmth, like looking through a window at a circus in the distance, while being tucked into a squishy bed while hugging a cute little animal. The colour after that has a very strong natural feel to it, sort of like trees. It's called "The Forest Glaze", by Laurence M.B. Looking into it is like looking into a beautiful walled garden, with a profound depth to it, the feeling of a deep forest path. It makes the Wizards contemplative as they look at it. Another picture on the wall is by Steven T. and feels like a drawing, even though it is a colour. The Wizards swear that there is a drawing, even though there isn't. The next group of colours are by the sisters Ruby Lee and Crystal Lee. They have a weird fun to them, looking crazy and distorted to the Wizards' eyes. The colours are cheeky, and the Wizards feel giggly at some of these. The last few pictures by the sisters contain an unbelievable beauty and dignity to them. The Adventurers walk around slowly, going back and forth, stopping to stare and soaking in the new colours. After this, they move on to the next room. Inside the room, the Wizards are greeted with several new colours that all seem to be related to each other.

Henna

The colours seem connected in some way.

Boden

Yeah, they do have something about them.

Navek

Let's have a look.

The colours appear to all be different shades or tones of a newly created colour. This colour has an autumnal feel to it and seems to be very diverse. The caption reads "Captured Colour of Autumn" "Created by nature". They look around the room, the colours giving the feel of falling leaves and windy afternoons.

Henna

Wow, this place is amazing.

They go from colour to colour, admiring the different Autumn feelings the pictures give them. Some giving a smoky Halloween feeling, while others giving feelings of bare trees under grey skies. They stay for a while in silence, just looking at the pictures of the Autumn colours. After a while, they move on to the next room, this has a wintery feel to it, with cold dim colours, that have an icy and snowy feeling, with some being whitish. As they go around this room, they feel colder. Some of the colours feel like cold snow lands, or wintery mountains. Others are warm and have a Christmassy feel to them, of warm houses and watching through deep snowy windows. In the next room, energetic spring feelings flow from the different colours. There are a few yellows, pinks, and whites among the other created colours. Some of the colours feel like fields of tulips, others feel like streams of petals or lands of flowers. After the Winter room, this room's colours begin to give them a warm vitality and feelings of hope. Into the next room, they find a very bright group of colours, that feel very summery, giving the Wizards a highly spirited and lively energy. The colours are very shiny, with a few blues and bright yellows and as they look through them, they get the feeling of sunny days, deep blue skies and fun exciting life. As they go, the Wizards note down colours they like for buying in the shop later. In the hall ahead, they turn to a door beside where they enter. In this next room, there is a Warden standing there. The canvases in the room contain pictures that are black. The Warden begins to talk to them.

Warden

This room is the shadow room or dark room. These colours or darks are very
rare.

He closes the doors and then covers the window in the ceiling, and the room
goes black. Inside the picture frames, a different type of colour appears, a sort of
shadow colour. With the light gone, some of them appear to glow in their frame,
others seem to be darker than the blackness of the room. The shadow colour in
the nearest frame is slightly greeny blue, it looks sort of creepy, like a quiet,
empty forest at midnight. The Wizards get strange fearful feelings while
inspecting it. The next shadow colour is inky dark and feels quite spirited, like a
party at night, with coloured lights hanging from trees, glowing through its
darkness. The Wizards smile as they are reminded of the Masquerade. The next
few shadow colours have a ghostly feel to them, looking slightly pale. Each dark
colour has interesting effects on their eyes. When they look away from staring at
a shadow colour, their eyes seem to retain the darkness and the walls in the
dark room look slightly darker. They move around the room and get to a shadow
colour that seems to suck their attention towards it, feeling as if it is pulling
energy out of the room. The colour's presence gives the Wizards feelings of
sickness, and scary thoughts creep from it, it draws their attention with hypnotic
darkness.

Warden

Don't stare at that colour at the end for too long, unless you want to be
depressed for the rest of the day.

The Warden says, as they head towards it. They heed his advice and pull away
from it, avoiding its sight. As they look at other colours, it draws their attention.
They go to speak, but stop in random bursts, feeling like the picture is
interrupting what they are saying with horrible dire thoughts.

Warden

Ok, I think that's enough.

The Warden opens the door in the ceiling and light comes flooding back into the
room. The pulling darkness recedes, and the frame seems to contain nothing
more than a matt black canvas. The rest of the shadows disappear too, their
canvas looking black as well.

Bethany

Thank you.

He smiles, and the Wizards move on to the next room, a room called "The Green Room", there they see different types of green.

Navek

This is weird.

Henna

Yeah, I didn't think there could be new greens.

Each of the greens are individual and unique, never seen before by the Wizards.

Boden

Wow, this is amazing!

The greens sit on canvases without frames, looking nice against the pure white walls. The Adventurers move around and the greens feel calming. As they stare at the colours, they get the feeling they are in a forest and a balancing energy flows through them, making them feel healed. There is a green that feels like leaves and another that feels like moss. Blues occupy the next room, which has a different kind of calming feel to it, sort of like sitting by the sea. There are several marine colours, a light greyed blue, a creamy blue and many others. On another wall there are sky blues, bright day blues and deep dark night blues. The room contains lots of other new blues. In the yellows they find lots of creams and daisy colours and a colour called solar yellow. The colours feel very warm and fun. They have a fresh shining glow to them, feeling very pure and light. The Summer yellows seem endeavourus and cheery. Next room and the reds they find are colours that give a strong passionate feel to them. Some of them feel deep, others feel thorough and elaborate. Some of the fiercer reds give a fiery feeling. There is a red that gives feelings of extreme passion, making the Wizards feel emboldened, another gives violent anger, making the Wizards feel like fighting. The danger reds make them feel afraid. The rage red look very threatening, and the lava reds seem very hot. The orange room feels very rustic and some of the colours feel bright and fruity, like orange peel, and others feel dark and earthy. The purple room contains indigos and violets. Some feel like plant colours. Other colours feel very royal. There are colours that feel like insects or beetles. There is a very dark purple that seems upsetting.

They travel to the next group of rooms, called "The Glow Colours". The rooms contain a rainbow variety of glowing colour, that have interesting colour glows in their picture frames. There are very strong luminous yellows and greens, glowing blues and reds. Some of the colours are new, and some of the colours glow different colours to the colour on the canvas, giving them a frame of glow around their edges. A glow colour called "Sharp Yellow" catches their eyes. It is very luminous and very shiny, making them pay attention and focus.

Henna

That would make a good pen for highlighting text.

Boden

That's a really good idea.

The room also contains several wooden handled glow batons. The Wizards wave them around in a fun fashion, leaving trailing glows through the air. After that, is a room marked "Natural Colours". Flowers and trees spread out through it. Henna walks over to a jug of flowers and touches them. They suddenly stretch out, shining lights all over the room, and colours start to dance over their surface.

Henna

Wow!

Bethany goes over to a herb and it puffs an amazing plume of coloured feather seeds, each a different colour, never seen before. With nowhere to go, the seeds gently head back to the flower. Looking through the trees, Boden and Navek catch sight of leaves that are so beautiful, with wondrously indescribable greens.

Navek

These greens, wow!

Boden

The trees are wonderous.

Bethany smiles as she stands beside them. The next room is called "Effects". The Wizards enter and see all sorts of weird colours on the walls. There are colours that look like they are really far in the distance when the Wizards stand in front of them. Another looks like it's spinning when you look at it, making the room feel like it's tumbling.

Boden

Wow, heady!

Another, if you move closer and further from it, the colour changes.

Navek

That's so creative.

Another colour makes the eyes jar suddenly.

Henna

Woah, that's hard to look at.

There's a colour that causes the eyes to flash like the light from a lightning bolt.

Bethany

Wow, it's snazzy.

Another gets darker and darker, then pings back to being bright again.

Henna

He, he. I like this colour.

While another colour in the background projects a shadow into the room, while glowing brightly itself. Some, when stared at for long enough, change how all the other colours look, making the room suddenly feel like it is a new colour.

Boden

Wow, that's very snazzy.

Navek

Ha, ha.

They find a colour that causes the room to pulsate. Some colours stay in their eyes, creating funny little shapes that run around their vision, doing funny little things. Henna chases hers with her hand. There are also colours that seem to not make sense when they look at them, some appear to not be sitting in their frames, others seem to be moving around or floating in odd shapes, coming out towards them from their canvases. At the back of the room, there are several colours that look like tunnels, looking at them feels like shooting along down them or exploring a cave. The Wizards go into another room, that is full of deep shades of rocky colours. Inside, there is a side door with another room that's full of lamps. They see some of the colours from before incorporated into the lamps. The lights dance around the ceiling of the room and the walls are full of little flecks of colour that mix and make the room look flowery. The room adjacent to this is full of all types of mirrors and glasses. The light is shone through them, either splitting up into new colours or passing through and getting distorted in some fashion. The mirrors reflect the Adventurers and make their skin and clothes look crazy with different colours.

Navek

Ha, ha, this is weird.

Navek says, as he looks at himself with dark green skin and bright red hair.

Boden

Yeah!

Says Boden, with his reflection of a squat body and giant long arms. Bethany sticks her tongue out, and in the mirror, it drops to the floor.

Bethany

Ha, ha, ha, ha.

Henna looks at her wobbling reflection mirror that squashes and twists her face and makes her body squeeze around, doing a weird dance. Boden and her move to the next mirror, that has a reflection of their backs as they look at it frontways.

Boden

We must get some of these, they'd be hyper handy.

Henna

Yeah, especially for your hair.

Boden

And eyeglasses would be fun too.

In the next room, they get a lesson on the history of light. Different pictures of people discovering different colours and uses for light. There is a picture that has a lighthouse in it, which Bethany reads.

Bethany

"The lighthouse has been used for ages to guide voyagers on their journey and help create paths. Some of the most interesting things about lighthouses are the types of light they use. A common source of light are port flames, which are cold to the touch but emit a light with amazing travel properties. When you are in their shine, you can create a path back to it easily from wherever you are. The light also makes the creation of different types of paths possible, including light paths."

Henna

Light paths, interesting!

In the next room, there is camouflage from animals. They walk around the room, almost bumping into animal statues, as they seem to appear out of nowhere. The Wizards are only able to spot them when they are very close.

Henna reads.

Henna

"Throughout the eras, many people have tried to create different types of camouflage. The whole idea of camouflage is to blend into your surroundings. It is different from invisibility, and each cannot be used as a substitute for the other. Certain super rare creatures have created forms of super camouflage, that allows the animal to move objects or make changes to things around people, without them ever noticing."

Bethany

Wow! Scary.

Boden

Yeah.

They move into the next room, which is full of pictures of colour and light in use, with signs full of information. Navek reads a sign near the door, next to pictures of people attacking each other and using light as a tool to blast at things.

Navek

"Light has been used as a weapon in many wars, especially amongst the wizarding community. Light Wizards from the past were a very sought-after commodity. They would mostly be self-trained wizards and there isn't any history of qualifications or passed down knowledge for light's use as a weapon. Some of the famous examples of light being used include the Damned Wars, where shadow and darkness were also used as a weapon, the wars against demons, who also had Light Magic and some of the neighbouring wars. Ever since the creation of the Castle Town Worlds and Heartwood Walls, there hasn't been much use for light attacks, and they have generally fallen into disuse."

In the middle of the picture is a Wizard using a light beam against a Damned Wizard who is using a shadow beam. Their beams clash in the middle in a bizarre disorientating energy.

Henna looks at another picture. In this picture is an artist creating a new colour.

Henna reads.

Henna

"The artist is using a crushing technique to create a fabulous colour for her painting."

The picture has a painting in it, made from all sorts of new colours and shapes. Bethany moves to the picture at the end of the room. Inside the picture is a woman with a sort of green glow coming from her hands, that is being projected onto the body of somebody in front of her, who is lying on the floor. Bethany reads the sign.

Bethany

"Light Healing is an ancient technique and used in many situations. It can also be used to give a boost to a person's health. Most Light Healers were wizards, but some of the non-magical races were capable of healing using light."

The Adventurers move on to the last hallway, which is narrow and bright. The sign on the entrance reads:

"Ethereal Room"

"The light in here is made from the heavens."

"All the colours inside the room are ethereal and can only be seen because of the light from the sun."

The first set of picture frames contain the rainbow colours and are pale pastel. The next are some custom colours created by people, which have a nice feel to them. The entire room makes the Wizards relax and feel at ease in themselves.

Henna

I like this room, it feels nice.

Boden

Yeah, sort of like stuff's going to be alright.

Bethany

Like bad things will never happen again.

Navek

Like power and weakness doesn't exist.

They come to the end of the room and there is a giant picture frame over the door. Inside the frame is a window looking out at the sun. It reads:

"Heavens Ethereal White"

"The King of all colours, the light of the sun."

The Wizards look at it and smile. They then leave the Ethereal Room and exit back into the main hallway.

Henna

Well, that was nice.

Bethany

We get some food before the class starts?

Navek

Yeah, I am famished.

Across the entrance hall from them, in the white wall, is a large window, stretching from knee height to above head height. They see people in the room, eating their food on small wooden tables while sitting on wooden benches. They go over to the room, and inside, the floor, walls and ceiling are all white. The walls have big white panels, giving off white light and the ceiling has a large, rectangular, opaque window that glows white, making the room very bright. They go in and sit down beside the middle of the window, behind the people they saw eating. A female Server comes up and hands them a menu. The food items all have different colour names. They order the food they think sounds the tastiest.

Boden

So, that was interesting.

Henna

They should start a colour museum in Olreon.

Bethany

Yeah, it's weird that we have nothing like that.

Boden

I guess we could suggest it when we get back.

As they chat, the Server comes back with their food. Henna's food is made of little round clear coloured gels. Navek's are little buns of all sorts of colours the Wizards have never seen. Boden has multi-coloured, chewy pastry twirls and potato shards. Bethany has a set of little coloured puddings.

Server

Have you been through the museum?

Henna

Yes.

Server

A lot of the colours in these foods come from those in the museum.

Henna

Wow!

Server

You might find something interesting happen when you eat them.

Henna

Hmm.

Boden's potato shards are all a glowing golden colour.

Server

We also add a special golden oil colour to make your shards extra crispy.

Boden

Excellent.

Server

Thank you. I hope everything is to your satisfaction.

Boden

It is, thank you.

They smile and the Server leaves. Henna's food looks so nice that her eyes and mouth seem to connect weirdly, and she can taste the food just by looking at it. She stares at her plate, and it feels like eating. Boden's golden fried shards are amazingly crunchy, with a dash of salt they taste extra nice. The flavour of his twists somehow taste like their colours, bright and chewy from the fruity flavoured fried pastry. Bethany eats her puddings, each of the flavours seem to correspond so perfectly to its colour that it seems that they were made for each other. The puddings have rich flavours, the darker colours tasting earthy and the bright colours tasting sweet. Navek's food also feels like this. The colour and the flavours feeling as if they were made from each other. Each bun has a different colour and different flavour. The pastel colours tasting like light from a meadow or chalk paintings, the darker colours tasting more savoury and special.

Bethany

Hmm, I wonder what we are going to learn.

Henna

Yeah, I would love to spend eras studying colour and light and shadow.

Boden

It's an amazing subject.

Navek

You not going to eat your food?

He says to Henna.

Henna

I just like looking at them.

They smile over at her as she just stares at her plate. After a while, she picks up the little round gels with a spoon and eats them. Her eyes explode full of the colours as she eats. The others look over and can see the colours swimming around her pupils.

Henna

Wow! Zingy!

They smile together and finish up their food. Afterwards, they pay the Server, with their gold hitting the pay tray and turning to different gold colours that glide across the surface like they are being painted along. The Wizards stare at the gold as it sinks into the tray, amazed. They then head out into the main hallway again. As they do, a Wizard with long, brown hair, full of big curls, with a wide, high cheek boned and slightly determined smiling face, comes through the door. She walks quickly, hands full of equipment, dragging a large chest with rollers as she goes. She wears a long coat, made of a patchwork of dusty light-coloured squares, with a round, thick, white edge that goes down her front. It frames her bright blue robes and continues around the bottom of the coat as it sweeps along the floor. Her hat has a white framed, patchwork rim, with a blue and gold, raised, round twist going down from the top, and her hands seem to be full of more things than any normal person could carry. She has large sheets and rolls of paper, lots of long sticks and paint brushes, several folded-up easels and long folder cases with handles. She wears a name tag saying Orio[(O-rye-o)].

The Adventurers go over and offer to help her with her stuff.

Orio

Thank you, thank you.

She says, smiling around at them.

Orio

I am just going into this room here.

She walks over to a side room and the Wizards follow, carrying her stuff.

Orio

Thank you, you can set it down over there.

The room they are in has chairs in rows, facing the front of the room.

Orio

I am giving a class on colours.

The sing-song sound of her voice makes the Wizards feel at ease.

Bethany

<u>She doesn't seem much older than us. Hmm, maybe just started into her Age of Adulthood.</u>

Boden

Oh, then we should give you these.

The Adventurers take out their tickets for the class.

Orio

Oh brilliant, then you're early, he, he. Well, my name is Orio, as you can see. How do you do?

Boden points around.

Boden

This is Navek, Bethany, Henna, and I'm Boden.

Orio

Nice to meet you all. So, what town do you come from?

Henna

We come from Olreon.

Orio

Oh Olreon, that's a lovely town, the wonderful lava lanterns. Yes, I must visit it again. So, what do you Wizards do with yourselves, are you still in school?

Boden

No, we've finished, now we're Adventure Wizards.

Orio

Adventurers!

A giant smile crosses her face.

Orio

That's brilliant, it's been such a long time since I've met an adventurer.

Henna

You met adventurers before?

Orio

Oh yes, I am still friends with some of them in my old eras. But sadly, that is an age of ages ago. So, are you training at the moment? It's always important for adventurers to train.

Navek

Oh yes, we are training in the park.

Orio

Brilliant, what kind of training are you doing?

Navek

Well, my father is a Wall Guard and he taught me all the techniques to train.

Orio

Fantastic! The wall guards have the most amazing training regimes.

Yeah, he's teaching us the techniques at the moment. It's hard to keep up with him though.

Orio

Sounds like you are very talented.

Navek blushes. In the background a Wizard walks in with her child.

Orio

Oh hi, nice to meet you. Ok, I'd better set up. Here, take these.

Orio hands the Adventurers a thick wizard pencil and stickers.

Orio

Name tags, so we all don't get mixed up.

The Adventurers take their seats and put their name tags on themselves. Orio unpacks her belongings and puts up an easel in front of them. As she takes out more stuff, the room starts to fill up with Wizards. When she finishes, the room is packed, and she looks around.

Orio

Ok, I think that's everybody. Hello, my name is Orio, I am a travelling artist. I've spent many an era travelling to learn this craft, and I still spend many eras training in it. Today, I am going to be teaching you the basics of colour and the magics involved in making original colours. So, to give you a rundown of the class. We are going to start with Original Theory. I am sure a lot of you have already learned it in school. For those who haven't, I will cover the basics. If you feel bored and don't want to listen, I have some books and magazines that you can look through.

She points to a set of books and magazines she has on her trunk.

Orio

Next, I will cover the more advanced topic of light. I am sure you will learn something. Again, some of you might have covered it, so the magazines and books are there.

Her voice has a soothing healing tone, which causes the Adventurers to feel really good as she goes on.

Orio

Next, we will go into techniques for creating colours, both magic and non-magical. Then colour roots. After that, we go into forms of light and colour, things like light used for different forms of magic and after that, we go deeper into darkness. Ok, any questions before we begin, I can cover subjects you like at the end of class.

Several people put their hands up.

Orio

You, Laratin.

She points to a boy from the audience.

Laratin

Will you be teaching us Battle Light?

Orio

Oh, Battle Light, no, I am afraid not. I am not big into harming people I've just met.

The room laugh at this.

Orio

Sandra.

She points to a curly haired girl.

Sandra

Is dark and shadow anything like Dark Magic?

Orio

Well, yes and no is my answer to that. Yes, dark and shadow can be used with Dark Magic and yes, they do have their connections. Dark Magic or Corrupt Magic has several types of shadow and darknesses. These are unconnected to normal shadows or darkness. Their form is very bad, and they absorb and destroy colour and light. I won't be teaching you anything corrupt, and the dark and shadow colours I will be teaching you through, are not Corrupt Magic either. They are quite good as dark and shadow, and can be used for extremely good deeds and very nice colours.

Orio points to Bethany, who has her hand up.

Orio

Ok, Bethany.

Bethany

Will you teach us about lighthouses?

Orio

Hmmm, it's not on the curriculum, but I'll cover it after we get through the class. For anybody who wants to stay after and learn other things, I will be more than happy to help.

Orio looks around and nobody else has their hand raised.

Orio

Ok, shall we begin.

Class

Yes.

The room says, in collective agreement. Orio moves her trunk with the magazines on it to the side of the group.

Orio

Ok, we will start with Original Theory.

Some of the Wizards move off and take a magazine. Henna, Boden, Navek and Bethany don't. They listen intently, even though they feel they probably know the lesson.

Orio

Ok, let's start with the Certancy of Originality. Now, a Certancy is what is known as a Romantic Nature, or Romantic Law. It is the soul of this Verse, Tream Heartaya, and all life that lives in it. It is also the way of your soul, the trees, the rocks, the lands, the mountains, the seas and all living things. Certancys are the natural laws of Tream, its heart roots, so as to speak. The wonderful Certancy we are dealing with is named the Certancy of Originality. With it, every creation is original. This means that there is no such thing as a copy.

It also means the person, creature or nature that creates a creation is the only creator that can have ever created it. It is made from them and only them. Nobody else could have created it or ever would be able to, this means they couldn't make it before or after its creator did. Nobody can create a copy of anything created. If I was to make something on a lathe, the shape I cut would be original to me. Say I made something on a colour lathe or song lathe, those colours and songs would only ever be able to have been created by me. Say I write a book, that book can only have ever been written by me. Nobody else could have written that book but me. It is a Creation of Originality and it is made from my creativity. No matter what people write or try, they could never have written my book. People may say that prints of my book are copies, but they are mistaken, and anybody who practices the art of printing, will agree with me, that the books people read are not copies. Those prints could not have existed before my book was written, and those prints are derived from the original work, grown from it, it is their root. The prints are created from the book, sort of like leaves are created from a tree. Having the printed book is like having a leaf from the original tree. So, remember, everything that you create is unique to you and your specialness. Your creations are made from you.

The group around the room smile at this.

Orio

Just to reinforce. The Certancy of Originality means your creations are all original and can only ever be created by you.

Orio brings her hands together.

Orio

Now, I will go into other aspects of creation, such as inheritance and making with other creations. So, any questions before we venture forth down that road.

A boy pipes up, with Aleon on his name tag.

Aleon

When my friend created a dance move the other day, he showed me how to do it and then I could do it. Is that not copying?

Orio

Well, that sort of leads on to inheritance and inspiration. What happens when you did the move, is you created your own form of the move. Making your move inherited from your friends. Sort of like a branch, growing from a tree.

84

Your move branched from his tree and your creativity. The moves, you could consider them a family. When he showed you the move, he was teaching it to you, which means you could create from it quite easily. If he didn't try to teach you it, it would have been harder to create a move inherited from it. In some cases, impossible.

So, my version of the move is my move?

Sure is, but it's common courtesy to call it his move. Also, he helped create your move with his, so he is partial creator, so it's only fair.

The boy nods with a big smile.

On to inspiration. Inspiration is another form of inheritance, it is creating with a creation. When you witness something amazing, and you marvel at it and care for it, it becomes a part of you, and you can use it for what is called Creative Inspiration. Say you fall in love with a song and listen to it a lot, and it inspires you to paint something beautiful. That song will become a new part of you and your creativity. When you paint, the song will become a part of the painting, part of its creation and the new song part of you will create the painting too. Creations themselves are not just creations, they are tools too. You can create creations that help you create other stuff, like different paintbrushes to help you create a painting. Your friends move helped you create your move, it was made from it. There are even creations that can create all by themselves, but they still inherit from their creator's creativity and this will be part of their creating. There are lots of ways to create with a creation. You can creatively grow creations into new forms, renditions and branches of the creation. All creation needs, is some loving care, a whole lot of effort, a mix of the mysterious and a little spark.

The group clap when she stops and Orio smiles.

Ok, onto light and how the eye sees.

Some of the Wizards around the room stop reading and start to pay attention.

Orio

Ok, the eyes see many things and can see in many ways. There are many ways your eyes work, and many ways light works, but I will be covering the main ways we know of today. When you look with your eyes, they connect to things around them through their Sight Fields. Your eyes project out of them a field, and you see whatever the eye field envelopes or touches. If you ever heard the term "Your eyes are windows to your soul", well it's correct, as the eye fields are part of your soul. When you close your eyes, the fields are still there, but they fade and become smaller. When you open your eyes, they grow and strengthen. Now, there are different main ways in which your eyes see things. Most things you see, come from your eye fields touching things, and when these things are lit with light, they are able to give off their own colour. Your eye fields absorb the colour and you can see them. Another way in which you can see stuff is by seeing their colour fields. Objects have a colour field around them, that when they, or the field from them are hit by light, they become stronger and are able to be seen. Now this colour field is how we perceive things from afar, as the colour fields can extend a great distance from the object. Sometimes these colour fields can have profound effects on people, depending on where they come from. Horizon Fields are a mysterious sight that we have yet to understand, but they help people a lot and also aid in thinking on deep and profound subjects. Your vision fields can see other things than colour and not all colours seen are seen as colour, if that means anything to you.

She pauses and smiles.

Orio

Ok, so what is light in all this. Light is a type of field, that when shone on an object's colour or a colour field, causes them to become stronger, to create their colour and churn with it. To shine a light on something means to envelope it in a light field. Light fields have their own colour too, so when you look at them, they appear as a colour. When Ethereal White Light, the light from the sun, shines on something and engulfs it, it causes the thing to form pure versions of its own colour, in a magnificent brilliance. It is the only light that can do this. All other light sources are coloured, and when they shine on other colours, they form mixture colours. Now there are other whites than Ethereal White, and they are all very pure and do very little change to the colour they light up. Our sources of light, such as the wood bulb, are very pure.

She stands a lamp on the table near her, it has a dark wooden ball at the top and ridged bell like rings down its outside.

86

Orio

These are some of the purest white light sources.

She connects to it via a streamer, and it lights up. The light shines into the room, making it ultra-bright.

Orio

This is a very powerful light. It would be able to comfortably light up a room much larger than this.

She turns the light down.

Orio

There are other forms of colour that can only be seen by certain creatures or special lenses. The lights based on those colours can light up visible colours. Some substances are able to give off a colour field without light needing to be shone on them, we call them glow colours. There is a section of the museum with them if you go through. There are other types of lights too. A firelight is what is known as a hot light, it gives off warm light that heats as well as makes colours glow. If you ever look at the blue of ice, you'll find that it gives off cold light or light that cools. Ok, so what is shadow and darkness and what has it to do with all this. There are many types of darkness and many types of shadow. Not all are understood and the study of them is very deep and intricate, full of blind alleyways and dead ends. The normal type of shadow and darkness is a lack of light. Things will look dark when they can't create colour. Your eyes won't be able to perceive them. This is a simple darkness that is common. The shadows from this form when things block light fields. Another type of shadow is cast shadow, lots of stuff gives off shadow fields when they are not in the light. Blocked light and cast shadow are the kind that make up your shadow when you move around in the light and see your shape silhouetted. These shadows can also have a colour to them. The colour fields in these shadows give off dark colours. You can feel these colours more than you can see them. Some though, are strong enough to be seen, like in these museum's dark colour section. Now, when night-time comes, another type of darkness called "Blanket Darkness" comes down from the sky and covers the land. This blanket of darkness is a field, like a light field or a colour field. When you look at it, your vision goes darker. You get the dark colours from it, and you get inky blacks from this field. It is actually a good field, as it blankets colours and their fields, stopping them from giving off bright colour and hushing them. It actually rests the colours and helps them shine when it leaves. In very, very black nights,

87

it can be hard for lights and colour to form big fields. So, things that are far off, tend to look very blurry or can't be seen. There are worlds which have very different types of night-time darkness. Some of them can be very bad for you and it's best to stay in the light in those worlds. They are very rare though. Darkness has a beauty to it. I remember when I was young, seeing somebody come to a porch. I was waiting outside with my father, it was very dark, and you could barely make out anything. As they came to the doorway with a lantern, they opened the door, and the light inside had no darkness running through it. I remember seeing the night darkness encroach around the edges of the door. It was quite dramatic. This type of darkness also shines shadows, and it can be very romantic when around a fire, as the fire at night will shine shadow and light, making them dance together, and form strange shapes. The writing ink colours are similar to the black colours of night, except they give off their darkness colour when light hits them. They are mostly made from darkness. Now, moonlight and starlight and the different lights you see in the night sky are very mysterious. They shine very strange light and colour fields that are very perplexing, they are hard to study and give curious effects. The moon and its phases are actually caused by it partly shining darkness and partly shining light. So, the crescent moon gets its C-like shape from shining a big ball of darkness near its middle. Some people speculate that this shape has special properties that it shines into the light. We do know though, that the full moon gives off a light with a special essence, as it turns werewolves into their hairier counterparts. Now, some inventive people that were inspired by starlight and moonlight, created colours and light fields that could shine great distances through the dark. These colours tend to look dull in normal light but thrive in the dark. Lighthouses, as Bethany mentioned earlier, have a light that shines like this, but this light loves the day as much as the night and can be seen great distances in both. From the dark section of the museum, you will see we have found a way to make dark colours. Some of the colours are made, most of them are found, and some are exceedingly rare. These dark colours are different from inks and black colours. They don't give off their colour in the light, but instead give off their colour while in shadow or when hit by a dark field. Some are similar to the night and give off darkness fields. There are a lot of different fields they give off. Some of the fields can be a bit morbid or off-putting. Now there is another type of darkness, that is quite on the grave side. This darkness is considered pure evil. If you were in the dark colour room, you were probably told not to stare at this darkness for too long. The darkness in this painting is a very tame version of the darkness I speak of. It is very, very evil, and it has given a bad name to other darknesses and is why we associate evil things with dark colours, and white light with good. It is the darkness of evil. It will consume colour and eats anything that it has in its power to devour.

It exudes terrible feelings and gives off horrible energies. It lives in the darkness. Now, there are plenty of types of bad darknesses out there, just as there are plenty types of bad whites or other bad colours, but this darkness is hideous, persuasive, horrible and used to do terrible things by evil people. It is the evilest darkness known. Avoid it like you would a rotten Zombie, for it is rot. Now, the only thing that has proven to be affective at stopping this darkness is Ethereal White Light. That is why, when light shines through the window in the ceiling, the darkness goes away. Now, there are other types of dark that we don't have here in the museum. There's a dark field that will shrink your eye fields, some that make light colours grow, cave darknesses that are quite nice. Other cave darknesses that are quite bad for you, darknesses that have been used as tools, and some that have been used as weapons and many others. Shadows in all this are either a lack of light, or a field in themselves, emitted from surfaces and shadow sources. On to our next topic, and why most of you are here.

Orio smiles.

Orio

The fun part, colour creation.

She picks up a white linen bag, with a symbol on the front.

Orio

Ok, we are going to go with a very early technique, used by ancient Wizards to create colour and probably some of the most difficult.

From the bag, she takes out a small white stone and starts to rub her hand across it.

Orio

Ok, here you go.

After she takes up her hand, there is a beautiful colour on the rock, original to all the eyes that see it.

Class

Oooh.

Orio

Ok, before we use this technique, what I want you to do is imagine a new colour.

Orio smiles a snazzy smile.

Orio

To imagine a new colour, first, in your mind, imagine any ordinary colour you already know. Close your eyes if you find it easier and concentrate on that colour.

Most of the room, including the Adventurers, close their eyes.

Orio

Ok, now take away the colour and you should still be able to imagine the vision of where that colour was.

Everybody concentrates on the task.

Orio

Got it?

They nod together.

Orio

Ok now, this is your canvas to create your new colour on. So, from here is the difficult part. Push with a lot of effort, trying to imagine your colour being created in this canvas.

Everybody now in the room concentrates, eyes squeezing with effort. The Adventurers push and pull, force and heave with their mind, their heads start to ache, but they continue on pushing against the pain and effort.

Orio

Imagine all the good things in you and pour yourself into your colour.

Feelings of colour wash through their minds and they endeavour on. Eventually and quite quickly a new colour floods across their minds' canvas, they get a shock as they see something that was never seen before. They can't help themselves, their smiles beaming out of them. As they open their eyes and look around, the room is full of happy faces.

Orio

Well, I can see from your expressions, that you all have created a new colour.

Now, because we are Wizards, all your colours are magical. So, you can use them in your magic if you wish. But for now, we are going to use the ancient technique I showed you.

She takes out the bag of little white stones and starts handing them around.

Orio

Ok, now imagine your colour again. Fill your mind with it, imagine it flowing into your hands till they are full up with the colour. Now hold your stone and imagine the colour being pushed onto the rock's surface and rub it hard with the pam of your hand.

Everybody in the room tries it for a while. Nobody's but Henna's has any mark on it.

Henna

Oh, look!

It comes out very faintly. Orio comes over and has a look.

Orio

Very good! I've never seen somebody get it on their first go. You must be a natural.

Henna

Oh really? My mum always said I was good with colours.

Orio

That's great and it's a wonderful colour.

Boden

Yeah, it's a beautiful colour, Henna.

Henna

Thank you.

Orio

Ok, for most of you, no colour has come up. So, I want you to imagine your colour again and try to strengthen it. That will exercise your colour and make it stronger. Try what you did when you created it.

Everybody imagines their colour again and tries to make it stronger. In their minds eye the colour becomes deeper.

Orio

After this round, the colours should be strong enough, and the simple answer to colouring your stone, is elbow-grease.

She takes another stone and begins to rub it with her hand.

Orio

Ok everybody, let's have a go.

Everybody in the room begins to rub the rock in their hands, checking it every so often to see if colour has come up. Eventually, most peoples' stones look like Henna's at the start, each a new colour and Henna's stone having become much deeper in her colour.

Orio

Ok, the colours you created now, are yours, and yours only. Nobody else will be able to create them. Now, you can give people the power to use these colours and create their own colour with your colour, creating through inheritance, like we talked about earlier, or a kind of growing of your colour, like printers do with books.

Orio's audience keeps at it and eventually everybody has a stone that is deep with their colour.

Orio

Ok, on to our next technique.

Orio hands around a bag of white, dusty clumpy, clay-like substance.

Orio

Ok, take this in your hands and break it apart while imagining your new colour coming out in between the cracks.

The bag is handed around and everybody takes a clump. As they have a go, it feels like pulling apart soft earth. Their colour appears inside the fractures and coat the newly formed surfaces created when the clay parts. Making the colours

92

this way is a lot of fun, and as they rip the clay apart every time, the colour appears. It feels like pulling apart clods of dirt and finding little nuggets of gold inside. The new surfaces are smooth, but by tearing it apart in different ways, the Adventurers can form different surfaces.

Orio

Now, this clay is a special substance that has been worked to make it accept colour. You can do this with a lot of different substances, but it will be a lot harder, as this clay is made from a special material. This method is used to create pigments, mainly for mixing colours. Now, some people are able to create colour as they craft. They do it naturally and how they do it is an utter mystery. If you have ever come across an object with a weird colour that you've never seen before, and you know the person hasn't done colour studies, you will find that they developed the skill all by themselves. Some people call these people Super Colourists, others think it's not that super. They are an interesting bunch if they are super or not. Their way with colour is beautiful, and some of the most amazing and sublime colours ever created are by them. Their colours are true works of art.

Henna nudges Bethany.

Henna

Our masks.

Bethany

Yeah.

Orio

Ok, so the next technique is a favourite of mine. A very magical technique.

Orio hands around a bunch of small black cauldrons. Next, she unscrews the lid of a square tin can and pours a colourless liquid into the pots, then she hands around sticks. After, she takes out her own small cauldron and a stick with layers and layers of different colours and pours the thick clear liquid into her cauldron.

Orio

Ok, for this, I want you to try a new colour.

She starts to stir the cauldron.

Try imagining your colour canvas in the stick, in the liquid and in the pot. You'll find it quite helpful. Ok, imagine the colour now coming off the end of the stick, stir and stir.

The group start stirring and imagining their colour canvas. As they stir, it becomes easier to imagine a new colour.

Imagine it coming out of walls of the cauldron, stir and stir.

The group imagine.

Imagine it coming from the swirls in the liquid. Stir and stir.

The group imagine.

I like to say a few words, like I am stirring an enchanted potion. Round and round the colours go, splish sposh, flish flosh.

She says, with a cheeky smile. As the group stirs, the liquids change to the new colours very quickly. Orio looks around the room, happily.

Ok, go around the room with me and show everybody your colour.

The group walk around to see the amazing new colours that all the others have created.

Ooh, that's nice.

Zingy.

Let me see yours, Boden.

Boden shows Bethany his.

Bethany

Wonderful! Very Bodeny.

The Adventurers put their colours together to show each other.

Navek

Wowza!

Oria walks up to them and looks at their collective colours.

Orio

There's something about them, something interesting.

Orio stops and stares.

Orio

Hmm, yes, you all have a similar wildness to you.

They smile at her.

Henna

Can we see yours?

She shows them the colour in her cauldron, and they get a similar feel as they do from theirs. She winks and moves on around the room. The other colours are amazing. Everybody's is unique and they awe the Adventurers as they look at them.

Orio

Ok, if everybody would like to sign the canvas behind me with your colours.

The class takes it in turns to sign her big white canvas with the newly created colours.

Orio

When you are done, you can have a go with my stirring stick. You will find it has an interesting coloury feel to it.

The stick gets passed around the room and everybody has a go. It feels like a rainbow of colours from the layers of paint on it. The Adventurers smile as they add their layer to it.

Orio

Thank you, I've collected many colours over the eras, and I'll show you my book of them at the end of class. Ok, time for some fun, we are going to do Colour Magic. Now we all know there are special opuses in which we use our magic. There's the Streamer Opus.

She lets out a glowing green vine with a wonderful shape running its length.

Orio

The Spark Opus.

She lets out a spark and jumps it up and down on the end of her wand.

Orio

The Arora.

She lets out an ambiance of sparkling light that fills the room around her.

Orio

The Field.

She lets out a translucent field that fills the room around her in a different way.

Orio

Shields.

She holds a thin shell in the shape of a ball of magic around herself.

Orio

Beams, Rings, Globs and many others. Now, for the younger members of the audience, I've brought you special wands, so you can do Colour and Light Magic.

She hands around wands that are somewhat shaped like paint brushes.

96

Orio

Ok, so we are going to start with the simple spark. Now, we all know we can change the colour of our sparks by creating them in our own version of colours we've seen. Remember how I said that all the colours a wizard creates are magical. Well, you can use your colour that you created as the colour of your spark. So, remember the colours you made earlier. I want you to imagine them in your head. Then imagine your spark is made from that colour. Ok, so now use whatever technique you are comfortable with to make your coloured spark and fire it out towards the ceiling.

As she says that, everybody's colour gets shot out of their hand or wand, leaving streaking trails and hitting the ceiling with puffy explosions of colour.

Henna

Wow!

Orio

Ok, so that principle and the next works for streamers and for most other magics. Now, this next principle you are going to do, is to create a light from the colour. It's a little bit harder and you may have to use your wand. Feel free to create your usual light forms that you use for light. If you have a hat belt, you can use that too.

A few of the Wizards in the audience with black belts around their hats, that have round golden brass badges in the middle, give a nod.

Orio

Ok, with this technique, you are going to have to create your own colour's light field. I want you to imagine your colour on its canvas again. I want you to imagine it in darkness, that no light shines upon it, that it is resting in that darkness and blanketed by it. Let the colour rest in your mind and let your mind rest with it.

As the Adventurers do this, their minds relax.

Orio

Ok, take your time and feel comfortable. When you are ready, I want you to create your light form out of the colour you created.

Around the room, the class make their magic opuses, some creating little fluffs of colour on the end of their wands or making the brass medallion in their hat belts change colour. The Adventurers form globules of magic in their hands as they look down into them. The kids say "Shreen Alara" and form light sparks on their paint brush wands.

Orio

Ok now..... SHINE!

The call hits them like lightning. Suddenly the effort seems immense, but it flows with ease. They shine bright their coloured light. Everybody smiles. Looking around, the Adventurers can see super bright streamers glowing, flashy wand tips shining beams of light, hat medallions glowing like torches. The Adventurers and Wizards around them seem to be part of their colour as they shine.

Orio

I always love this.

She smiles at them as they glow.

The light dies down, with big grins on everybody's face as they look around.

Orio

Brilliant.

Orio smiles.

Orio

Next, to create a new version of a colour, it's quite a simple thing, if you want to try, what you do is imagine a colour, say any colour you like from the rainbow, imagine it sitting there on the colour canvas you created in your mind's eye. Now, instead of creating your colour in your empty canvas, you create a colour with your chosen colour in the canvas. The colour is created from you and the colour you picked. It should spread across your mind's eye and be easier to create than your own colour.

They give this a quick go. Boden creates a new red that feels quite inventive, Bethany creates a new green that feels like a hug from a big warm blanket, Navek creates a blue that sort of sings in his head and Henna creates a yellow that reminds her of the cute ducklings in a pond.

Orio

You all manage that?

The group nod in confirmation.

Orio

Brilliant, well this topic brings me onto creative roots. Now, when you create a new type of some colour, you use what is known as a "root" in its creation. If I was to make a type of green, it would be using the green root. If I see any type of green colour, I can use its green root rather than the colour itself to make my creations. All your colours can become roots too. Now, there are many types of roots and branches. Say I wanted to create a new type of salad fork. Salad fork would be the root I would use, salad fork's root would be fork and the fork's root would be cutlery. Creations can have many roots and can branch into many creations.

She makes a tree gesture with her hand, her fingers being the branches and her wrists being the roots. A sort of magical tree appears over her gesture.

Orio

Now, there are several natural light roots, and they make up most of what we see in the world around us. There's whites and the colours of the rainbow: red, orange, yellow, green, blue, indigo and violet. There are also colours from rocks: greys and shales. There is the earth browns and specialist colours: silvers, golds and pinks. There are also optical colours like reflective or mirror and specialist colours used to make telescopes, called lenses or see throughs. Glass tends to fall in these categories. Telescopes also tend to need special shapes or colours, but not all do. Light has many forms for use. Light and colour has been used in healing, weapons, food preparation, exercises, language and many more. Hopefully after this class, you will come up with your own uses.

The class smile to each other and whisper a few words.

Orio

Ok, so let's talk about the things you want to learn about. So, first off is Lighthouse Magic, as per Bethany's request. Lighthouse Magic was very popular in the past, before the use of Road Worlds, Tunnel Roads and Road Magic. It still has a use at sea, but now with shipping lanes, that has fallen away. It was used as a safety net. If you carried a Lighthouse Staff or had Lighthouse Energy imbued in you, you could travel out and use the Lighthouse Beacon as a way of creating a path home if you were lost. The other way it was useful, was for its

99

enhanced path creation, so it was easier and faster to go where you wanted. People used them when travelling very far or very deep. Lighthouses have had a lot of uses over the past and it would take eras of class just to teach it.

Orio looks around.

Orio

Are there any other things you would like to ask me about before we finish?

Bethany raises her hand.

Orio

Yes, Bethany.

Bethany

What about Healing Magic?

Orio

Oh yes, Green Colour Magic. The colour green is the main Healing Light, that's why trees and plants are green, they are always looking out for others. In fact, it is said that the green part of the rainbow comes from the trees, that they created the colour. Now the subject of Healing Light is another area that would take eras and eras to teach. Its main principle is balance, just like most other forms of healing and green is considered the colour of balance. It is the center of the rainbow, balanced between its sides. The Healing Light used in medicine is created from or with herbs mainly. They can be used to create very powerful cures. Some of the Light Healing techniques range from hand torches.

Orio shines a green light out from her hand and across the audience. From it, the Adventurers suddenly feel super healthy.

Orio

To orbiting sparks.

She shoots little green sparks that circle around them. Glowing, and making them feel well and happy.

Orio

Colour and Light Healing are a very creative branch of medicine. If you want to study healing, I suggest you endeavour to make Light Healing a part of it. Anything else you want to learn?

Henna puts up her hand.

Orio

Yes, Henna.

Henna

Do animals create their own colour? Like, is a duck's yellow their yellow?

Orio

Brilliant question. Yes, they do. That is the natural colour, created from who the animal is. If you look at a little yellow duck. The colour he creates is part of him, it comes from his soul. A duck's yellow is his own. The yellow made from him would have roots in his parents, who would have roots in duck yellow, and duck yellow has roots in yellow. The colour of your blonde hair comes from who you are. You create it naturally as you grow, decide and create the you that you are. Everybody's hair in this room is an original colour, just as everybody's skin colour is an original colour. That form of creation is a natural form of creation that we all have.

A few more people ask questions. Orio runs through them, giving detailed and in-depth answers. When all hands are answered, she smiles around at the people.

Orio

Ok then, that's the end of our class. I'll be here for a while if you would like to go into any more stuff. Here is the book of colours, you can pass it around and have a look.

Orio goes and cleans up her stuff, packing it away. Boden, Navek, Henna and Bethany go up to her.

Henna

I would love to learn more about colours.

Orio

Brilliant!

Henna

How would I go about doing it?

Orio

Well, I have several books.

She takes out some from her bag.

Henna

Oh great, how much?

Orio

Hmm, you can have them for free.

Henna

Really?

Henna says, face astonished.

Orio

Yeah, consider it a present.

Henna

Are you sure?

Orio

Yeah, they might come in handy.

Henna

Wow, thanks!

Boden

Really, yeah! Thanks!

Henna

Wow, look at this!

Bethany

We can use it for training.

Henna

Is there anything we can do in return?

Orio

Training, hmm, maybe there is a favour I could ask of you then.

Henna

Yeah, sure!

Orio

Would you let me train with you?

Henna

Really?

Orio

Well, it's been such a long time since I have met Adventure Wizards, I would love to train again with them.

The Adventurers look at each other.

Boden

I can't see why not.

Navek

Yeah, I don't mind sharing some of the wall guard techniques.

Orio

You don't have to show me any top secret Olreon stuff.

Navek

Well, I will go through the stuff that is common to most wall guards.

Orio

Brilliant, and I can show you a few of my trainings.

The Adventurers' eyes go wide.

Henna

Oh yeah, definitely!

Orio gives them the books and continues to pack up her belongings.

Henna

Thanks for the class.

Boden

Yeah, it was brilliant.

Orio

Oh, my pleasure. Yeah, it's great when you have such a nice group to teach, such as yourselves.

The Adventurers talk a little longer with Orio. Telling her where they are staying, so she can send a letter for training. After, they head back onto the street. From the outside of the building, they notice that the black hedges now are full of new colours.

Henna

Wowza!

They stand outside admiring the flowers.

Henna

I wonder has our vision changed to see them.

Bethany

Yeah, we couldn't see them before we went in.

Navek

It must be.

They look through the flowers, seeing all the nice new colours. Happy at the sight, they head down the street, watching the blanket of colours on the black hedgerow as they go. They smile to themselves before finally turning off the street.

Navek

Where to now?

Boden

I guess we go back to the inn.

The Adventurers walk together through the busy streets and back up towards the inn. The street outside is full of horse carriages.

Boden

I wonder if they are all going to the show.

Navek

Yeah, looks interesting.

They get back to their room and sit on their beds.

Henna

It's amazing now, what we can do with colours.

Bethany

Yeah, we would never have learned that if we were still in Olreon.

Bethany takes a small jigsaw from the room's cupboard, and they take a small round table from the other end of their room. Each of them has a small chair beside their bed, which they use to join Bethany.

Bethany

She's an interesting Witch.

Henna

Yeah, I wonder why she wanted to train with us.

Navek

Well, the wall guard are very strong, maybe she wants to become more powerful.

Boden

I don't think it was that.

Bethany

Yeah, she doesn't seem the sort.

Henna

I don't know, she does know a lot about light.

Navek

Maybe we shouldn't show her everything.

Boden

She did say that you don't have to.

Navek

Might have been a ploy.

Bethany

Gosh, why so paranoid?

Navek

I'm not paranoid. I'm just cautious about giving away our secrets.

Henna

Anyway, I don't think she would be into Corrupt Magic.

Navek

I guess you're right.

They start piecing together the jigsaw. The Adventurers work on it till dinner, and after eating, they go to bed early. The next day, they go down to get breakfast in the inn, to find it as loud and heavily packed as ever. They order their food and are squeezed in across from a group of Sprites. The Sprites are thin, long, strong and elegant looking. Their skin is pale yellow and their hair light purple. They have small dark violet horns sticking out of the front of their hair and fangs in their teeth. They have dark yellow, curving vine patterns framing their faces and going down in a thinner pattern over the side of their necks, across their arms and spreading out down the side of their chests. They wear loose white tunics, seamed with a gold stripe. Out behind them are large see-through wings, full of spiralling translucent colours and shapes, with a bright

106

golden strip at their edges. The wings seem to stick out through a mound of grey fluff. The Sprite in the middle has mostly clear translucent wings, while the pair either side have blue or green translucent wings and sit sideways, facing the clear winged Sprite.

Blue Winged Sprite

Oh, interesting, Wizards.

Boden

Hi, how's it going?

Clear Winged Sprite

We were just talking about you.

Bethany

Us specifically?

Clear Winged Sprite

Nooo! Your kind.

Bethany

Well, I hope it's good news.

Clear Winged Sprite

Well, yes and no. We were just talking about races that might come close to being able to fight a Sprite.

Green Winged Sprite

So, why are you Wizards in town?

Boden

We are Adventure Wizards, we travel from town to town.

Blue Winged Sprite

Interesting.

Clear Winged Sprite

Yes, very.

Green Winged Sprite

So, what do you do to make a living from town to town?

Bethany

We do odd jobs from town work centers.

Clear Winged Sprite

Interesting, yes, a good way to scrape together some coin.

Navek

What do you do then?

Clear Winged Sprite

We are storytellers.

Blue Winged Sprite

So, do you Wizards have any interesting stories?

Bethany

Yeah, a few.

Blue Winged Sprite

Well, I bet Salner here would be willing to trade you a story.

The blue winged Sprite says, nodding to the clear winged Sprite in the middle.

Blue Winged Sprite

I'm Tammis and this is Nairis.

He says, pointing to himself and the Sprite on the other side of Salner.

Boden

I guess we could tell them a story about Roarden and Sierra.

Blue Winged Sprite : Tammis

Roarden and Sierra?

Henna

Do you know of them?

Tammis

No, who are they?

Boden

Well, they are a group of Adventurers.

Clear Winged Sprite : Salner

Well, I am sure they are an interesting bunch.

Salner says, with a hint of disdain.

Salner

My story has quite a lot of gravitas to it. So, I'm sure you'll want me to go first.

The Wizards look at each other and smile.

Boden

Ok, fire away.

Salner

In a world of rock and clay, there lived a Sprite called Skulp, who was a very good sculptor. He would say to people "Hello, I'm Skulp the Sculptor". He would travel around from town to town, and everywhere he left would be more beautiful than when he arrived. Now, on a sunny day, he was travelling through a huge kingdom called Pearl, full of riches but very little beauty. People would ask him to make sculptures of this and that. Eventually he got so popular in the kingdom, with his sculptures popping up everywhere, he caught the eye of the Princess. So, she sent for him, and he was drawn to the court in front her. He walked up and bowed. He noticed that she was extremely pretty. He became smitten with her immediately.

Salner puts on a light calm voice for Skulp.

Skulp

How may I help you, my lady?

Salner

He asked.

Salner puts on a female accent which is quite high-pitched and girly.

Princess

You will make the most beautiful sculpture ever made, so as I can look upon it and admire it.

Salner

He bowed to her and promised he would. So, Skulp set out and started to search the beaches. He got some Sprites to help him try and find the perfect piece of granite washed up on the shore. After a long time searching the beach, he came across a rock which had streaks of marble running through it. Over the next days and nights, he worked tirelessly, carving his statue into the granite. Eventually it was finished, and a party was arranged for the great unveiling. On the day, all the Princess's friends were invited to see the unveiling. The statue arrived and was held under a giant cloth to be revealed to the party. The Princess would pull the curtain at the end of the evening. As the party proceeded, Skulp stood in the corner, nervous, and not wanting to talk to anybody. A food Server with a cheeky smile tried to reassure him.

Salner puts on an even girlier voice for her.

Food Server

I am sure it will be lovely. From what I see of your statues, they are the most amazing thing I've seen in all my life.

Salner

Now, Skulp, not knowing where to look in this party full of important people, took his food and didn't look up, muttering a "Thank you" under his breath and watching as the cheeky smile disappeared. Eventually the party was full and quite merry. So, the Princess decided it was time to unveil her statue. She tapped her glass, and the room went silent. Over to the sculpture she went and pulled on a long golden rope connected to the sheet covering the statue. The cloth hit the floor, revealing a statue of the Princess herself. It was perfectly crafted, the skin was soft and elegant, and the green marble that cut through the granite edged her face with beautiful highlights.

Salner smiles.

Salner

Silence, utter silence filled the air.

Then suddenly, the room erupted with applause. Nobody there had seen such a work of art in their life. The Princess was overjoyed with her statue. At the end of the party, she went over to Skulp.

Princess

I am going to put this in the courtyard in front of my castle. I am happy with what you have done. Please join me for a late dinner tonight.

The food the Wizards order arrives, and they begin to dig in.

Navek

Please continue.

Salner

Well, Skulp was so delighted, he said yes immediately. That night they dined together. Skulp saw such beauty in the Princess's face, he convinced himself that someday he would marry her. All they talked about that evening was things they liked. Fun conversations about foods and stories. So, as the dinner closed that evening, the Princess decided she would have another statue. This time it would be of her favourite animal, the Unicorn. So, Skulp would set out and find a piece of marble. Eventually he came across a big piece in the rose garden inside the kingdom. He got permission for its use and started creating a Unicorn. The rose petals from the garden over the eras had washed into it, creating veins of beautiful reds and pinks. So, another party was held by the Princess. Skulp stood nervously in the corner again as the party went on. Eventually it came to the time of the unveiling. The Princess pulled the drape, and the most beautiful Unicorn was shown to everybody in the room. After the event, Skulp and the Princess talked again about what they liked. The Princess went on about carriages, and interesting animals. So, she asked him would he carve a Lion. To this reply, Skulp said he would. The only thing was, that he needed gold, because the last sculptures were presents and Skulp never charged much for his other works. Instead of asking for pay, he said he would have to take a longer while to carve the sculpture. He would use his spare time to carve for others, so he could make a living. So, as he carved the head of the Lion from a spectacular piece of sandstone with sparkling gold dust in it. He also worked around town, carving small statues of rich people and the things they liked. Eventually, the unveiling

111

came and Skulp stood nervously watching from the corner again, as the Princess pulled the veil to her statue. The room was impressed, and the Princess invited him to dinner again. This time the Princess and Skulp went over their favourite things. Eventually the subject of marriage came up. The Princess said she would like to find a man that worshiped her. To this, Skulp nervously replied.

Skulp

I worship you my lady, you have such beauty, such depth.

Salner

This made the Princess laugh.

Princess

I can't marry a worker.

Skulp

But I think you are divine.

Salner

Skulp replied.

Princess

Ok then, if you make me a sculpture that takes my breath away, I will marry you. Since you have already done a sculpture of me, it can't be that.

Skulp

Ok, I'll try my best.

Salner

So, the next day he found a piece of quartz that was blue and translucent. He decided to carve some of the Princess's favourite flowers. It took him less time, as he barely ate and didn't do any odd jobs on the side. On the day of the unveiling, the Princess was watched by everybody, as the news that if her breath was taken away, she would marry a commoner. Skulp took up his usual spot, waiting. Eventually the statue was unveiled, everybody in the room was amazed at the beauty of it. When the curtain finally dropped, each person looked at the Princess, but she simply smiled.

It is truly a wonderful piece.

That evening, the Princess and Skulp had their usual meal.

I am sorry Skulp, it is an amazingly beautiful piece, but it didn't take my breath away. Maybe on your next piece. I will have to leave early, you are welcome to finish up your dinner without me.

Skulp sat there in deep thought. How could he come up with a statue that would take her breath away? He looked around the room, but there was nothing there to give him a clue. He racked his mind and couldn't think of anything. As he was thinking, something started to percolate in his mind, then suddenly he was interrupted by a noise. He thought:

<u>What is that?</u>

It was like a whimper. He looked around the room. It was coming from the serving chamber to the rear side. He got up and walked over to the sound. Inside, was a woman dressed in a serving outfit, with her head in her hands.

Are you alright?

She looked up, startled.

Oh, am, yes, I'm fine.

She said, wiping her eyes.

Food Server

Sorry to have disturbed you. I'll let myself out.

Skulp

No, it's quite alright. May I ask what you were crying about?

Food Server

It's fine, the story is my own, I am just a bit weak, that's all, don't mind me. Am…
so you're trying to create a statue that will take the Princess's breath away?

Skulp

Yeah, we seem to get on quite well. We talk about what we like, a lot.

Food Server

That's lovely, if there is anything I can do to help you?

Skulp

Well, I need to find the perfect stone. I think that's my problem.

Food Server

Well, there is a place I know of with a lovely rock.

Skulp

Yeah? What kind of rock?

Food Server

It's a beautiful moon blue rock. Meet me at moonlight tonight, outside the
castle gate.

Skulp

What's your name?

Food Server

Alea.

She said, a cheeky smile climbing over her face, the cheekiest smile that Skulp had ever seen. So that twilight dawn, they met outside the castle gate and walked through the fields, up to a spot on the edge of a cliff, overlooking the sea. There, she showed him a giant blue Azurite Rock.

Food Server : Alea

You are lucky.

Skulp

How so?

Alea

It is said that whoever breaks this rock, gets to make a wish.

Skulp

Silly superstitions.

Alea

I guess so. My dad would bring me out here and we would look at the stars. He said only those with a noble wish could break the stone.

Skulp

Well, I don't hope to break it, I only hope to carve it.

Alea

Isn't that what carving is?

Skulp

No, people think that, but you shape the rock, you don't ever break it in any way.

Alea

Well, I don't really understand carving.

Salner

Skulp sighed and looked up.

Skulp

Ahhh, the moon.

Alea

It's a beautiful gem, isn't it?

Skulp

I would love to carve it. It's what old sculptors would make their wishes on.

Alea

Do you ever?

Skulp

Yes.

Salner

They talked till morning, sitting on the rock, watching the stars and moon. They would argue passionately at times, other times they'd laugh, and sometimes sit still, lost in each other's words. Skulp wasn't sure if he liked her or hated her. When morning came, she had to go back to work, and he had to organize people to transport the stone. So, to his studio he took the blue Azurite Rock. But he was at a loss to what he would make the statue into. That night, he dined with the Princess, to try and gather information on what she liked. Well, she did like an awful lot of things. He felt ill talking to her as she kept on going on about what she liked, it seemed harder and harder to pick something to sculpt his stone to. So, he changed the subject onto the Staff.

Princess

Oh yes, I do like to gossip, specially about the Staff.

Skulp

<u>Great, another thing she likes.</u>

Salner

He thought. So, she began with the Waiters.

Princess

Oh yes, there's Kattello, who was an inventor, but now he makes our cakes. Think he still yearns to be an inventor. Silly profession.

Salner

According to the Princess, most of the Staff were slackers and didn't deserve the pay they were getting.

Princess

There's Alea, she cries a lot at night when she thinks nobody is watching. I just leave her at it. I reckon she slacks off a lot, too.

Skulp

Why does she cry?

Princess

Oh, her brother is sick and she's the only other person left in her family. She looks after him and buys his medicine. Mother says she doesn't work very hard, so she tries to keep her on her toes. So, I try the same, making her undo jobs she has already done, so she can redo them. There's Dawltin, he was a woodworker, but his customers dried up.

Skulp

Really?

Princess

Yeah, he owed a lot of tax gold to us, so he couldn't afford to buy wood or tools. There's a few more, but we can talk about them tomorrow night. I have to go now for another banquet, please feel free to finish your dinner.

Salner

At the end of his meal, he noticed the door to the servant quarters was open. Inside, there was a servant that was washing the dishes, cursing under his breath.

Skulp

Hello, is the girl I talked to last night, here?

Server

You mean Alea?

Skulp

Yes, that would be her.

Server

Some family emergency, left me to do the dishes, this is supposed to be her job.

Skulp

Where does she live?

Sever

In a little house on the edge of town.

Skulp

How do I get there?

Salner

The Server gave him directions.

Server

It shouldn't be hard to find, it is full of little decorations.

Salner

At this, Skulp set out to seek out her quarters. After looking around for a while, he found it, a tiny house on the outside of town. He knocked on the door and Alea came out.

Skulp

Hi, I heard you were staying here.

Alea

Well, my brother is very sick, I haven't been able to afford much food or medicines since the Princess cut my pay.

Here.

Skulp handed her all the gold he had earned doing extra jobs.

What is this?

Just take it, save your brother.

This is.... I'll help you make your statue.

You don't need to.

This will be enough to save him. I can never repay you. I will help you carve that statue, that's a promise.

Skulp spent the next few days musing over his sculpture. Alea didn't show till later. When she finally arrived, they started talking about what to make the sculpture. Alea was very smart and even though they argued, he had fun talking to her. She had an ace card, she knew the family's secret crest. Which was also the Princess's favourite secret, for she hoarded its image.

How did you come by it?

Well, before my father died, he used to make little butterflies for the royal family, that only they knew about. He made me a butterfly, but I had to sell it for my brother.

Salner

So, over the next few days, Alea helped Skulp create his masterpiece. As well as working at the castle, she also made him meals and cleaned up his room and washed his dishes. This left him able to do nothing but sculpt. After a lot of work on both their parts, they were happy, and it was finally ready to give to the Princess. At the next unveiling party, he didn't feel so bad, and his nervousness didn't seem to come to him, which he didn't quite understand, but he was thankful for it. Alea was there, serving food. She had told him about how, at the first party, she had said he would do great, but he seemed more happy now. She smiled her cheeky smile when she gave him his drink and walked off. That evening, he chatted with a bunch of other kings and princes from surrounding lands. A stern looking Prince offered him a job on the spot. His kingdom was a democratic kingdom, and he wanted to have a head of sculpting, to make giant statues of their favourite heroes and carve the people's houses till they looked elegant. Skulp politely refused, but the man said if he ever felt like it, the job would always be there for him. Finally, it came time to reveal the Butterfly. The Princess took up her position at the rope and made her announcement to the room.

Princess

I am a Princess of great influence and wealth, but even I may have my heart turned by a commoner. Like my great-grandmother before me, if I am impressed by a noble deed. I will bestow my love, the most cherished prize of all, to whom is worthy.

Salner

She pulled the cloth to reveal the most beautiful sculpture Skulp had ever done. The Princess almost fainted at the sight of it. Everybody in the room stood there, not breathing. Its beauty had taken everybody's breath away, not just the Princess's. Then and there, she agreed to marry him. Alea was so excited for him, she came up and congratulated him, while smiling ear to ear. The whole room was mesmerized. Afterwards, the Princess and Skulp had their usual meal. As he was talking, an old memory of his dad popped into his head. They were walking together along a coastline.

Skulp

Why are we walking, Dad?

Salner puts on another accent for Skulp's father.

Skulp's Father

I just need to let off steam.

Skulp

Why are you and Mum always fighting?

Skulp's Father

Hhh, my son, there's people in life that you will meet, and you will have nothing but good conversations and good times with them. There are other people who you will share your life with. Their happiness will make your heart sing, but you will suffer with them, they will suffer for you, and you will suffer them because you love them.

Princess

What's on your mind?

Skulp

Oh, just something my father said.

Princess

Speaking of what people say.

Salner

The Princess went onto another of her barrages about how she likes this and that.

Princess

Oh, here's some good gossip.

Skulp

Yeah?

Princess

Do you know that girl who helped you with the statue?

Skulp

Alea.

Princess

Yeah, Mother fired her tonight.

Skulp

Oh no, why did she?

Salner speech grows with anguish as he talks in Skulp's voice.

Princess

Yeah, you can't work for the kingdom and work for somebody else at the same time. She was working at nighttime to earn extra pay. She was cleaning some sort of filth. So, I told Mumma. I'm sorry, I know she was handy to have around, and I know it's a bit harsh of Mumma, but I agree, it sends out the wrong message.

Skulp

Wrong Message!!!

Princess

Don't worry now, you can have any of the other servants help you out, now that you will be royalty.

Skulp

But what about her?

Princess

I am sorry, we can't hire her back. I can't see why you would hang around with her, she is beneath you. Besides, it wouldn't do.

Skulp

Wouldn't Do!!!! If it wasn't for her, that statue wouldn't be.

Princess

I still think you could have done it without her, probably would have taken a little bit longer, that's all.

Skulp

But she'll starve without a job!

Princess

Ah, who knows, it's not our job to look after the little people. We are much too important to let it rob our minds.

Skulp

Rob Our Minds!! This is a good person.

Princess

I don't like it when you disagree with me Skulp, it doesn't suit you.

Skulp

Suit me, Suit Me!!! I'll tell you what Suits Me!!!

Salner

Rage boils over into Skulp's body.

Skulp

I'll show you.

Skulp gets up from the table and storms out of the room.

Princess

Skulp, come back, I'll tell you anything you want, don't get angry.

Skulp

Just like her to agree with me when we have an argument.

Salner

Skulp walked the halls till he found what he wanted. He grabbed it from the wall, stuck between a shield and sword, then he came back. The Princess was in shock.

Princess

Skulp, let's talk about the things we like again. Never mind that silly serving girl.

Salner

Skulp stood across from the Butterfly, revealing a mace from behind his back.

Princess

No, not my butterfly, no, please Skulp, STOP! GUARDS, GUARDS, COME, PLEASE
COME.

Salner

Skulp closed his eyes, ran at the sculpture and hit it with the mace, breaking it
into rubble. The moment he destroyed it, he disappeared.

Bethany

Disappeared?

Salner

An era passed and nobody could tell what ever had happened to Skulp. There
was a reward sent out for his arrest. During that era, Alea managed to just
scrape a living and keep her brother fed. Every full moon, she would go to her
spot on the cliff and wish that Skulp would come back, wishing on the moon as
Skulp did. As she watched over the era, the moon started to look a little
different, like it was slowly being transformed. Then, during a full moon, it was
there, clear in sight, the moon had been carved into a beautiful butterfly. That
night, like all the others, she wished that she would see Skulp again. When she
woke in the morning, a knock came at the door. She opened it to see Skulp. He
was standing there. He got down on his knee and proposed to her. The ring he
gave her was made from the moon and was a small, beautiful butterfly, just like
the butterflies her father made. They fled the kingdom and Skulp was given the
job of carving heroes with his new wife Alea and her healed brother. With
Skulp's help, they both became sculptors. Their statues where amazing and as
beautiful as Skulp's and they quickly became rich.

Henna

What happened to the Princess?

Salner

She had sought out Skulp, as she thought the moon statue was for her. Only to
find out from a very stroppy servant, that it was for Alea. Well, this didn't do,
and the servant was fired and well, there was an uprising in their country, led by
that very servant and the Princess ended up working for a living, instead of
being a lady of leisure.

Bethany

What happened to them afterwards?

Salner

Skulp had a family with Alea and they all lived happily ever after.

As he finishes, he pauses to take in the effect of his story. The Wizards look around, slightly teary-eyed and full of smiles.

Salner

I see you all really enjoyed the story.

The girls look at the boys and smile. Navek and Boden try to wipe away their tears before they are seen, but the girls each put an arm around them.

Salner

Well, we have to go, but when you're ready to tell us your story, we'll be waiting.

Boden

How will we contact you?

Nairis

We will be staying at this inn for a good while, send a letter to our name and we will join you with a meal.

Salner

Until then, we have other work to attend. So we probably won't be here if you leave it too late. It'd better be good.

Boden

We'll try.

Nairis

Don't mind Salner, take your time, we practically live in this inn.

The Sprites take their leave.

Bethany

That was such a nice story.

125

Henna

Oh, it was!

Boden

I hope they publish it, if they haven't already.

Bethany

That would be a great present.

Henna

So, which story do we tell them?

Navek

I'm not sure, we will have to leave that to later, we got other things coming up, the carriage show is soon.

Henna

I wonder what that will be like.

Boden

Yeah.

Bethany

Carriages are so rare in Olreon.

Navek

I would love to drive a carriage.

The Wizards wipe their eyes from after the story and finish up their meal. They head back up to their room. Boden takes out his diary and starts writing down stuff. Navek looks out the window at the end of his bed.

Navek

Still busy.

Bethany

Do you guys want to take a look at the Work Guild?

Henna

I suppose so, guess it would be more interesting than staring at the ceiling.

They get up off their beds and head out into the bustling streets below. The Work Guild on its outside is a large, circular, grey dome, with the edges of the dome leading to a short wall on the ground. The whole dome is grey and the short wall a slightly lighter grey. The name on the front is written in flat yellow. They head inside to find queues of people for every service inside the shop.

Bethany

Do you want to wait around?

Navek

Nah.

The Wizards walk back out onto the street.

Bethany

Where to?

Navek

I don't know, there's not many places we could just amble without being trampled.

Henna

I guess it's back to the inn.

Bethany

We could check out a library.

Boden

Yeah, good point.

The Wizards set out to find a library. They travel through several streets before they come across a place, hidden on the edge of a sharp bend in a thin cul-de-sac road. It has a flat square shape and is hidden from the road by the buildings close by. It has tall windows leading from the ground up to head height on its side. Only a small corner of the building sticks out into the laneway leading up to it, with a green railing running beside its path. Inside, there are a lot of

127

people reading away. The Adventurers split up and go to their respective sections. Boden goes off to the tools, buildings and invention section. Bethany and Henna head off to different ends of the craft section, and Navek off to the music section. They find books they like and take a seat at a long desk with wooden dividers between people. Boden opens a book titled: "Wonderful Digging Machines". Bethany takes out a book on stitching: "The Invisible Art". Henna picks a colour mixing book and Navek a book titled "Writing Music in Verso". They sit beside each other as they begin to look through their books. Boden looks at a machine with rotating buckets, kinda like a waterwheel, but in reverse. Navek looks at a song, written in a verso style with big swirls and curls, while Henna reads about how rainbows are made.

Henna

<u>Rainbows were thought to be caused by water droplets in the air, it was found not to be the case. Rainbows are created by an unknown vitality.</u>

As Bethany reads about knots, she leans in and notices something out of the corner of her eye. It's a section of the library, titled: "Dark Arts".

Bethany whispers.

Bethany

Look at that section.

The others lean and look over.

Bethany

I wonder would they have anything on the Legendary Abominations.

Navek

Let's have a look.

They go over to the section, as they do, the librarian gives them a concerned look.

Navek

Ok then.

The titles on the books are quite obscure, most of them are just named, with very few having a description of what type of book they are.

Some of these might be stories.

I guess we should explore them as much as we can.

They each take a book and sit back down to read it. Boden's is about poisons. Navek's about grave robbing. Henna's about parasites of the skin. Bethany's book has no title, but an interesting picture of a wild creature on the cover. They each look through their books, first checking the chapter names, then checking the index.

Bethany

Hey look, it says, "Legendary Abomination".

They come over to Bethany's book.

Bethany

It's in the index.

She goes to the page the index says. On it, there is a small part titled:

"Legendary Abomination"

Bethany reads.

Bethany

"Taming the Legendary Abomination"

"My technique was to use creatures that have Corrupted Magical Powers and see do any respond to them."

He goes on explaining the virtues of his technique and his experiments.

Bethany

"Legendary Abominations do not mix well with other creatures. We have put several creatures of corrupt nature in with them and they have not responded well. The creatures have mostly ended up being killed by the Abominations.

We may have to postpone the use of this technique, as the creature seems to be becoming more powerful the longer it's around here. The chance of it escaping again seems lightly."

They read through his suggestions about the project, till they come to a diary statement. Bethany reads.

Bethany

"Researching the Abomination has become a serious problem. I have tried to take myself off the case. I, and everybody else on this project have been suffering from serious depression. We have lost several team members... friends, to this hideous creature. Some lost from the depression itself, others, when it escapes and roams around the corridors, casually killing us. After a while, it always comes back of its own accord, and we try to imprison it again. It seems escape is a game to it, and we have to replace members of the team every time. Sightings of it killing are rare and strange, witnesses don't explain them clearly, saying odd and bizarre things, they usually become very addled while describing it and then trail off into gibberish or just stop talking mid-sentence. All other times, the team member simply vanishes, never to be seen again. Its intelligence is insidious. I don't like it, I don't want to be here."

The writing stops there.

Henna

Does it say anything else?

Bethany

Let's have a look.

The Wizards scour the book but find nothing.

Bethany

It seems to be a scrapbook on dark creatures. A collection of found information.

Henna

Hmm.

Boden

Well, that answers the question of there being more of them.

They look through other books, finding nothing. Eventually, dinner time comes around and the Wizards leave.

Bethany

I guess we come back and see what we can find.

The Wizards spend the next few days going and coming back to the library, reading through different dark art books. As they finish on a black evening in the library, they find that there are no other sources of information to be found of Legendary Abominations. As they go back to the inn, the sky bursts with rain. They manage to just get in before being drenched. They go up to their room and look out over the street. Below them is a beautiful sheen. The road is reflective and shimmery as the street below is drenched by the rain. The streetlights reflect off the dark ground and are surrounded by glowing drops. The window they look through is enriched with the little droplets and rivulets going down its front. The sound of rain and trickling water feels deep, as out on the street the coloured lights blur and a couple kiss below the lamplight. Most of the passers-by have umbrellas unfurled, and a different type of black is given off by the clouds and night together.

Navek

Still as busy as ever.

Bethany

You would have thought the rain would have slowed people down.

Henna

It's a beautiful sight, though.

Boden

Yeah.

The Wizards dress and get into their cosy beds. The shadow of the rain and window frame stretching across their ceiling.

Boden

I can't believe none of those books had anything more on the Legendary Abominations.

Bethany

Well, least we know a little more about the dark arts.

Navek

Ha, like that could help us in any way.

Boden

It's a pity, I was hoping to find something on the Death Wands.

Bethany

That would be worthwhile to know.

The day finally comes round for the carriage show and the wet weather hasn't changed. The rain still floods the streets in torrents of downpour. The Wizards get up and dress in special rain gear, with hats that are wide and act like umbrellas.

Navek

Hopefully this thing will be indoors.

They look at the address on the pamphlet.

Bethany

Ok, we have to go up to Canter Street. It's a bit of a walk.

As they go, the air smells cold and damp from the giant downpour. The crowds on the street seem a bit more sparse because they are holding umbrellas, causing gaps between the people walking by. They finally make it to Canter Street and to the address on the pamphlet. The place is a giant hall, running the length of the street and into the distance. The front is flat, grey pebbledash. The roof looks like the shape of barrels, cut in half from bottom to top and lain down on their side, side by side. The middle entrance is up a few steps and inside a low-ceilinged square room. They walk up and pay at the round ticket booths, their gold turning to little carriages whizzing around the pay tray. They walk through the brass turnstiles and into the exhibition hall. The inside is tall and full to the brim with people, bustling about between the stalls of parked carriages.

Boden

Wow, it's packed.

132

The Wizards walk through the hall and over to the first stall. They see a group of open-top horse-drawn carriages on show. The carriages each have different soft linings, with a big brown carriage having a massively thick bed of straw. Boden goes over and climbs in.

Bethany

Aaaa, Boden, I'm not sure you're allowed to do that.

She says, embarrassed and waving her hands.

Henna

Yeah, what do you think you're doing?

The men beside them, dressed like carriage workers, speak up.

Carriage Seller

It's fine, you'll actually find most of the stalls are allowing people to try out the carriages.

Boden is lying back in the carriage, staring at the ceiling, when the others join him. The whole carriage consists of a straw bed running down its inside.

Boden

Wouldn't this be great for a Sky Circle.

The others lie beside him and look up.

Henna

Snazzy.

Bethany

Sure is comfy.

They get off and thank the stall holder and move on to the next stall. There are several enormous Clydesdale Horses here. They crane their necks up at the giant horses, which look amazing with their white manes and thick hair at the bottom of their legs. They pass by, admiring their strength and sheer size. The man at the stall hands them a brochure and starts talking to them.

133

Stall Holder

These horses are used to pull very heavy loads and carriages. They are also trained to use horse-cycle carriages. They are exercised daily and are able to withstand being loaded directly without a carriage.

In the background there is pictures of a gigantic horse with a big boulder on its back. There are also pictures of the horses pulling wagons with huge weights in them. The Adventurers smile and take a brochure. The next stall, in contrast to the last, is full of little ponies, the size of dogs. They munch at small bales of hay scattered around the booth.

Stall Keeper

These ponies are excellent for people looking to buy their child a pet. They don't grow any bigger and can be ridden by young children.

The Adventurers run over and pet the ponies.

Bethany

They're so cute.

Henna and Bethany pet the smallest pony.

Henna

Can we get him?

Navek

Yeah, I would love to have him around.

Bethany

We could make him a summoning animal.

Boden

I don't think he would appreciate it.

Bethany

But he's so cute.

Boden

I don't think non-magical animals like summoning.

Bethany

Hhh, I guess you're right.

They hang around, petting lots of different ponies, the Wizards giving them all names. Then they return to the crowd, looking back over their shoulders longingly as they move on to the next stall. As they go, several groups of girls go over and pet the ponies. The next booth has more tools and equipment at it. The carriages all have special attachments for different things. Boden takes a chisel and carves on a lathe, while Navek uses a large spinning fan to blow air at passers-by, who smile back, bemused.

Stall Owner

The power for these tools comes directly from the horse.

At the center of the stall is a horse, pushing a rod connected to a large wheel in the middle. Onwards to the next stall, there they meet the Carriage Workers they met in the inn.

Hector

Oh, it's you, how goes your stay?

Bethany

Interesting so far.

Hector

Would you like to look at our carriages?

The stall they have is quite large, with a small roadway beside where the carriages are parked. Each of these carriages are large, with either tall, thin wheels or short, thick wheels. Some of the wheels are on wooden beams that are sticking out in front and behind the carriages, while other carriages have their body over the wheels.

Navek

Sounds good.

Tarver

Come on, let's take a ride.

They all get into the front section of the nearest black carriage. Inside, it has two rows of seats. They find a horse sticking its head out from the wall in the center of the back row. The girls sit either side, petting it.

Hector

The reason we keep the horse like this, is that we don't have to have several people to operate the carriage.

Tarver

The horse pedals the carriage and gets to look where it's going.

Hector

It is also easier to feed it this way and it is kept out of the elements, like most horse cycles.

Tarver

The horses have been trained to respond to mechanical signs.

Hector

So, here we go.

Hector pushes the foot pedal down in front of him, and the horse sees a mechanical dial above the front window. The horse's head starts to bob up and down as he cycles and the carriage lurches slowly forward.

Hector

This cycle is really comfortable for the horse to use.

Hector uses the steering wheel to turn the carriage onto the road beside their stall. They go around the track at sauntry speed, people watching from the crowd as they pass.

Hector

So, what do you guys think?

He asks, as they pull back up.

Tarver

Before you say something, look at how we feed the horse.

Tarver pulls on a lever and a food basket opens up under the horse's nose. The horse takes a nibble at the food inside.

Henna

Snazzy.

Bethany

Well, it's a very well-made carriage.

Henna

I like that the horse can see the road. I don't think I have ever come across a horse cycle with that in it.

They get out of the carriage.

Tarver

Well, it means you don't have to have a separate person in back, looking after the horse.

Henna

So, do you have any load carriages?

Tarver

Ah yes, come with us.

They go around a corner to find carriages which are each as nearly as long as a house, that have big wide wheels underneath them.

Tarver

Here they are. We are trying to find a buyer for these. They are some of the largest carriages there are.

Hector

Also, we are in talks with the Clydesdale stall over there.

He says, pointing to the stall they had just visited.

Hector

To get the right horses.

Tarver

We have quite a range on show, if you would like to see some others.

Hector

We also do luxury carriages, if you would like to take a look.

The Wizards are shown over to the few of their carriages that are painted white and have intricate carved window frames. The doors have lace patterns running between the frames and pillars. The carriages sit on tall, thin wheels, that are on long curved suspending arms sticking out the front and back.

Tarver

If you would like to get into the passenger seats, we will take it for a spin.

The Wizards go over and get in behind the horse cycle bit of the carriage. Inside, the carriage has soft white seats that face each other and feel squishy when they sit on them. The carriage starts to move as they close the door.

Tarver

Hey, will you set up the bumps.

As they go, his helpers lay out several small bump shapes onto the road. The carriage takes them easily, leaving the Wizards barely feeling them as it goes over each.

Hector

So, what do you think?

He asks, as the Wizards get out of the carriage cabin.

Henna

Excellent.

Boden

Yeah, amazing.

Hector

Thank you, it's great to finally show them off.

Some of the people who were watching as the Wizards got out of the carriage come over to their stall.

Hector

Better get going.

Tarver clasps his hands together.

Tarver

Well, when we are getting ready to go, we will leave you a message in the inn, so we can do the Job.

The Wizards bade them a farewell and move on to the next stall. At this stall there are human powered carriages, they are made of a dark brown wood and are generally smaller. Each carriage is pedal powered. Some have trunks at the back, and others have several places for people to pedal, most having large areas for carrying luggage. They hear a stall worker speaking to a potential client.

Stall Worker

The mail guilds tend to use these to transport mail around the worlds. They are cheap and a great alternative to having to buy a horse. They are made from the Daner Tree, whose branches are as strong as iron.

The Wizards go over and have a look at the pedal carts. They see a small set with small wooden boxes at the back for luggage. The cycle sections have frames of square wood, with black spoked wheels. The seats are big, soft, squishy and run the length of the crossbar, stopping under the handlebar connection. The Adventurers each take a cycle cart, Boden taking a cycle with a small basket at the back. They head out onto the path behind the stall. Boden whizzes around, quick as lightning, pulling wheelies and donkey kicks. The others cycle around at a leisurely pace.

Navek

These are nice.

Bethany

Very comfy.

Navek

Ha, look at Boden.

Navek says, as Boden does a really big donkey kick.

Bethany

Yeah, zingy. What do you think of buying some of these?

Henna

If there was a foldaway cycle it would be handy.

Navek

These are made for transporting goods along the Road Worlds.

Boden stops his whizzing around and comes up beside them.

Boden

These are great! Pity they don't have any off-road cycles.

Bethany

Yeah, would help us get from place to place.

Navek

I don't think the off-road cycles could handle the places we go.

Bethany

Yeah, you're probably right.

They leave the cycles back at the stall and head on to the next area. Here there are warthogs instead of horses.

Stall Salesman

These warthogs are excellent for somebody looking to travel from town to town in a small-sized cycle.

The man shows the cycle with the warthog in it.

They are very comfy inside the frame, and they love to run. They have powerful legs and can outrun most other cyclists on the path.

After that, the next booth has experimental fire cycles.

Boden

I wonder have they got any further with these.

The Wizards look in the booth. A downtrodden man greets them as they walk in. Around the room are silver, brass and black contraptions, with lots of wheels and odd shaped pipes and cylinders emitting streams of smoke or steam. Gears and cogs are running in odd directions in them and interlinking in odd paths.

Man

Hi there.

Boden

How's the research coming into fire cycles?

Man

Well, we have been working on steam for an age and still haven't made any progress. It has the most power of all fire-based engines and still isn't enough to compete with horse or man. We have worked with firework powders and explosive gasses, but these seem impossible to turn into any form of useful energy. What we hear from the different people working on it, as well from what we have done ourselves, it looks like there might be a Certancy that means travel powered by fire and fuel will never happen. That man and beast power will always be the way carriages and carts work.

Boden

Aww, are you sure?

Man

Well, we haven't seen any major progress. And the Certancy looks like it may indeed be there. You Wizards wouldn't have any tips?

Navek

Not really, most of our stuff is magic powered.

Boden

Yeah, our firework powders all contain magic as well.

Man

I see, well, it may just be a dead end.

Boden

Is there anything that shows promise?

Man

Sail power might be competitive, but only at sea is there any form that can be used. But no, engines that run on fire, I'm afraid not.

Bethany

Hmmm, it's tough.

Boden

Yeah, we wish you the best!

Henna

Good luck!

Navek

Hope you find a use for it.

Man

Thank you.

They move on.

In the next area they find a ship and some small boats. There is a sign that reads:

===

"These ships are cycle ships, and they are the fastest of their kind."

"We are hoping they will be able to surpass the sea's wind power for transport."

===

Navek

I wonder will they be able to compete.

Boden

With the wind, ha, I think not, on land, yeah, no problem, but on the sea, wind sailing has never been beaten.

At the next stall, there is free food and brochures for events in the hall they are in. There they see a Wizard they recognize.

Chandrin

Hi.

Henna runs up and gives her brother a hug.

Chandrin

Hey Henna. Ah, you guys have made it here, brilliant! Hey Boden, Navek, Bethany, how are you all? It's lovely to see you.

Boden

Hey, Chandrin.

Bethany

We're great.

Navek

Yeah, nice to see you, Chandrin.

Chandrin

So, how goes the adventure? Done anything interesting? Gotten into any trouble?

Henna

Oh, you wouldn't believe what has happened. We saved a Prince and got into a big water fight.

Chandrin

Interesting, I would really love to hear all about it. I am kinda on business at the moment. Maybe you lot would like to come around tomorrow to my offices, and you can tell me all about it.

Henna

Awww, but we wanted to hang out with you.

Chandrin

Ok, well you can come around with me to the stalls, but I will be talking business at most of them.

Henna

Brilliant!

Chandrin

Ok, but I warned you.

They eat the tasty finger food at the stall together.

Chandrin

So, Boden, how's the inventing going?

Boden

Oh, well, last thing I made used Glink Magic.

Chandrin

Glink Magic, really? You managed to do something with that?

Boden

Yep, Henna was a big help.

Henna

Yeah, it's an amazing Staff.

Chandrin

Well, I must say I am impressed.

Boden explains the Staff to him.

Wow, I might be able to trade them, if you get back home for a while and fancy making more.

That would be good.

How about you, Navek? Got any new Defence Magic moves?

Well, I've been working on some to defend against the stronger spells.

Any headway?

Well, not at the moment, but I am hopeful with the Wall Magic training.

Oh brilliant, you have started that training. Can't wait to see how you get on. What about you, Bethany? How's the healing going?

We went to the colour museum and met a Witch that taught us about Healing Light.

Ah yes, I must go and have a look at that.

You haven't been?

It's funny, but all the eras I've been here, it never occurred to me to take a break and have a look around.

Chandrin takes out a notebook.

Chandrin

I have to go to the next stall, you are welcome to join me. If you get bored, you
don't have to stay.

Chandrin says, as they begin to walk around.

Henna

What are you looking for here?

Chandrin

Well, I was hoping to expand my trading into the Road Worlds. So, I am looking
for carriages.

Henna

Have you taken on any new goods?

Chandrin

At the moment, we are looking at some more preserved foods. As you know,
certain herbs only grow in certain worlds and certain towns. So, we are opening
them up to other villages as much as possible. We are also looking into some
heavy goods. Some of the carriages here have sparked me a bit of interest in
that area. Also, I'm looking at some new minerals. The knight groups have come
across a new metal called scun metal.

Navek

They have opened up a mine for that in Sunlin.

Chandrin

That's some useful information, thank you.

Henna

Have you seen the stall where the horse gets to see out the front? Hector and
Tarver run it.

Chandrin

Oh yes, I was quite busy talking to them. It seems like an ideal way to transport
goods. I am still unsure if I'll go with them, though.

Henna

Why?

Chandrin

Well, there are still a few wizard carriages I haven't seen.

Henna

Wizard carriages, brilliant.

Chandrin

Well, there is a problem with them.

Henna

What's the problem?

Chandrin

They tend not to be made to carry heavy goods. Because most wizard towns are self-sufficient, there is no incentive to build big carriages. I know they are probably better in most other ways, using magic and magical horses, but they aren't made for the heavy stuff. If there is some way I could get the companies to co-operate, it would make things quite handy.

Henna

Yeah, you'd be stiff competition.

Chandrin

Precisely, you always have to see what other people don't see. Well, that carriage company that you were talking about are willing to do a deal with me, if I can find a wizard carriage builder for them to work with. I was thinking of buying both companies and bringing them under my umbrella.

Henna

Wow, will it cost a lot?

Chandrin.

Not too much, I have budgeted for it.

Navek

Look at that.

Navek gets distracted by a big battle carriage nearby, with all manner of spikey things sticking out of it.

Boden

Wow!

Chandrin

So, what are you guys planning to do while you are here?

Henna

Well, we are going to join the Card Tournament.

Chandrin

Oh, interesting, you should get to compete with some of your fellow Olreoners in that.

Henna

Well, maybe.

Chandrin

I saw a big bunch of them arrive from a carriage the other day, and I transported another bunch via my ships. I took part in a Spirit Game Tournament eras ago, too.

Navek

Yeah?

Chandrin

It was great, I got the bronze medal.

Navek

Ohh, very good.

Chandrin

Well, it isn't gold, but considering I was starting my company at the time, I was quite pleased with it. The game wasn't as popular as the Cards, though.

Boden

Well done!

Chandrin

Thanks. So, here we are.

The Adventurers and Chandrin come to a stall with magic carriages. Chandrin goes off and starts having a conversation with the stall holder, a stocky looking man with a serious face. Beside them, they hear another member of the stall, who has a wide face, and is explaining how the carriages work to an old looking Human.

Stall Holder Wizard

Well, you see most wizard machines have globe handles.

He says, pointing to a set of round balls that are sticking out of a table at different heights in front of him, sitting on top of elegantly carved rods.

Stall Holder Wizard

They are made like wand handles and are imbued with magic. A wizard can power them simple by holding them.

He puts his hand on the nearest, and light flows down through the rod's carvings.

Stall Holder Wizard

But most wizards prefer to send out streamers, so their hands are free.

He takes his hand off it and sends out a streamer from his chest. The glowing, flowing, colour tendril connects to the orb, and it lights up again.

Stall Holder Wizard

Inside each of the carriages, you'll find a globe like this.

The Adventurers come over to have a go at the globes. There are shiny brass-coloured globes and dark brown wooden globes, some with rings of light brown wood or bright scratched brass. Some have fiery dark red inlays of rings or flowery lace shapes running through them. There's some made of wire-like cages, that when they are fed magic by the Adventurers, fill with little lightning clouds. There are large shiny mahogany handles with brass stars, and some globes with magic that raises up off their surface and flows across them, massaging the hand.

Old Human

So, what materials do you use in these globes?

The old man says, holding up a pair of glasses with the frame arms closed across the back and a little beaded chain hanging down to his pocket.

Stall Holder Wizard

Like a wand, we use wood.

Old human

And?

Stall Holder Wizard

Nothing else, all the handles are made from wood.

Old Human

But isn't that brass?

Stall Holder Wizard

No, it is a type of wood that looks like brass. You will actually find that most wizarding brass comes from a tree.

Old Human

Interesting. So, how do the magic horses power the carriages. Do they have streamers as well or do they use those spark fellas I heard all about?

Stall Holder Wizard

Only wizards are able to create streamers or sparks. The horses can send their magic through their hooves and power the carriage that way. But we are able to create connecting streamers that can join the horse's magic to a handle.

Old Human

I see. My client is interested in fast carriages. What can you tell me about them?

Stall Holder Wizard

Well, you will actually find the fastest carriages powered by wizards are Cycle Magic carriages. We use both a handle globe and foot powered linkage. The magic flows out through our feet and into the pedals as we cycle, creating a form of magic cycling. The fastest carriages overall are a combination of Horse and Wizard Magic, with the horse also magically pedalling the vehicle. If you like, I can show you around them.

The Adventurers leave them and go take a look at the carriages themselves. They head over to a small, wide carriage, that is coloured dark purple and has gold stars dotted over it. They duck their heads to look inside. There they see several rows of soft, squishy, deep looking seats, made from a lighter purple, that are also dotted with gold stars and a globe handle in the middle, that sticks up between the front seats.

Navek

I wonder what it's like to live in a town that needs these to get around in.

Bethany

Maybe we'll find out.

They walk on through the wizarding carriages, very few of them come close to the size of the first carriage that they got a ride in with Hector and Tarver. They pass the man and stall holder again.

Old Human

So, very few of these have steering wheels or columns. How do they steer?

Stall Holder Wizard

We are able to control steering through our streamers, but some have steering implements, like wheels or handles, especially the fast cycle carriages. We use Steering Magic to create our way.

Old Human

You certainly do a good job on the design of your carriages. Of all the carriages I've ridden in, none have been as comfortable as a wizarding carriage.

151

He runs his hand over an elegantly carved Lion face on the carriage in front of
him.

Old Human

Nor have any had so much attention or hard work gone into them. Your
carriages are so full of carvings and decorations. It soothes the eyes just to look
at their beauty.

Seeing the carriages in front of them from a fresh perspective hits the
Adventurers. Those around them are full of intricate carvings, blacks with
shimmering night sky designs, glossy whites, pale pastels, and fantasy colours.
There are large flowing carvings that draw the eye across them and feel deep
and comforting. Some carvings are like the surface of a brackish swelling sea,
others have incredible forest scenes with animals running through them. They
stand around, looking at the carriages as if they were just dropped into the
middle of an art exhibition.

Chandrin

Ok, well I am going to have a little look around.

Chandrin says, coming up behind them. He smiles, looking at their faces and
their grins.

Chandrin

They certainly are beautiful.

After a while of looking through the lovely carriages, they go out and Chandrin
says goodbye to the stall holder.

Navek

Hey, can we have a look at this stall?

They travel across to the stall that had caught Navek's attention earlier. At the
stall, a band of Knights sit in front of their carriages.

Knight Stall Holder

Hello Wizards, may we interest you in our battle wagons? They have been made
to transport people through rough terrain and areas known for their raids and
safety issues.

152

The carriages behind the shiny armoured Knights are large, thick, grey metal wagons, that are full of spikes, looking like castles on wheels. Some with rows of the spikes around the top and bottom, others looking like a porcupine, completely covered in them.

Chandrin

Interesting, very interesting.

Henna

What do you think you'll need them for?

Chandrin

Well, I was thinking, if I start a transport service, I might branch into people carrying. The upcrust tend to be frivolous with their spending and love their security.

Chandrin

Do you have any luxury class battle wagons?

Chandrin asks, as he takes a Knight to convers over at the side. The boys ask a pair of the Knights if they can have look inside. They go over together and open a carriage door, made from a thick heavy armour. It swings out slowly and Boden and Navek get in.

Knight Stall Holder

As you can see, there are several crossbow slots and spear areas.

Boden and Navek look through the thin slots that have sliding hatches.

Knight Stall Holder

You can fire out, but they can't fire in. These here are special slots that allow you to reach your arm and sword through.

Boden and Navek look at them, smiling at the thought of a wagon having a sword fight with a person.

Knight Stall Holder

Would you like to have a go?

Their eyes light up.

Navek and Boden

Yes, please!

The Knights smile, each pulling out a short and shiny sword and handing them to Navek and Boden. The boys' faces a joy, they take the swords, sticking them in the slots and sliding them through. The carriage keeps their arms sealed from the outside as they push through. Armour unfolds in a fluid motion, feeling like smooth clockwork metal bands enveloping their arms, covering them in a new way they have never come across before. The armour makes their arms feel strongly comfortable, like their skin is made of metal. As the girls watch on the outside, the arms fully unfurl out of the carriage. The sharp points of their swords raises out and their armoured arms form a taper. Square and rectangular shapes form interlocked scales that coat the surface of the boys' arms.

Henna

They're having fun.

Bethany

Heh, heh, they sure are!

Navek

Wow!

Boden

Zingy!

Navek

En garde.

Boden

Ha, ha, take that.

Knight Stall Holder

Ha, I've never seen Wizards enjoy armour so much.

Navek

It really feels good to wear.

Knight Stall Holder

Our next carriage will be made from scun metal from Sunlin.

Navek

Oh interesting, scun metal, yeah, we heard about that.

Knight Stall Holder

Do you think you wizards would be willing to buy armour?

Navek

Well, our guard might.

Knight Stall Holder

Hmm, interesting.

Navek

It would probably have to be like robes, though. Wizards hate wearing non-robed outfits.

Knight Stall Holder

I think we could do that.

Navek

What town are you from?

Knight Stall Holder

We are from Creedin Town, and you lot?

Navek

We're from Olreon.

Knight Stall Holder

Ahh, Olreon, fairest Wizard World in all of Tream Heartaya.

Navek

Ha, that's very kind.

Knight Stall Holder

Well, you did help us out in a time of trouble. For that we have never forgotten.

Navek

How did Olreon help?

Knight Stall Holder

Your town lent us Guards against the War Of The Vamperish.

Navek

I've never heard of that war.

Knight Stall Holder

Those were dark days. We drove them back though, and they have never bothered us since. With the help of Olreon's magic towards the end, there was peace.

Navek

So, there is no sign of them?

Knight stall holder

Well, since we used the Knight Walls, we haven't heard sight nor sound of them.

Boden

Knight Walls?

Navek

They are like our walls, practically indestructible.

Boden smiles.

Boden

So, what else you got on this carriage.

Knight Stall Holder

Well, we've got a monster ball and chain. I can't really show you it in action, as it might kill somebody.

He pulls a lever in the ceiling of the carriage and a ginormous bright silver ball with small square spikes, and a thick, shiny, curled up chain is revealed.

Knight Stall Holder

This is mainly used to take out other battle carriages.

Other Knight Stall Holder

It also makes the carriage hard to get at.

Outside, the girls stand beside Chandrin, engrossed in his conversation.

Helmless Knight Stall Holder

If you would like to buy our company, we would more than welcome a Wizard at the helm, given the right price.

Chandrin

Well, I am a pacifist, so, your carriages would be used more for royalty that wanted to look powerful or up their security. That's why I was suggesting teaming you up with the builders of the luxury carriages.

Helmless Knight Stall Holder

Well, it does sound interesting. If that's where the market is, we will adjust.

Chandrin

Brilliant, I will take your details and contact you over the next while.

Helmless Knight Stall Holder

Quite right.

The boys come over to them with large smiles on their faces.

Bethany

So, did you boys have fun?

Navek

Yeah, it's amazing, this cart!

They walk to the edge of the stand.

Bethany

I thought you didn't like hurting people.

Navek

Of course, we're all pacifists too, but it's still fun to look at.

Henna

You boys and your toys.

Navek

Man, I wish this tournament was Castle Crashers, rather than Spirit Cards.

Henna

Ha, well, you're still unbeaten in Cards.

Navek

True, but Alvay and I had that near match.

Bethany

Yeah, I think she thought she had you.

Navek

Well, hopefully she won't come to the tournament.

Henna

Alvay was a force, she scared me.

They walk on to the next stall, which has holiday carriages. All the carriages have rooms that fold out and their insides have ovens, chairs, beds and little pot belly stoves. The furnishings seem thin and light, made from tea coloured wood.

Henna

Wow, look at them.

Boden

Do you ever think of travelling by carriage and living like this?

Bethany

Maybe someday.

The Wizards walk on, and Chandrin catches up.

Navek

You couldn't get over a mountain or go through a deep forest.

Bethany

True, but it sure looks snug.

Henna

Do you think you'll be buying that knight company?

Chandrin

Maybe, if I can get some people into rich social circles, I can pedal them.

Henna

Nice pun.

Chandrin smiles.

Chandrin

I Just want to look at the wagon carts before I go.

Bethany

What's the difference between a wagon cart and a carriage?
I always thought they were the same thing.

Chandrin

Well, a wagon cart tends to be very cheap and a great way to carry a lot of
goods. The idea is to use them in trains. Basically, wagons carts are designed to
be attached to each other to amplify storage. But they are not the safest form of
transport. I only plan to use them on private roads.

Henna

You are going to buy roads?

Chandrin

Well, we will see, maybe someday. There are toll roads I will use to start with. You have to be a reputable trader to use them.

Chandrin brings his hands together.

Chandrin

So, I will see you guys in the morning. I gave myself the day off tomorrow, so we will be able to spend the day together.

Henna

Brilliant, we can feed the ducks.

Chandrin

Yeah, like old times. Where are you staying, so I can call in?

They tell him the inn's name and their room and with that, Chandrin says goodbye and heads off.

Bethany

So, what do you guys want to do now?

Navek

I guess we check out some of the other stalls.

The next stall they check out has a chart on the wall. It says, "Animals used for carriage and wagons". On the chart, there are horses, hogs, elephants, rhinos, bears, camels, wolves, ox and plenty of others. To the end of the chart it has cycle carriages, and there it has wizards, demons, sprites, knights, vampires, humans and horses again. They walk on, and the next stall has the mail service carriages. They listen to the man at the stall.

Mail Representative

The Inner Mail Guild is owned by several kingdoms and runs with heavy-duty carriages. In a lot of kingdoms, we use our own private roads to deliver mail. We also own several seafaring ships. Our service is the fastest way to communicate in the known world.

160

Navek

Well, I guess they are confident in themselves.

Henna

Yeah, well, they are the best mail service out there.

After that, they move on to a group of large, luxury carriages. A sign above them says, "Win The Grand Prize Of A Grand Carriage". A man in the middle of the stand above, on a podium, begins shouting out.

Show Man

All you have to do is enter your name for a draw, and you could be the proud winner of a beautiful grand carriage.

Henna

A grand carriage, I wouldn't mind travelling in that.

Boden

What's a grand carriage?

Henna

Well, it is a giant carriage, commissioned by a king or queen. It's ultra-luxury. Some of them are as big as the biggest delivery carriages.

Bethany

You gonna enter your name?

Henna

Yeah, definitely, god, travelling around in that, I would feel like a princess.

Boden

Ha, you and your princesses.

Henna

Hey, I don't say things about your pirateyness.

Navek

Ha, pirateyness.

Boden

Shut it.

Boden says, with a smile. Henna and Bethany go over and enter their names into the draw, for a small fee.

Bethany

Well, it can't hurt.

Bethany says, when she returns.

Henna

I don't think we'll win, but hey, it's just a little dream.

They move out to the center of a junction.

Navek

I think that's everything.

Boden

Well, it was very interesting.

Bethany

The stuff about the magic carts was zingy.

Boden

Yeah, I knew some of that already.

Bethany

I kinda thought you would.

The Adventurers leave the show and head back out onto the streets, where the rain has stopped. The convention hall looks bright and cheery in the shining sun. They go to a little dining hall to have dinner. They sit in the widow and watch the busy street pass by.

Bethany

Hanging with your brother tomorrow?

Navek

I hope he has something exciting in store for us.

Henna

I don't know, when he's not working, he's thinking about work, and he will always talk about business. Hmm, well, maybe we will do something exciting. He was always good when he organized things for us to do.

The Adventurers all eat a dish with tape-shaped noodles and a clear, pungent, vegetable broth.

Bethany

Well, I guess we call it a night.

Henna

Yeah, we want to be up early if we are hanging with my brother. He's an early starter.

The Adventurers travel back through the rain washed streets and head straight for bed.

In the morning, they wake early to a knocking on their door.

Chandrin

Hey you guys, are you awake?

Navek

What's going on?

Navek say, tiredly and Henna gets up.

Henna

It's my brother.

Navek

What, why? The sun isn't even up.

Henna

It's Chandrin, he's always up well before sunrise.

Boden

Uuugh, what's going on?

Henna opens the door to let her brother in, she pulls on the oil lamp in the ceiling to open the shutters in its sides, so as to let out the light.

Chandrin

Sorry, I'm a bit early, am I?

Henna

We're all kinda still in bed.

Chandrin

Oh, I'm sorry, well, if you would like me to come back later. I just thought we could watch the sunrise at my docks.

Chandrin says, quietly, as Henna rubs her eyes.

Henna

Wait outside. I'll get these lazy bones up.

Chandrin goes and waits in the hall.

Henna

Ok, up you guys, time to rise.

Navek

Aww, it's so comfy.

Boden

Yeah, cosy.

Henna goes over to the boys and grabs their blankets and pulls them off their beds.

Navek

Aaaah!

Boden

Come on, Henna.

Bethany gets out of her bed, face scrunched and joins Henna. The Wizards change separately in the bathroom. They join Chandrin in the hallway, gloomy eyed and hands in their pockets. The morning air is dense and dusty.

Chandrin

Brilliant, let's go.

The Adventurers follow in a tired silence. As they go, Chandrin acts like a tour guide to the city, explaining how he had to do this for some of his clients.

Chandrin

The inn you're in,

He smiles as he makes the pun.

Chandrin

was used as an old bank, that's why the room doors are very hard to break into, not that I've tried, but the inn itself uses that fact as a selling point.

They go down the road.

Chandrin

The streets of this place are always busy, day in, day out. The traffic consists of traders, merchants, entertainers, people going and coming from work and because most places are open all day, It's usually shift workers. Jobs can start at any time. There is also a lot of traffic from other towns because Trader City isn't just a merchant hub, it's also a traffic hub. A lot of the other towns don't have direct connections to each other, so they use Trader City to get to where they are going. Most traffic at night isn't from other towns though, it is usually locals and some tourists. People love Trader City because it's always open.

As they go through the city, Chandrin points out some old buildings with marvellous features and interesting back stories. There are tales of feuds and accounts of people making names for themselves. They travel on to his company building, the outside of which is wide and squat, with many storeys and is shaped like a wide loaf of bread, seen from the front. Its walls are a pale sandy colour, with a pale pink hue on the band of skirting along its bottom and on the fat mantlepieces below the small, square windows.

Chandrin

I've given most of the Staff the day off.

The Security Guard greets them as they go through the main door.

Guard

Morning, Chandrin.

Chandrin

Morning, Tal.

They walk into the large bright hall, full of desks and little white dividers. The floor is light wood, and the walls are like the outside, pale sandy yellow.

Chandrin

Ok, there isn't much to look at in here. The building is mostly offices and stores. The brilliant thing about this building, though, is the size of the underground store house, it's the size of several warehouses.

They follow him upstairs and into a room with a few desks around and over to a table near a window with a picture of Chandrin with Henna and their family, framed nicely. Chandrin picks up a basket and they leave.

Chandrin

Ok, let's go out and watch the sun rise.

They travel out back, which is a lot darker and only lit by the grey morning and faint starlight. The place has a stone ground, leading to a huge dock that has lengths of decking and boats rigged up.

Chandrin

I have several other warehouses along the shore here.

He explains, as the boats shift slowly up and down, and a low ding is let out by a buoy.

Chandrin

Ok, come on.

They travel out along the coast path at the side of his docking area, on its dark, weather-worn, differently sized, square stone slabs, that have a dusting of sand and crabgrass. Chandrin takes out a thick white blanket from his basket and they sit on it, overlooking the sea. He also takes out some sandwiches that he prepared earlier. They eat away at them, the chewy salady taste, full of interesting new leafy vegetables, little cubes of cheese and vegetable chutneys.

Navek

These are good.

Chandrin

Thank you, I made them up from some of the foods I deliver. We usually get samples before we decide on trading them.

As they sit there eating in silence, a ray of light streaks across the sky. They watch as the rays burst forth and the sky's blue starts creeping across. Then the tip of the glowing orb peeks out into the morning sky. As the sun rises, the water turns a deep blue, and the sky around the sun glows golden. The Wizards sit there in awe of the beauty, silent and contemplative they watch it for a while, nibbling on sandwiches. Warm yellow light glowing on their faces and the cold, salty salad sandwiches washed down with freshly squeezed orange juice from the basket, they feel vibrantly alive.

Henna

So, what do you have in store for us today?

Chandrin

Well, a grand day out with your older brother.

Henna

Yeah, but anything exciting?

Chandrin

Isn't that exciting enough for you?

Henna

Well yeah, but I thought you would have something else planned.

Chandrin

Maybe I do, maybe I don't.

Henna

Come on.

Chandrin

You'll see, later.

As they look out to sea, Bethany notices a lighthouse off in the distance.

Bethany

Oh, look over there.

Navek

What is it?

Bethany

A lighthouse.

Navek

Oh yeah.

Bethany

We found out a bit on lighthouses in the colour class.

Chandrin

Yeah, they are handy.

Bethany

What do you know about them?

Chandrin

Well, we use them to navigate. They make course creation very easy, and they make path creation very simple. They also have their own small Sea World.

Bethany

Their own Sea World?

Chandrin

Yep, it helps for navigation. We can use them to create a Lighthouse Path directly to the lighthouse. You interested in lighthouses?

Bethany

Yeah, they kind of feel cosy. I like the idea of living in a lighthouse.

Chandrin

Well, they used to have them for the land, until they came up with the Road Worlds.

Bethany

Pity.

Chandrin

They could still use them for the Road Worlds, it would be handy if there is flooding or subsidence in the roads, but I guess that's rare enough these days.

Chandrin turns towards the group.

Chandrin

So, you lot going to enjoy the Card Tournament?

Henna

Hopefully, it will be a bit of fun.

Chandrin

Well, the Cards have become quite popular with the wizarding community, so, a lot more people are travelling to see it. The stadiums are huge.

Henna

Scary! A whole stadium.

Chandrin

I heard you were the guys who got it banned in school.

Boden

Well, I didn't mean to.

Henna

Gosh, you should have seen their match, it went on for an age.

Bethany

Yeah, I didn't think you and Jared would ever finish.

Chandrin

Jared, I remember you told me he was called "The Assassin".

Navek

Yeah, he is like the anti-Boden. He was known for taking out the hardest players.

Boden

He also likes to pick on the weaker cards. That's what had me take so long. It was hard to keep my pack alive while he put all his time into trying to kill the weakest cards.

Chandrin

So, what were you guys called?

Navek

I was "The Hammer".

Chandrin

Yeah, I can see that.

Navek

I didn't really think I was a hammer, though.

Henna

Well, your style is very powerful.

Navek

I guess so.

Henna

We gave you that nickname before you played Cards, he, he.

Chandrin looks at Henna.

Henna

"The Mystery"

Navek

Yeah, you should see her play. The opposition never knows what hits them.

Henna

I did the best I could.

Chandrin looks at Bethany.

Bethany

I didn't play.

Chandrin

Ah, I see.

Bethany

Well, I have a lot of Spirit Animals. But I never like competing. I played some of the nicer Spirit Games.

Chandrin

Yeah, the tournament I played in was a different Spirit Game. But the Spirit Cards seem to be all the rage nowadays.

Navek

Yeah, I actually prefer the Castle Crashers Game.

Chandrin

I wonder is there a way that we could get non-wizards in on the Spirit Games. Might make some gold there.

Henna

Ha, you're always on about gold.

Chandrin

Sorry, I said I wouldn't today. So, Boden, what do they call you?

Boden

"The Survivor"

Chandrin

Interesting name, why do they call you that?

Henna

It's because he hasn't lost a single card in battle.

Navek

Yeah.

Bethany

And he also hasn't destroyed a single card in battle either.

Chandrin

How can you win without destroying cards?

Navek

With great difficulty.

Henna

Yeah, they were gonna call him some slow nickname, but when they realized they were fit for another game after losing to him, they called him "The Survivor".

Chandrin

It's funny, I remember when Henna first met you.

Boden

Me?

Chandrin

Yeah, she seemed to brighten up, it was like she found herself.

Boden smiles quizzically at this.

Chandrin

Beforehand, she seemed so lost, like she was stuck.

Henna

I suppose I was stuck before I met Boden.

Bethany

Boden is great at getting people unstuck.

Chandrin

Rule of business, surround yourself with good people and they are worth more
than all the gold at the end of the rainbow.

Henna

You and your rules of business.

Chandrin

I find them to have served me well.

Henna

He read this book when he was in school, all about proper business people and
since that, he's had all these rules from the book.

Chandrin

Well, yes and no. I've made some of them up myself. Well, after she met Boden,
she was full of go.

Bethany

Ha, really?

Chandrin

Yeah, it was like she was a changed person. She also gave up those poisonous
friends of hers. I think that helped too.

Henna

Yeah, they were quite horrible to me after I made friends with Boden.

Chandrin

Well then, you were better off.

Henna

Much better.

Chandrin

But after meeting Boden that day, you were changed.

Boden

Wow, I didn't realise I had such a profound effect on people.

Bethany

You do a bit.

Henna

I was a bit dispirited alright.

Chandrin

Ahh, we were all worried about you.

Henna

Really?

Chandrin

You seemed all alone.

Henna

Then Boden comes along with his crazy notions.

Boden

I suppose my notions are a bit crazy, ha, ha.

Henna

They are wonderful, do you remember the first thing you said to me?

Boden

That you could create who you wanted to be?

Henna

It's because after that day, I realized I wasn't who I chose to be, I was driven by my fears. And from that day forward, I would design who I wanted to be and try and become it.

Navek

Yeah, I had a similar experience when I met you lot.

Chandrin

Well, you are a wonderful group of friends.

Chandrin looks up into the sky.

Chandrin

My friends are all a bit different.

Henna

Ha, ha, they are mad about business and love that way you have of treating people.

Chandrin

What way is that?

Henna

You always treated everybody like how that book told you to treat business people. It used to get on my nerves.

Chandrin

Yeah, I do that a bit, don't I. Sorry.

Henna

That's who you are, it's more endearing now.

Henna kisses her brother lightly on the side of the cheek.

Chandrin

Well, you guys could do motivational speeches about friendship, have you ever thought about that? You'd be very good. I'd say it would pay very well.

Henna

Chandrin!

Chandrin

Sorry ha, ha. I always have business on the mind. So, would you like to look around the port?

Henna

Yeah, sure.

They get up and take a stroll around the docks. The moored ships look strong and stable. Their hulls are made from a mild brown wood and have thick, black wooden beams running around their edges.

Chandrin

These ships here, are all wind powered. We do have some fast ships that are wind and horse powered. You can't see the sails because they have been taken in for improvement. On the very fast ships there are also kite sails, but they tend to be used less often because of stability.

They walk up onto a small ship. Its hull is as thick as a tree trunk.

Chandrin

When the ships are full of cargo, they sit further down in the water. You have to make sure you don't over-stock them, or they might sink.

They look into the center of the ship, there is a big cargo hold, which is a huge hole in the floor, covered by a purple force shield.

Chandrin

We use a special type of storage to improve the cargo as it's transported.

They walk around the ship, looking at the massive thick anchor and the large round steering wheel set inside the captain's room.

Chandrin

Wheels on the outside decking of a ship provide more powerful steering, but we prefer our crew to be indoors as they sail.

Below deck, they see that the rooms have either hammocks or beds, and each of these have a thick blue blanket and white pillows.

Chandrin

Most of the crew prefer hammocks, some still use beds that are magicked to stop them rolling out.

They head back to the shore. The coast running along and connecting to either side of the port, with waves lapping as they go. Chandrin takes them inside the closest of the large wooden warehouses.

Chandrin

Inside, we store different goods.

Inside, the warehouse is full of wool from floor to ceiling.

Bethany

Wow, that's a lot of wool.

Chandrin

Yeah, we send it on to the woollen mills of several companies. The robes I am wearing today were a present of the Ashland Spinnits' mills.

They head back out to the dock.

Chandrin

I was hoping to connect a pathway to my docks, as part of my roadway business.

Henna

Brilliant.

He shows them a crane next to the warehouse. It has a plain blue, square cabin, sitting on tall, thin, square legs that bend midway, forming a mild outward bendy zigzag, like a tall insect's legs. The crane's arm is made from several long, strong beams, with zigzag metal bars going in between them, forming a lattice structure.

Chandrin

It's human made. We usually use a horse to power it, but it has been modified so we can use it too.

They go up a ladder inside the leg.

Boden

Glad this is inside and not on the outside.

The cabin at the top is plain, with a square window in the front and before the window is a small round stool with a cushion on it. In front of them is a lever with an orb at the top of its handle. Chandrin uses his magic on it, and the crane lurches and moves around. He lowers the lifting wire and lifts it back up again. He then moves it over a boat and shows them how it would work with it. The Adventurers have a go moving it around.

Chandrin

It, like all cranes, causes things to be in a lifted form. The crane moves the lifted form through a lift scape. This crane's lift scape being different from a wizard's crane.

He parks the crane and they come back down and go over to the offices. They head around to the front and go through the customer entrance, which has a large, sandy, semi-circular counter, a white roof, small chairs, and light-yellow grey carpet.

Chandrin

Here's where we deal with customers. The main desk usually takes most transactions, but it will also send somebody to an office desk to organize a bigger delivery or deal with somebody who has certain needs.

They go to the tearoom in the building and sit in a big cushy seat by the window.

Chandrin

It's funny that you're all Adventurers now.

Henna

I never thought I would be an Adventurer.

Chandrin

You, Henna, gosh. I thought it was the only job that would have you. Do you remember how we used to play Knights and Queens?

Henna

Yeah.

Chandrin turns to Boden, Bethany and Navek.

Chandrin

Well, she'd be the Queen and I'd play the gallant Knight. Except, I never got a chance to be gallant. Queen Henna would always have some adventure that she would go on and save the day. I was usually left looking after the running of the castle.

Henna

You loved the taxes and all that stuff.

Chandrin

Oh, I did, but I swear, you were more in love with adventure than you were with being a Queen.

Henna

I loved the outfits and celebrations, but I would like the royal life done my way.

Chandrin

Yeah, you were always running fast and climbing trees.

Henna

Ha, well, you were always there too, making games of this and that.

Chandrin

You liked my games?

Henna

Remember the leaf gold?

Chandrin

Yeah, that was fun.

Henna

We used to have pretend shops and pay each other in leaves.

Chandrin

I remember your school shop.

Bethany

Oh yeah, Henna's shop, gosh, that's a great era.

Chandrin

I remember you all running around at home, working on the store.

Henna

Bethany had her teddy and dolly healers, and she also made a few too and Navek had his magic toys. Boden sold fireworks, under the table of course. It was your leaf shop that inspired that and all those other funny business games that you came up with for us as kids. That and your food cart.

Navek

Food cart?

Henna

Yeah, he had a food cart he worked near some of the heavily trafficked gates, he would work at it after school.

Chandrin

That was a lot of hard work.

Henna

Well, it paid off. You wouldn't have all this if you hadn't started the stall.

Chandrin

Business Rule of Growth: Start small and if it works, the business will grow.

It's funny, looking back you were always my brilliant older brother.

Chandrin smiles at the compliment and leans over in his seat, putting his arm around her shoulder and leaning his head against hers.

Chandrin

So, you lot want to get some breakfast? My treat.

Bethany

Yeah, sounds good.

Navek

Thanks, Chandrin.

They wander out onto the streets, which are full of traffic, going this way and that. He brings them to the entrance of a very fancy looking street, where there is no traffic. The street is cut off from the other roads by a black iron railing that has a guard booth at the side. Chandrin goes up and pays the Guard to let them in. The road is black cobble, and the path is paved in white-grey granite, with streaks of light white. The buildings are all redbrick, with white pillars and white carved window and door surrounds. There are thick green hedges running in front of the buildings, each behind a black railing. Some of the buildings have vines running up their walls, and the street gives off an expensive aura.

Henna

Wow, fancy.

Chandrin

Yeah, I don't eat here often, unless I have a rich guest in town.

They go up to a dining hall called Mullgreins. It has Guards standing by the door and a man standing behind a little, raised, round tabled podium. Chandrin tips him with a gold stud on his cufflink. They are brought into a fancy room and seated by the Steward at a fine, round, white linen table, with tall stem glasses that have napkins in them. They are each given menus.

Chandrin

So, do you have any gossip from Olreon?

Henna

Well, the Guard have decided to pursue some Damned Wizards.

Chandrin frowns, with a quizzical look on his face.

Henna

Mom hasn't told you of the Damned Wizards?

Chandrin

No.

Henna

Or anything about our adventure so far?

Chandrin

No, but you've only been to Sunlin so far and you just arrived here.

Henna

Wow, yeah, am, ok, well we can tell you about the Damned Wizards.

They tell Chandrin all about the Orb in the forest and how it attacked a Wizard and how the King's nephew had been used as bait to catch it, and how the Guard had come to take over the search for the creature, and how it was called a Legendary Abomination.

Chandrin looks stunned as Henna finishes the story.

Chandrin

Wow, that's amazing, Legendary Abominations. Yes, I can't say that I have heard of them, but they do sound interesting.

Henna

Apparently, there are others too.

Chandrin

Hmm, I know a little about the Damned. I did a small history project on them.

Bethany

What are they like?

Chandrin

Well, they used a special type of magic, they called it Voranic Magic.

Bethany

What was so special about it?

Chandrin

Well, it was based on death, sacrifice and torture. It infuses the soul and makes you hideous.

Bethany

Terrible.

Chandrin

It is, and so were they. Power is all they craved, they wanted to destroy anything that they could not control. They would fight wars and then use the deaths and pains of war to feed their magic. If they had their way, there would never be peace.

Navek

How were they stopped?

Chandrin

Well, they fought amongst themselves so much that their power was brittle. There was also an age of Wizard Champions. To see such a creature in the ages of peace we've been having, isn't good.

Henna

How do you mean?

Chandrin

It was thought that the Damned Wizard faction were extinct, a relic of an older age, but to hear that there might be more...

He slowly shakes his head.

Boden

Do you think they are connected to the Damned Wizards of old?

Chandrin

Most certainly, the Damned tended to guard their teaching with religious ferocity. Some people even consider them another race.

Henna

Oh really?

Chandrin

I am not sure how closely we are related, but people like the idea though, because it detaches us from them and makes it so that wizards seem a lot less cruel. I also think the Damned like it because they think they are the ultimate race.

Bethany

I hope the wall guard can cut this off before it gets any worse.

Henna

Sounds like we need more Champions.

The Steward comes over and they order their food.

Chandrin

Well, the Age of Champions is long past, and a Champion is a rare thing now.

Navek

Father wants to bring back the Champion Training.

Chandrin

He's a good man, your father.

Navek

Yeah, I guess so.

Chandrin

Only a handful of Wizards have made Champion in this age.

Navek

He did it before I was born.

Chandrin

I remember, it made big town news. Mom and Father were very impressed.

Henna

Wow, you remember that?

Chandrin

Indeed, it was in all of the newspapers. He was the first in Olreon in a long, long time. It's not something you do lightly.

Navek

He has taught me some of the training used to become Champion.

Chandrin

Oh really, is it difficult?

Navek

Yes, it's incredibly hard.

Henna

You should see Navek train, he's amazing.

Boden

Yeah, he will make Champion.

Navek

Ha, I don't know about that, I kind of want to be an Adventurer more.

Boden

Sierra was a Champion.

Navek

True, but that's a long way away for me, and I reckon you will all catch up with me soon in the training.

Henna

The woman who taught our colour class will be giving us lessons.

Chandrin

Interesting. I really have to have a look at that colour museum, it sounds so intriguing.

Henna

If you could start a colour museum in Olreon.

Chandrin

You might make a pretty penny.

Chandrin and Henna smile at each other.

Chandrin

So, what kinda training do you think she'll teach you?

Henna

We were hoping to create more colours and learn some more Colour Magic.

Henna lets out a streamer in the colour she made in the class.

Chandrin

Wow, it's beautiful! Did you create that colour?

Henna

Yeah.

Chandrin

That's amazing.

Henna makes a little light show out of the colours she has. The Steward comes in from the background with their food, interrupting Henna's show. All the plates contain tiny, elegant food. There are little whirls and dollops smeared over the lace patterned delph, small beads scattered across it, and food rolled up in an interesting shape or with swirling contours.

Navek

Well, this isn't exactly a big meal.

Henna kicks Navek under the table.

Navek

Hey.

Henna

Don't be rude.

Chandrin

Don't worry, it's quite filling, besides, I want you guys hungry for dinner tonight.

Henna

Oh, where are we going tonight?

Chandrin

It's a surprise.

Navek

Well, least it tastes nice.

Navek says, as he eats his meal. The Wizards savour their food as each bite is a new taste experience. The food is very hearty and the round savoury flavours are very filling.

Bethany

So, what areas are you expanding into?

Chandrin

For now, I'm concentrating on land-based transport. I think when I have done that, I will start looking at other businesses and help them out with their attempts. I would like to get into some manufacturing. For now, though, I am going to concentrate on getting the carriage side of my business going.

Henna

You're gonna be great.

They talk away and finish up breakfast and move back out onto the street. They walk back to Chandrin's offices and spend most of the day talking about different business ideas and stories from Henna's childhood. There are lots of fun ideas and chats about games they would play and the things they would do.

Afterwards, Chandrin takes them to a park on the edge of town and pays them in. He and the Adventurers carry picnic baskets full of food with them as they head through the park.

Chandrin

Here we go.

They walk out beside a giant lake that is full of ducks.

Chandrin

We've brought enough bread to feed the whole lake.

The Wizards sit on a blanket and start to unpack their dinner. Chandrin takes out the paper bags full of bread. Each of them takes up a handful and starts throwing it into the river. As they do, flocks of ducks come over to eat the bread. The Wizards throw more, and some of the ducks catch the bread on the wing.

Boden

Ha, that's brilliant.

Each of the boys start throwing it further and faster to see if the ducks can catch them. Even the hardest throws are easily caught by the ducks.

Navek

Wow, that's amazing.

Some of the birds come up, and Henna and Bethany feed them directly.

Chandrin

So, do you guys know Henna's secret spell yet?

Navek

She has a secret spell?

Chandrin

Yeah, it's this weird cool power.

The Adventurers look at her and Henna frowns.

Henna

I don't know what you are talking about.

Chandrin

Remember when we were in Faltya?

He says, with a wink.

Henna

It's nothing, I told you to never tell anybody.

Navek

Oooh, it's embarrassing.

Chandrin

Well… no, it's kinda brilliant.

Henna

Well, he thinks it's brilliant. I don't.

Chandrin

Why don't you show them?

Henna

No, because it can backfire.

Chandrin

Oh yeah, that was funny, that time when it backfired.

Boden

This is interesting, you gonna have to tell us now.

Henna

Nope.

Navek

Come on.

Henna

No way.

Chandrin goes to say it and Henna launches herself at him and clamps her hand over his mouth.

Henna

If you tell them, I'll tell Mom about the time when you dressed...

Chandrin

Ok, ok, get off, heh, heh.

Boden Navek

Ha, ha.

Bethany

Siblings.

Navek

Reminds me of Roary and me.

Henna

So, what were we talking about?

Chandrin

Well, I think Autumn is soon to be around the corner.

Henna

Yeah, Summer is looking a little bit duller every day.

Boden

How does the Winter effect your trade?

Chandrin

Well, the seas can become very choppy, and storms can cause it to slow down drastically. But the need for fuels and food goes up, so it kinda balances out.

Navek

Have you ever lost a ship?

Chandrin

No, thank goodness, we don't go along any unknown routes.

Boden

I would love to explore the sea.

Chandrin

You still hankering after being a Pirate?

Boden

Ha, well, it's kinda like Adventuring.

Henna

You should have seen our side era, we were on a giant flying ship.

Chandrin

Side era?

Henna

Yeah, we created a side era to save the Sunlin Prince.

Chandrin looks at them with shock.

Chandrin

That's some seriously powerful magic.

Henna

Really, I thought it wasn't that big a deal.

Chandrin

Well, I've never heard of a side era being created by somebody. I mean there are naturally occurring side eras of course, but not made intentionally by a person.

He looks at them with admiration, shaking his head in disbelief.

Boden

It's a part of Adventure Magic, the side era creates the magic we used to save him.

Chandrin

Well, it sounds amazing. Maybe I should look into this Adventure Magic, might be good for business.

Henna

You and your business, I don't think it would help much.

Chandrin

Still, can't hurt to study up on it.

Bethany

We need a story for the Sprites when we get back.

Chandrin

Oh, you met some Sprites?

Henna

Yeah, you've met Sprites too?

Chandrin

Yeah, the Sprites we work with can be arrogant and they will talk down to people.

Henna

Yeah, sounds like the guy we met.

Chandrin

But they are some of my best customers.

Henna

He wasn't too bad, just a bit arrogant.

Chandrin

Yeah, they can be like that, some are friendly. I shouldn't generalise, though.

They continue to feed the ducks at the pond and chat away until it gets dark.

Henna

I think it's time we head home.

Chandrin

Yeah, I have a lot of letters to send, and I also have to organise to buy these carriage companies.

They get up and head together to the gate of the park.

Chandrin

Well, I will probably see you during the Card Tournament.

Henna

Yeah, that would be nice!

Bethany

And we can treat you to dinner.

Chandrin

You're too kind Bethany, but it isn't needed.

They reach the entrance to the park and say their goodbyes.

Chandrin

Can't wait to see some of the card battles. Been an age since I've seen a Spirit Game.

Henna

Brilliant, you can see me win.

Navek

You're not going to win, I am.

The group laugh together and bid their goodbyes. They take leave head back to where they are staying.

Bethany

Well, that was a lovely evening.

Henna

Yeah, it's great to see him again. He rarely returns home now, he is just so busy. I wonder what he will do with the carriages.

Boden

Knowing your brother, he will turn it into a gold mine.

Henna

Yeah, well, he will work hard on it.

Bethany

I love his rules.

Henna

Yeah, he's been spouting them off since I can remember.

Bethany

He should write a book with them.

Henna

Don't tell him that, he'll end up going into publishing.

Boden

What's wrong with publishing?

Henna

Nothing, he just doesn't need any more distractions. Sometimes he is amazingly focused, other times he would chase a squirrel if he heard it stores gold in its cheeks. Some of his crazy ideas!

Henna shakes her head.

Bethany

I think that's behind him now. Besides, he doesn't need to do business anymore, it's more of a passion of his.

Henna

Exactly.

The Wizards walk up to the inn, with the traffic somewhat calmer around them. When they get back to their room, there is a letter left for them in the room's mailbox.

Bethany

It's Orio.

Boden

Oh, interesting.

Bethany

She's training in the park tomorrow and has invited us.

Henna

Oh, excellent.

Boden

I want to do some card training. I know the tournament isn't for a while, but it's still good to get some exercises in.

Bethany

Well, it's not really a big deal. I mean it doesn't matter who wins.

Henna

Yes it does.

Navek

Yeah, it will finally seal who's the best Card player in the yard.

Bethany

Ha, you lot always took that way too seriously. Besides, there will be other players there from different towns.

Navek

True, but all of Olreon's contestants will be in the same branch.

Henna

There are other schools in Olreon as well as ours that played Cards.

Navek

Damn, yeah, we might not get to face each other.

Boden

The tournament might be structured so we won't face each other till the end.

Henna

I don't want you guys to find out my moves, I think I'll train separately.

Navek

Ha, always the mystery.

Bethany

I think I'll hit the hay, you guys have fun.

Bethany goes to bed and the others stand there looking seriously at each other.

Boden

I think I'll put up the tent so you guys can't see me train.

Henna

Yeah, well, I'll do the same.

Navek

Oh good, then I can train outside.

Henna

Good, then we can peek out of our tents and see what you're up to.

Navek

Damn you.

Navek, Henna and Boden put up their tents around their beds so they can train under them. They work into the night, with sounds and whispers coming from each of them, until Bethany gets annoyed and gets up.

Bethany

Guys, this is ridiculous, we won't be up to training tomorrow.

Navek

Right, training.

Henna

Yeah, I want to do some more colour stuff.

Boden

I guess I'll call it a night too.

Bethany

Thank god.

They leave their tents and Henna looks over to Navek.

Henna

And I thought you preferred Castle Crashers.

Navek

True, but Spirit Cards are still a really great game, and Boden is gonna be a hard opponent.

Henna

Hey, what about me?

Navek

Well, in truth, I am less scared of you.

Boden

Hey, The Mystery Girl hasn't lost a game.

Navek

True, but still.

Henna

Still what! Navek?

Henna sticks out her tongue.

Henna

Well, least I'm not a blunt hammer head.

Navek

Hey I...

Bethany

Enough, it's time for bed.

Navek

Oh, ok.

The Wizards get dressed and hit the hay.

Bethany

Thank god.

Henna

Night, night, blunt headed hammer.

Navek

Night, night, annoying mystery girl.

Henna

Ha, night slow poke.

Boden

Ha, night.

The Adventurers wake the next morning at sunrise. Bethany is first to get up.

Bethany

Come on, time to rise sleepy heads.

They each get up and dress, then afterwards, Boden, Henna and Navek just stand there, still tired from their card training the night before.

Bethany

Come on, we have to be early, or she might leave before we get there.

The Adventurers skip breakfast and head down to the park. They meet Orio waiting at the entrance.

Orio

You're early, that's good.

She looks the Adventurers over.

Orio

Are some of you tired?

Bethany

They were up late last night, training for the Card Tournament.

Orio

Card Tournament?

Bethany

Yeah, there is a Spirit Card competition coming up.

Orio

Interesting, in my day, Spirit Animals were the big thing.

Bethany

Oh, you played with Spirit Animals, they're what I like.

Orio

Yeah, we would spend eras in the Spirit Realms, earning their favour and playing with them.

Henna

I suppose cards are a bit easier to make.

Bethany

Cards are different alright, but still hard to earn and make.

Orio

So, you lot going to be up to training today?

Boden

Yes, definitely!

Navek

Don't mind us, we are made of stern stuff.

Henna

Yeah, I train like a champion.

Orio

Ok then, let's go.

The Wizards all pay into the park and head up to the deserted field where the Adventurers trained before.

Orio

Ok, so who has the exercise plan?

Bethany

Well, we each have an exercise we do, and we teach them to each other.

Boden

We can do my exercise first, it's the same as last time. I'll show you before we all do it.

Boden shows her the exercise.

Boden

I created it to target every muscle in the body. There are several variations for speed or muscle growth or endurance.

Orio

Interesting, I like that, very inventive.

Boden smiles.

Bethany

Inventive, now there is a word Boden likes!

Bethany smiles over at him.

Bethany

He loves inventions, he's always inventing.

Orio

Oh, an Inventor, inventers are amazing people. I've studied a lot about them.

Boden blushes.

Orio

This exercise is so clever. You don't mind if I use it as part of my regime?

Boden

No, go ahead.

Orio

Thank you dearly.

Boden

There is also this.

Boden also shows her the streamers made to resist his movement.

Orio

Oh, nice idea.

They spend the next while doing different forms of Boden's exercise, while people stop to stare or watch as they walk by. Orio choosing to do the speed exercise with Boden.

Orio

Wow, that's a full workout in itself. You are very fast.

Boden

Yeah, you're not bad yourself.

Henna

Boden has a family trait.

Boden

Yeah, speed is part of who I am.

Orio

A really good trait to have.

Navek

He lets us use his speed too.

Orio

Oh, I have a neat trick, if you would like to learn it?

Boden

Yeah sure, what is it?

Orio

Well, have you guys grown and imbued yourselves as a group?

Boden

In Adventure Magic, yes.

Orio

Well, you can pass magic through your Adventure Magic connection. If you can cast your enchantment or power on somebody, you can connect it into the Adventure Magic, so others in your group can use it.

Boden

Snazzy!

Orio

You guys are gonna have to stand in a circle, facing each other, to do this.

The Adventurers comply to her command and Orio takes out her wand of swirling colours.

Orio

Ok, encase yourselves in your Adventure Magic field that you created.

They send out the field around themselves, and it encircles them. Little orbs of their created colour dance among red, green, blue and yellow glowing marbles.

Orio

Ok, I want you to place both your hands in the middle, stacked together, so you are each touching.

They place their hands there, smiling around at each other as power surges through them.

Orio

I want you to create a ball over your hands from each of your own Adventure Magic.

A sphere of bright light forms over their hands, creating a new colour as though all their own colours were mixed together. It swells and convulses.

Orio

That's good, you're doing really great.

As they watch, golden bubbles boil out, oozing and dripping off like molten sugar. Next, a red lightning shoots across its surface, giving thundering sounds.

Then a blue fire engulfs it, flowing around its surface like a stream of smoke over rocks. Then green tendrils form thin lace-like herbal plant patterns across its surface. Orio comes over and sticks her wand and hand over the ball, the wand's tip glowing with her colour. The orb bulges with energy, little comets with exploding trails of their colours come off their chests and start to orbit it. Inside the sphere, the colours flow into elegant swirls, forming strange and beautiful endless shapes.

Orio

Great, now I want you to imagine this as a magical connection to your friends. They and you are a part of it. Now use these sparks.

Orio backs off and sends them the most beautiful, long, twisting sparks, made of endless shapes too. As they do as she says, the orb explodes out a shower of bright embers.

Orio

Now hold the orb and imagine your friends, imagine your friendship.

In their head, they see each other, the fun they've had, the games they've played and the times they've stuck together.

Orio

Now, imagine the orb and draw in its energy.

As they do, the orb starts to shrink and translucent pink ribbons with beautiful shapes flow out of it and around them in the air. The orbiting comets start dripping beautiful drops and blobs into the orb and along the ground, others flying out and shooting lightning into the sphere. Spinning rings of different coloured flames stream out and encircle the orb. The comets start to rain with drips as the rings get thicker and thicker. Eventually, the rain turns to curtains and the sphere forms a new, amazing colour. They look at each other, smiling, then BANG, everything collapses. They stand there and laugh.

Orio

There you go now.

The feeling is effervescent and flows through them.

Orio

I presume you can make others faster, Boden.

204

Boden

Yeah, I have an enchantment for that.

Orio

So, if you would like to imagine the sphere that you held together and send your
Speed Magic into it. Just think of your enchantment and connect it to that inner
sphere, then the others in the group will be able to use it.

Boden

Wow!

Boden imagines the ball of colour they created together, like outside, lightning
storms through it, rings of fire encircle it, lace-like ribbons weave its surface and
boiling dripping shapes orbit it. In his imagination, he sends a powerful burst of
Speed Magic into it, turning it red.

Orio

Now, if the rest of you would like to access it, just imagine the globe and use the
magic from within it.

They close their eyes and suddenly take off at full speed, running around as their
eyes open with surprise.

Navek

Ha, ha.

Henna

Oh my god, it's too fast.

Bethany

Boden, this is so zingy.

Orio smiles at Boden.

Boden

There's something you don't learn every day.

Orio

Well, I had a lot of friends who were Adventure Wizards, so they showed me how.

When they come back and stop, they smile at each other.

Navek

Wow, not even out of breath.

Orio

If Boden needs to, he can disjoin his magic from the orb. It's as simple as imagining it being detached.

Bethany

You sure know a lot about Adventure Magic.

Orio

Well, when you've been around as long as I have, you learn a few things.

The Adventures nod their heads in slight confusion.

Orio

With the spell, you can create a variety of orbs to send each other magic and other useful stuff too. You can also colour each orb to what you want for organization. When you go to create your next orb, try to give it a colour while you are making it. That way, you won't get mixed up and the others can tell that it's a different magic. If you look at the core globe you created as a whole, you will see those smaller globes you created as part of it, as they are grown from it.

Bethany

Thank you so much!

Boden

Yeah, it's really amazing magic.

Navek

Seriously snazzy!

Henna

Fun too.

Orio

So, what exercise is next?

Boden

Well, Bethany was doing this thing with her Healing Magic.

Bethany shows the pin trick to Orio. The group give it a shot, and Orio is able to do it on her first go, like Bethany.

Bethany

Wow, first try, I haven't seen that before.

Orio

Well, it's not my first time with medicine to be honest. I have had to learn a lot of first aid in my travels.

She smiles at Bethany.

Orio

Here is a quick tip if you'd like. Now in truth, you should practice first aid without this, but your standards are probably high enough to take it on, Bethany.

Orio goes over to Bethany, she runs a small blade from her pocket across the back of her own hand, leaving a small cut.

Orio

Ok, I want you to imagine some of your favourite trees.

Bethany imagines the trees down a long winding river, with long drooping thin branches and elegant leaves.

Bethany

Ok, I've got it.

Orio

Now imagine the green from that trees as vividly as you can.

Bethany

Ok.

Orio

Now push and grow that green into your Healing Magic and heal the cut.

Bethany places both hands over the cut on Orio, and suddenly a burst of green
light emanates from her hand, healing faster than the pin prick.

Bethany

Wow, WOW!

Orio

And that's why green is the colour of trees, they invented it. It helps to be
around them, like we are in this park, but you will always be connected to trees,
no matter where you are.

Boden

Wow, let us try.

They try to heal their pin prick with it, but it only speeds it up a little.

Orio

You need to practice with what Bethany gave you first.

Henna

Aww.

Orio

Is there another exercise?

Navek

Well, Henna taught us all how to do this.

Navek shines a shadow from a coin-shaped streamer in his hand, that causes a
small patch of ground near him to go grey.

Orio

Wow, a Shadow Torch, that's really impressive magic.

Henna

Yeah, I created it for fun, playing shadow puppets when I was younger.

Orio

Well, I am very impressed.

Henna teaches her the spell, and they each use the Shadow Torch like a puppet show. As Orio does hers, she is able to change the colour of the shadows.

Henna

Wowza!

Orio

Yeah, it seems to be able to accept dark colours.

Henna

How do you create a dark colour?

Orio

With great difficulty, it took me an era to make them.

They shine the shadow around, making interesting shapes. After a while they stop and move on to the next exercise.

Navek

Ok, so that leaves me.

Orio

Show us what you got.

Navek

Well, I was showing them my father's exercises.

Navek flings a fireball through the air, then an iceball and they connect, causing a small explosion, which causes a person walking by to jump.

Navek

So, the idea is to keep this up to strengthen your fireball and iceball.

Orio

Very good, that is a nice exercise technique.

They begin the exercise together. Boden, Bethany and Henna get tired after a while, having to stop, but Navek and Orio continue doing the spell for long after the others. The tired lot look on in amazement at the stamina of Orio and Navek as they continue the exercise. Navek's competitiveness shows in his face as they continue. Eventually he starts to show signs of fatigue, causing his spells to get smaller and then causing him to stop. When he stops, Orio stops. He bends double from his tiredness. Orio comes over and puts her hand on his shoulder.

Navek

You're as bad as Pop.

Orio

Ha, ha, sorry.

Navek

He would always outpace me with the fireball exercises.

Orio

Well, I have a lot of experience behind me.

Navek

But you look very young?

Henna

Yeah, I thought you were the same age as my brother.

Orio

Well, age is a funny thing. Sometimes you find it doesn't age you at all. Anyway, would you lot like to learn Magic Missiles?

Boden

They have their own opus form?

Orio

Yes, they do. They are not as powerful as a fireball, but they can follow targets.

Boden

Let's have a look then.

Orio

Here we go.

She picks up a stone and throws it through the air and then sends out a small little comet-shaped Magic Missile, that starts to follow the stone as it falls, hitting it before it lands and letting out a small explosion, breaking it apart.

Orio

You can also create missiles that can daze an opponent. So, let me teach you, and you'll be able to do both.

The Adventurers stand around her.

Orio

May I connect a streamer?

Navek

Sure.

Orio

The opus is simple enough, should only take a little while to learn.

Orio connects them up via a streamer from her hand, made from her own colour. A coil of energy whirs around the streamer. As they are connected, little fiery Magic Missile shapes dart over its surface. They spend most of the afternoon learning the Magic Missile Spell and its opus. Orio talking them through it, showing them the magic, and connecting them up every so often with her streamer to feed them magic and understanding. Eventually, they all manage to make the missiles. After everybody has it down, the Adventurers look tired, so Orio calls a stop to the training.

Boden

That was a good work out.

Henna

Yeah.

Orio

So, would you guys like to have lunch, my treat.

Henna

Sure.

Bethany

That would be great.

The Adventurers follow her out of the park and to a tall lunchrooms, with a mostly glass front, framed in blue, on the junction of several streets. Inside, the lunchrooms has mosaic floors that are composed of sandy yellow colours, and the walls are green, with golden stripes.

The lunchroom's Waiter greets them with a smile.

Waiter

Hi Orio, how's your day going?

Orio

Oh great, been training with my friends here.

The Adventurers each give a small wave.

Waiter

Nice to meet you all. So, any plans coming up?

Orio

I will be leaving soon for new lands.

Waiter

Ah, what a pity.

Orio

Yeah, I will miss it around here. Are there any seats upstairs?

Waiter

Oh yes, lots, the lunch trade hasn't come in, so it should be empty.

Orio

Me and my friends here will have the buffet.

The Waiter hands them plates and they go up a thin stairs in the wall behind the counter. They turn around on a landing and go further upstairs, leading them back out from the wall. This floor is completely empty of people and has a dark carpet full of thin stars. Around the room are low, rectangular, squishy chairs. The whole front and side of the room is completely glass, and along the wall, just outside of the stairs exit, is a stand with a small fire in a black grate and piping hot trays of meals that are self-service. There's mashed potato with fried crusty bits running through it and beautiful foods with new colours.

Orio

I taught the chef who works here. He's very good with colours.

Orio says to them, as she ladles mounds of rushels, which are little white doughy balls. There are falafel cakes beside pickle salads and sesame creams. Up above the food trays are hot beverages.

Orio

I really like the hot chocolate here.

She says, as she lifts the lid and ladles some into a cup. The Adventurers each choose food of their liking and go sit in the corner of the window, around a short square table, their seats looking down out over the street.

Bethany

It seems extra busy today.

Orio

Oh, this junction is seriously busy.

They look out and passers-by flow through the junction like a river, so thick that the ground isn't even visible.

Henna

So, you will be leaving soon?

Orio

Well, I wouldn't mind training every day with you, until I leave.

Bethany

Do you not have any more classes?

Orio

No, I am finished with them for the moment.

Navek

So, what will you do in the next town?

Orio

Oh, probably teach some other subject.

Boden

So, colour is not your only specialty?

Orio

Oh no, a travelling artist must know how to teach other kinds of art too.

They each take a sip from their piping-hot hot chocolate.

Orio

So, what kind of mischief have you been up to?

She asks, cheekily.

Henna

Well, we were part of a Masquerade, we started a water fight that is now a town event, and we saved a Prince.

Orio

Amazing, oh do tell me, I'd like to hear the whole story.

The Adventurers recount the events of the previous town. Orio marvels at the story, especially liking the tree swing and the water fight closing the town. When they tell her about the Orb creature and the Legendary Abominations, she grows more serious, but lets them finish the entire story.

Orio

Well, for the start of an adventure, you lot have seriously gotten yourself into a lot of mischief.

Boden

Well, we try our best.

Orio

Hmm, so you used the Arboura Narakabyss spell to save that man?

Henna

Yeah, it was very difficult.

Orio

It is an amazing magic. I am surprised you were able to do it at all.

Boden

Really? You know about the enchantment?

Orio

Yes, and I've only ever heard of very powerful Wizards willing to use it.

She looks at them, concerned.

Bethany

Yeah, I don't think we will be doing it again In a very long time.

Orio

I would seriously advise you to never do it again.

Navek

Really?

Orio

It's not a spell you do lightly.

Henna

Yeah, we were asleep for days after it.

Orio

I can imagine.

Henna

Have you ever done it?

Orio

Me, no, I am not an Adventurer. I'm not connected to Adventure Magic.

Boden

How do you know so much about Adventure Magic, though?

Orio

My friends were Adventurers. I would travel with them on occasion, and they would teach me the spells.

Orio stares off into the distance.

Orio

They wanted me to join their company, but I declined. Adventuring is a dangerous business, there is a reason there is so few of them left.

Navek

Yeah, the King of Sunlin warned us of the same.

Orio

Wise man. But the world needs Adventure Wizards, and I am glad that you have taken it on. Just stay safe.

Boden

We will, thank you.

Bethany

So, what do you know of the Damned Wizards?

Orio

Not as much as I'd like to know.

Oria looks contemplative for a while.

Orio

I wonder does it have something to do with the Temple of Grace.

Boden

Temple of Grace?

Orio

Yes, it is said that the Temple has changed.

They look at her, surprised.

Orio

I don't know what has happened, but the surface has changed again.

Boden

How so?

Orio

I don't know, that's all I've heard about it.

Boden

Hmm, nobody seems to know a lot about the Damned.

Orio

From what I do know, the Damned Wizards were thought to have all been wiped out, but I guess they survived.

Bethany

I wonder if there are many.

Orio

I will have to look into them. They were nearly completely wiped out when the Demon Wars began. Since then, they have never been heard from.

Navek

The Demon Wars were ages and ages ago. You are talking ancient history. How could they be connected if they were before that?

Orio

I know, but something must have survived over that time. It's most unsavoury.

Boden

Seems like an odd mystery.

Orio

Hmm, yes, this will be an interesting time for you lot. New Adventure Wizards, who would have thought it.

Navek

Do you have any more adventure stuff for us?

Orio

Well, I have some more Adventure Magic tricks to teach you, but first I want you lot getting stronger.

Henna

It's amazing how much Adventure Magic can do.

Navek

It's funny, I didn't think it could be so powerful. I mean, there wasn't much we could do spell-wise, other than that side-era enchantment.

Orio

Well, when you get to grips with Adventure Magic, you'll be surprised, most of its power comes from being a team. I do know some Adventurers that have used it on their own and it has really helped them, but it is rare for a lone venturer to use Adventure Magic.

Henna

So, what you gonna teach us?

Orio

You'll see when you're strong enough. I will add some of my personal exercises to your training.

They finish their food, talking about training exercises and Spirit Games.

Orio

Ok, so, I have some letters to send and places to be. We start early again in the park tomorrow?

Boden

Yeah.

Orio leaves and the Adventurers decide to head to bed early, so they are not tired for the training. They join her again in the park the next day.

Orio

Ok, so I want to show you the training I am going to have you do.

They stand around her, waiting for instruction.

Orio

I want you to encase yourselves in the Adventure Field again.

They back off a little and envelope themselves.

Orio

I need you to try and resist my magic.

She lets out a flat, knife-like streamer, and the end glows brightly as it starts growing into their field.

Orio

You are going to have to use only Adventure Magic. I'm going to need you to stop the streamer from invading your field.

The Adventurers comply and begin to try force her streamer out, using only Adventure Magic. They raise their hands and push hard with the magic. The streamer just sits there.

Orio

Push harder.

The Adventurers concentrate hard and put as much force in the magic as they can. Eventually, after a lot of effort, her streamer starts to recede.

Orio

Very good.

The streamer leaves the field and Orio looks at them, satisfied.

Orio

Now, try and counter this.

Orio lets out a cluster of knife streamers, like an array of sharp tentacles. They all pierce the Adventure Field. The Adventurers look at each of them and start to try and push out individual streamers. Orio watches, and no matter how hard the Adventurers try, the streamers sit in their field, not budging a tiny bit. They spend a very long time at it, till eventually, Orio stops them.

Orio

I know it's hard, but until you beat it, we can't move on. Start again.

The Adventurers grow their Adventure Field and Orio sends another cluster of knife streamers into it. After a while of pushing, Boden looks around.

Boden

We need to do this together.

The others look at him.

Navek

How?

Boden

Try and amplify each other's pushing.

Boden puts his hand on Bethany's shoulder and starts sending his Adventure Magic through her, and Navek does the same with Henna. With great effort, they are able to push the individual streamers out.

Orio

Very good, you were very quick on that exercise.

Orio creates a big fat spike streamer, as the last of her smaller tentacle-like streamers gets pushed out.

Orio

Ok, try and beat this.

She sends it in, and it pierces the field easily.

Boden

Ok, like before, except we boost in a line.

Boden boosts Navek, who boosts Henna, who boosts Bethany. Bethany raises her hand to the large streamer and pushes with all her might. The magic cascades through the Wizards, getting amplified much more than if they had each boosted Bethany individually. Bethany pushes and Orio's streamer dies away. After this, the Adventurers gasp at the air.

Orio

Ok, you can break now.

They let the Adventure Field down and bend double to catch their breath.

Orio

Great work. Very quick on working together.

Boden

Will we need to train more without each other's help?

Orio

Yes and no. You were supposed to work together. The gains you made from teamwork far exceed anything you would get by working alone. The enchantment I am going to be teaching you at the end of this training will require you to be strong in Adventure Magic. As I said, Adventure Magic is a Team Magic and you can train alone, but it won't strengthen you as much. There are still some benefits to it though, but nothing as big as team exercise.

They continue their training over the next while, each day getting stronger and stronger. As they go, each of the Adventurers start to get more of a feeling for Adventure Magic. On a bright sunny day in the park, while Boden is resting after he has finished the days exercise, he decides to try some innovation. He starts with a blob of magic and mixes it in the air.

Henna

What ya doing?

Boden

I was just wondering if I could invent something using Adventure Magic.

Orio

Have you been studying innovation long?

Boden

I have, well my dad and mum were inventors, so it kinda runs in the family.

Orio

That and Speed Magic. They're some nice family traits.

Bethany

Yeah, his parents are ultra-fast runners.

Boden

They both worked as Running Wizards in their youth.

Orio

Interesting.

Boden

Bethany's family has a lot of herbalists and healers.

Bethany

Also, my dad's side has mining magic.

Henna

And I have a lot of entrepreneurs in mine.

Navek

I inherited Arcane Magic.

Orio's eyes go wide.

Orio

You are from the Arbine Tribe?

Navek

Yeah.

Bethany

You know of them?

Orio

Yes, they are a seriously powerful Tribe.

Boden

They have quite a lot of powerful Inheritance Magics.

Orio

I can imagine.

Navek

Well, your Tribes are powerful too.

Boden

Still, Arcane Magic is incredible.

Orio

Ok, back to training. I want you to be able to get this spell before I go.

The Wizards go back to training hard. Over the days, they train in Orio's spells and theirs, becoming proficient in Bethany's healing, shining bigger shadows, doing Navek's for much longer and combining the different types of Boden's exercise into an even harder lone-style training. Orio's techniques start out easy, with them learning new ways to access their Adventure Magic, create a new opus with it and also some tips and tricks for combining their magics. Then she starts teaching them gruelling exercises that make all the other exercises seem mild. They train so hard that they go straight to bed after each session and wake up tired the next day as they go down to train again. Eventually, after many days of training, she decides that they should only do her training, otherwise she won't be able to teach them the enchantment. The days start to get shorter and hints of the change to Autumn start to show. She gives them a few days off to rest. Eventually, on her last day, they arrive together in the park.

Orio

Ok, today we're not going to be doing any training.

Henna

Really?

Orio

Yes, it's gonna take the whole session to get this enchantment right, so I don't want you worn out. We need to get ready. What spell language do you know?

Bethany

We were all taught Arillion[arr rill e in].

Orio

Brilliant, Arillion is the language I've seen used in this enchantment.

She takes them to a large, empty field and lays down several blankets far apart, for them to sit on.

Orio

Ok, this requires some spell work and chanting. So, I want you to sit on these blankets and put yourselves into the Adventure Magic Field again.

Bethany

We are very far apart.

Orio

You need to be able to project the field. My training has strengthened your magic so you can do this.

They go to their respective blankets and encase themselves in Adventure Magic.

224

Orio

Ok, project it out further.

She watches as their fields jump in size.

Bethany

<u>Wow, her training really did work.</u>

Orio

Ok, where your fields connect in the middle, create the new opus I taught you.

Inside the center circle, made of their overlapping fields, they create an orb. It takes the shape of an endless structure, made of patterns within patterns, flowing frames of vaulting shapes twisting inwards in spirals and branching throughout.

Orio

Ok, I want you to expand it.

They expand it as hard as they can, its endless structures flowing as they do. They manage to make it about the size of a person.

Orio

Ok, bigger.

They try harder, and the orb becomes bigger than a horse in size and starts to glow in their colours.

Orio

Not big enough!

She shouts at them.

Orio

Bigger!

The orb grows to the size of an elephant, the colours washing over the surface and the structures disappearing completely.

225

Orio

CONCENTRATE HARDER!

Eventually the orb becomes the size of a house, glowing very brightly in their combined colour.

Orio

Brilliant, now hold it there. I want you to project after me.

Orio stands on her tippy toes.

Orio

Ha va na do kan a.

Boden, Bethany, Navek, Henna

Ha va na do kan a.

Orio

Tor vo lo ca.

Boden, Bethany, Navek, Henna

Tor vo lo ca.

As the Adventurers speak the words, shining light surrounds their mouths, and it draws black symbols which fly over to orbit the orb.

Orio

Ok, now start to chant.

Orio starts to glow.

Orio

Valakor moralnor soralanor vorasha mashana.

The Adventurers begin the chant, and more symbols start to layer up. They continue chanting as ribbons of black symbols start flowing out. Eventually the orb is entirely encased in them.

Orio

Ok, now push the symbols into the orb.

The Adventurers continue to chant, and the symbols start to push in on the orb surface. They cause streaky fingers of black shadow to shine out where they sink into the orb. Near the edge of the clearing, a crowd has formed around them of passers-by, everybody seeming to wonder what is going on.

Orio

HARDER!

The letters dive into the surface, and suddenly the orb balloons out in size, encasing the Adventurers inside it. The letters now glow, giving off a liquid golden colour on the surface. The people in the park take a step back, some running as the orb expands out. It spins around slowly, getting faster and faster. The surface appears to roll in the oddest of ways, as if it is not travelling, even though it is. Inside, a wash of bright light shines out, giving off dusty wavy rays. The shapes of the Wizards can be seen, as their own colours engulfs them, shining through it. Suddenly, the orb collapses in towards each of them, and a loud explosion sound resonates through the park. They lie back, exhaustion overcoming them.

Orio

Brilliant, Brilliant!

The crowd around them begin to cheer, as if they had just seen an amazing theatrical show. Then they suddenly stop and disperse on their way to wherever they were going.

Orio

Great job guys, brilliant.

The Adventurers catch their breath, stand up and walk slowly to Orio.

Bethany

So, what was that?

Orio

It's an Exercise Magic Field. You now have an aura of Exercise Magic running through you.

Henna

Wow!

Orio

It basically means that you are always training now.

Boden

Always training?

Orio

Yeah, you'll never lose out and you'll always be exercising, no matter what you do. Do you know the way if you stop training for a long while, you can silt up and gain weaknesses?

Navek

Yeah.

Orio

Well, no matter how long you leave it between exercises, you won't suffer any losses. Not only that, as you go about your day, you will be exercising.

Boden

So, we will always be gaining.

Orio

Exactly. If you ever want, you can stop the field. But you won't need to unless you are very injured or near death, as the field is self-supporting.

Navek

So, how will it affect our normal training?

Orio

It will enhance your training and the exercises you do will become incorporated into the aura and you will always be training in them.

Henna

That's pretty amazing.

Boden

Yeah, hyper training booster.

Boden bends over, then the others follow, their breath caught in their chests.
Orio gives them a while to catch their breath.

Orio

Come on, we will need you to eat up. No more efforts for today.

They head off sluggishly and as they travel, they slowly emit little fizzling embers
of their colour.

Bethany

What's all this?

Bethany says, pointing at an ember.

Orio

Oh, that will be gone in a few days. It's just part of the magic.

They go to the lunchrooms on the junction and Orio sends them up to sit down.
They each take a big plate of food and some hot chocolate and sit by the
window, emitting small fizzles.

Boden

I don't know about you lot, but I feel like I could sleep on a pile of rocks.

Navek

Yeah, I could just nod off here.

Orio comes up and joins them after grabbing a small plate of food.

Orio

So, I take it you're tired?

Bethany

Yes, I feel almost asleep.

Orio

Well, I am glad I could give you something before I left.

Boden

Who came up with that?

229

Orio

I did.

Boden

You did? But I thought you didn't do Adventure Magic.

Orio

I don't, but it doesn't mean I can't create magic in it.

They look at her, tired and confused.

Orio

Ok, me and my friends invented it together.

Boden

Oh, so they provided the Adventure Magic?

Orio

Precisely.

Henna

So, where are you going to go now?

Orio

Oh, I'll probably wander on to some of the college towns. There's a non-magical art class I'd like to teach.

Henna

Well, we'll miss you.

Orio

Aww, thanks, I'll miss you guys too.

Bethany

Is there any way we could stay in touch?

Orio

Hmm, I don't see how, but I reckon I'll see you guys again.

Henna

Well, we could give you our address, if you would ever like to send mail our way.

Orio

That would be great.

The Adventurers write down their home addresses on a sheet napkin and give it to Orio. She smiles as she seals it with magic and puts it in her bag.

Orio

So, what are you guys up to next?

Henna

Well, we need a good story for the Sprites we met in the dining hall, and we are gonna help out these Horse Carriage Makers, they found a gem cave.

Orio

Oh, a gem cave, it's been an age since I've visited some of those.

Henna

Have you been to many?

Orio

Yes, they are quite fun to find. It's very rare, but they can still be very dangerous.

Navek

We will be cautious.

Orio

An important thing to be.

Orio smiles.

Bethany

We don't really need the gold at the moment. The last town we were in left us flush, but still an adventure's an adventure.

Orio

Spoken like a true Quest Wizard.

Bethany

The old term for Adventurer.

Orio

The gang I hung with preferred that term.

Orio cleans off her plate as the rain starts to drip outside.

Orio

Well, I have to prepare now. I have done most of my packing. I hope you don't
mind if I leave early. I was eager to be out on the road before sundown.

Bethany

No, we don't mind.

Orio

I'd take a little nap here before you walk back. I talked to the store owner, he
said he wouldn't disturb you.

Boden

Brilliant, thanks.

The group get up and hug goodbye and kiss her on the cheek.

Henna

Thanks so much.

Orio

No, thank you. It is so great to hear there is a new generation of Adventurers.

Henna

We will repay you someday.

Orio

Pass it on.

They stand there, slightly teary-eyed of their goodbyes.

Orio

Well.

She smiles, a hint of sadness behind the smile.

Orio

I wish you the most amazing adventures and the greatest of challenges.

She turns and leaves.

Boden

<u>An adventurer's goodbye.</u>

She leaves down the stairs. The Adventurers watch out the window. The sky grey as she takes to the street and pulls her coat across her chest. She walks off down the road, disappearing into the crowd. As the Adventurers watch out the window, the sky grows greyer, and it begins to rain. The people in the streets begin to become blocked out from view by umbrellas. The Adventurers watch the window as it begins to flow with droplets of water, creating a twinkling bubbly shimmer. Eventually they lay back into their long cushy chairs and gently fall off to sleep. Boden wakes after his snooze and opens his eyes. Behind him, people are starting to fill into the lunchrooms, and the night is black outside.

Boden

I think it's time we get up.

The others slowly open their eyes and sit up.

Henna

Yeah.

They get up, rubbing their eyes and stretching. More and more rain-washed customers start to come up the stairs and fill the dining hall. Quietly the Wizards shuffle out past them, down the stairs and onto the street. Outside, the rain is coming down in torrents. The Wizards pull off their pointed hats and walk under the canopy of umbrellas from the people marching the street. Eventually the canopy breaks and they find themselves getting wetter and wetter. They reach the inn, drenched. Inside the entrance, they ring the bottom of their cloaks dry and are given a set of dry slippers to put over their shoes. They walk up to their room, open the bright oil lamp in the ceiling and change into their bedclothes. Outside, the water makes a trickling noise, as well as a pitter-patter.

Navek

I think I'll light a fire.

Boden

Not even Autumn and we are lighting fires.

Bethany

Yeah, it's weird.

Navek gets up and opens the fireplace grate. He pulls a little lever to open the chimney up. To its side is a stack of logs and coals. Above on the mantlepiece are balls of cotton, soaked in vegetable oil and sitting in a little glass tinderbox. Navek takes out the cotton balls and places them in the fireplace, then he places logs around them and coals on top. He lights the cotton with a small magic flame and the fire starts to smoulder into life.

Henna

So, Orio is gone.

Bethany

Yeah, it's kind of sad.

Henna

I wonder how she stays so young looking.

Boden

You reckon she's really older than she looks?

Henna

Yeah, not sure how old, though.

Navek

I reckon she's as old as our parents. She just seems so powerful.

Bethany

I thought she was about Chandrin's age when we met her.

Navek

I wonder what he is getting up to.

Boden

Yeah, and what it would be like on those boats in the rain.

Bethany

You and your pirates.

Boden

But don't you think it would be romantic, the sky opening up, the waves crashing against your boat and rocking you in all sorts of directions?

Henna

Sounds cold and wet, ha.

Bethany

I like it.

Navek

It wouldn't be bad.

The fire starts to heat up, throwing yellow and orange flames up the chimney. Navek gets up and closes the spark guard on the front. Boden goes over and takes a book out of his bag.

Henna

What ya reading?

Boden

I was just looking for a story to tell the Sprites.

Navek

Good luck.

Henna goes over to the window and leans against the side frame and Bethany comes over and joins her. Outside, the rain blows to and fro as it falls, being stirred by the wind. The ground and surroundings don't give off much of a shine, as the dark weather dulls the street. Navek, feeling dozy, gets under the covers of his bed and closes his eyes.

Henna

I wonder how Olreon is at the moment.

Bethany

You feeling homesick?

Henna

A little, but since I met with Chandrin, that's kinda subsided.

Bethany

It's nice that he showed us around.

Henna

Yeah, it's great to see his business first hand.

Bethany

Do you think your homesickness will grow?

Henna

No, I had a bit at the start in Sunlin, but then it went away, cause I loved Sunlin.

Bethany

Sunlin was great.

Henna

When we arrived here, I wasn't as bad as when we arrived in Sunlin, so hopefully it's fine. I definitely don't want to go back, I love adventuring.

Bethany

I was feeling a little homesick in Sunlin before we had the water fight. But now I am glad I came.

236

Bethany smiles and puts her arm around Henna's. They look out the window as the rain trickles down. As they watch, the storm grows heavy. They each get into bed and listen to it blowing fiercely outside.

The next day, Boden rises early and gets out of bed.

Navek

What are you doing? It's too early! We need to lie in.

Boden

I am going to find the Sprites and tell them a story about Roarden and Sierra.

Henna

Roarden wha?

Boden

It's ok, forget it, go back to sleep.

Boden leaves the room and goes down to inn's dining hall. People are sparsely seated, and he finds the Sprites to the side, talking animatedly among themselves. They look up as Boden approaches.

Salner

Oh, it's the Wizard.

Boden

Hi.

Salner

Where are your friends or do we only deserve the delight of just you?

Boden

They're sleeping.

Salner

So, why do you bother us with your presence?

Boden

Bother, oh well, I can tell you the story another time then.

Boden goes to get up and leave.

Tammis

Stop! Come on Salner, don't be like that.

Salner

Ok then, sit, tell your story.

Boden

You sure?

Salner

Yes Wizard, now start.

Boden

Ok, you have never heard of Roarden and Sierra?

The Sprites shake their heads.

Boden

Well, there was a Witch named Sierra and Demon named Roarden. They had spent a long time travelling together and had been on many adventures. Sierra was an interesting person. She was an Inventor before she was an Adventurer and Roarden was an Adventurer most of his life, famed around the Lava Catacombs as the saviour of the Demons that resided there.

Salner

Before we begin, does your story have a title?

Boden

Oh yeah, am.

Salner

Story has to have a name, otherwise it's not a story.

Boden

Ok, yeah, I have a good name.

Salner

Well?

===

Boden

"Roarden and Sierra, a Whirl with Vampires and Deadly Death"

===

He pauses for dramatic effect and Tammis and Nairis nod and smile.

Boden

Thorten was a new friend that Sierra and Roarden had made. He was a Skarling Vampire. You know the race that don't kill by their bite, but can make Necrolings, almost mind dead servants?

Salner

Yes, of course.

Boden

Well, Thorten had gone on an adventure with them. They had gotten a large mound of buried treasure from some forgotten King. They were on their way to a Vampire World, where they were going to stay with Thorten, meet the town's King and return to him an artefact from the treasure. Because Thorten couldn't be out during the day in their world, it was late evening when they passed through the portal tree to the Vampire World. As they passed through, they were enveloped by a much higher darkness.

Boden puts on a vampire accent.

Thorten

Hhh, feels homely.

Boden

Thorten said, as they came out from around the trees. Up above them they were greeted with lots of white sparkling stars.

Thorten

Now, that's my sunlight.

Boden puts on a female accent for Sierra.

Sierra

So, it's never day here?

Thorten

There is a large black star that crosses the sky. Some people think it to be how the sun shines in our world. But the stars are out day and night.

Sierra

Mesmeric.

Thorten

Come, let's travel, it is still very far.

Boden

They walk along through meadows that are full of dark green grass and wide green leaves. Thorten stretches as the starlight reflects off his greyish white skin.

Thorten

Sunlight may burn, but starlight is so rejuvenating.

Boden

They walk through the fields for most of the night, till they see the large black star rising on the horizon. It appears as a different colour of black to the rest of the sky, but seems to make no noticeable difference to the world around them. Up ahead, on the road, they see a light red castle, surrounded by a large town.

Boden puts on a gerring sounded accent for Roarden.

Roarden

Looks pretty quiet.

Thorten

You're right, there should be a few people coming and going.

Boden

They look at Thorten as he suddenly walks forward with a concerned look on his face.

They follow him into town, where they find lots of black timber-framed houses, with white walls and stone wall bases. Most of the houses have doors broken down or signs of damage.

Thorten

What's happened here?!

They walk up the street.

Thorten

Stay away from the houses. I'm not entirely sure we're safe.

Boden

They continue through the streets, looking for people. As they go, the moon sneaks up into the sky. They march out onto a long street. In the distance, they see a lone figure, standing with his legs somewhat apart and his arms dangling in front of him. The moonlight casting a long shadow towards them. Thorten signals for them to stay behind. They edge forward, the man has his face down, looking at the ground, his tattered hood up. Thorten stops a stone's throw away. He stares, concern growing.

Thorten

Hello there.

Suddenly the man's face rises, full of blood and green patches.

Thorten

Damn!

Boden

Hissing and spitting, he takes off towards Thorten. Roarden and Sierra raise their magical shields, while Thorten raises an energy barrier in front of him. The man barrels towards him.

Thorten

Get him.

Boden

Sierra and Roarden shoot fireballs at the man, blasting holes in him, but he keeps coming.

Thorten

RUN, DAMN IT!

Boden

They shoot off down the street and notice as they run down, that a large group of Vampires, hissing and howling, are flooding into streets around them. They dodge down a side alley and sprint on.

Roarden

What the hell is going on?

Thorten

Just run, we need to get to safety.

Roarden and Sierra send blasts of energy behind them, that hit their pursuers and do nothing.

Sierra

Those are strong.

Thorten

They're stronger together. We have to lose them.

They dive down an even thinner alleyway. They round a corner, and a door opens up in front of them. They are waved in before their pursuers turn the corner. They barrel through and hands are held over their mouths.

Woman

Don't make a sound.

Boden says, in a whispering hiss of a womanly voice.

Boden

The Vampire woman holding her hands over Sierra and Thorten's faces says, as a male Vampire holds his hand over Roarden's. As they listen, they hear the hissing and screaming get louder as the Vampires pass. The sound of a river of thudding feet and angry noises can be heard. After a while, it dies down.

Woman

Ok, I think it's safe.

Boden

The woman lights a lantern, and a grey light washes out the room, revealing the male and female Vampire, wearing matching rings that indicate they are a couple. The woman wears a pale cardigan and long dress. While the man wears a black suit with a red tie. They both look extremely old, their round faces full of wrinkles.

Thorten

What happened here?

Man

We don't know, it started to spread through town before we knew it was here.

Thorten

It's a Zombie Virus?

Woman

Yes, Zombie Vampire Virus.

Sierra

Then we might be safe from it.

Man

I wouldn't risk it. They might still be able to make your mind damaged.

Boden

The couple sit down in front of them.

Woman

You won't be any match for them when they're together, anyway.

Thorten

Horde Powers?

Woman

Yes, together they are incredibly strong.

Man

They also have a mystical ability.

Thorten

So, doesn't look like we will be fighting our way out of here soon.

Woman

Why did you come here?

Thorten

We have an item to deliver to the King.

Woman

We don't know what happened to them, or if the infection has been brought into the castle.

Thorten

What about food, how are you surviving?

Man

We ran out of blood root, we have been drinking, in a manner.

Boden

The woman and man lift their hands to show that their arms are full of the marks of vampire teeth.

Thorten

You can't survive like this.

Woman

We can't go out there, they'd slaughter us.

Thorten

Hmm, what are your names?

Woman

Nairneen.

Man

Einin (eye nin)

Thorten

Well, we are going to have to find a way out of here.

Woman : Nairneen

The edge of town is full of them, we saw them go after people who fled.

Man : Einin

They came back with them, they were all turned to Zombies.

Thorten

Ok, well, we need to feed you up first.

Nairneen

Do you have food on you?

Thorten

No, I ate my last supply before we came into town.

Man

Then how?

Thorten

You may feed on me.

The couple look at each other.

Nairneen

But.

Thorten

No buts. Now do it!

Einin

Where will we go then?

Thorten

We will make our way to the castle. They may still have blood roots planted.

The Vampires look at Thorten with concern.

Thorten

Come on now, we don't have time to watch the horde grow.

Boden

The old couple get up from the table and come over to him.

Nairneen

Where should we feed?

Thorten

The neck is fine.

Boden

Thorten leans down. As the couple stand before him, their faces contort, changing into horrible, sharp, angular, violent looking forms. Their fang teeth extend down, and they bite into his neck. Thorten stands there, looking unfazed. The blood gets drawn up into their teeth as they feed, and they suddenly seem stronger and less old looking. Thorten nods to stop, and their faces change back to their roundy shape.

Sierra

Wow, you look a lot younger now.

Nairneen

It's amazing how starvation can age you.

Boden

They still appear older than Thorten, but all their wrinkles have disappeared.

Thorten

Ok, so, we are going to have to head back out.

Nairneen

Yeah, ok.

Boden

Thorten opens the door a smidge and looks out.

Thorten

Ready?

Einin

The best we can be.

Thorten

Make sure you don't get bitten either.

Boden

Thorten says to Sierra and Roarden.

Thorten

A Demon and a Witch is much handier to have on our side.

Boden

Roarden and Sierra smile at this.

Thorten

Ok, the coast is clear.

Boden

They step out onto the street and go slowly. At the next junction, they peer around the corners. Nothing there, so they proceed down the road.

Sierra

Is the castle locked?

Nairneen

We're not sure.

Boden

They peek around the next corner and see a group of the Zombies, wandering silently.

Nairneen

We can't go that way.

Boden

They go inside the nearest house, which has its door broken open. Sierra and Roarden magic the door so it will stay closed. From inside, they hear a hissing noise.

Thorten

Damn it!

Boden

They stalk through the house till a door bursts open and a Vampire Zombie charges out. Sierra and Roarden shoot fireballs at it, while the Vampires slice the air with energy slashes that cut into it. Together, they manage to cut it down. It fires off a bolt of energy before it dies, cutting into the wall near them.

Roarden

Lucky there weren't more.

Boden

Roarden says, looking at the sliced-up wall. They pass through the halls till they come to a side door. Back outside on the street, they see more Zombies wandering aimlessly. Thorten picks up a stone, charges it with energy and throws it into the distance behind them. It starts giving off a racket of noise, which causes all the nearby Zombies to run towards it. They go through the now clear street and into another set of buildings. Inside is empty and they close the doors, then head upstairs. There they find large windows in the side of the hall.

Einin

Will they see us up here?

Nairneen

It should be fine, the back entrance leads onto a much safer street, very few people go on it.

Boden

They cross the windows, and the Zombies below start to take notice. The first few seem docile and start scraping and moaning below the windows. But as more show up, they start to send energy bolts at the building.

Thorten

Grack, RUN!

Boden

They jump out of the corridor, just as the floor caves in. Frightened, they look back and forth at each other with startled expressions as they check if they are each ok. They run on down the hallway and down the stairs. The wall caves in at the end of the hall and they dive through the closing gap. At the back, they leave through a door into a set of gardens. They use magic and Vampire Energies to lock the door behind them, then head through the back alleys. Suddenly, as they go, a Zombie jumps out from a bush, grabbing Nairneen and shoving her into a wall. She holds it off as it snaps at her viciously. The others spring over, trying to rescue her. The Zombie lunges in to bite, just as Sierra blasts it in the face. It rolls off and falls to the ground. Nairneen sighs.

Einin

He didn't get you?

Nairneen

No, I'm fine.

Boden

They come to the street with the main castle. It is hefty and made from dim red stone and appears to be deserted. They go over and ring the bell. A voice projects from a nearby wall.

Voice

Is somebody out there?

Thorten

Yes, let us in.

Voice

There are Zombies attacking the town.

Thorten

Yes, we know, they aren't on the street here though, are they?

Voice

No, ok.

Boden

The voice disappears and they wait. They look up and down the town, ready for something to come crawling out of the woodwork. A face, clad in armour, appears over the battlements.

Guard

Hello, I'll let you in.

Boden

He pops his head back and a little later a massive thick door opens from the side of the tower. They go inside and he shuts it behind them.

Guard

How did you get through town, it's swarming with them?

Thorten

With a lot of luck. Do you have any food?

Guard

Yes, come, I'll lead you through. My name's Rowken. Ever since this started, they have been trying to find a way in here.

Thorten

You say it like they are intelligent.

Guard : Rowken

They are, or at least from the stories I've been told.

Thorten

So, what's the plan then?

Rowken

Well... when they horde, it strengthens them. So far, we have no plans to leave. The castle is safe enough. They can't get us, and we can't get them.

Thorten

But you'll have to leave eventually.

Rowken

We have all the food we need growing in the castle. We don't have anything with flavour in it though, but that isn't important.

Thorten

What about for my friends here?

Rowken

Hmm, I'm sure some arrangement can be made.

Boden

Thorten drops back to Sierra and Roarden.

Thorten

Don't worry, we won't be staying here forever.

Sierra

Come on, let's drop your parcel off with the King and see what we can do.

Rowken

Ok, I'll take you to King Rawtorn, you can drop it off and we will see what to do
next.

Boden

The Guard brings them before the Royals in the area. In the room he takes them
to, they see King Rawtorn, who has a broad face and stately armour and is
sitting in front of the townspeople and nobles, who are bickering about different
things.

Rowken

Sir, I found these people out on the street. There were no Zombies around when
they were near.

Boden

The King silences the crowd of Vampires. He looks at Sierra and Roarden with a
strange desperate glint in his eyes. The rest of the crowd also seem to give them
off-putting stares. The king stands up and bids them to come to the fore of the
crowd.

King Rawtorn

What news of the town and outside world do you have?

Thorten

We finished an adventure you had in your local town job shop and came here. It
was for the treasure that was at the end of the Varren Caves.

King Rawtorn

I would congratulate and pay you, but it seems a more pressing issue has come
to our attention.

Thorten

Yes, it does seem dire, doesn't it. The news of the Zombies is that they are very
powerful, and we don't stand a hope of beating them when they are together.

Boden

The crowd's faces become very grim.

Roarden

We did destroy a few on our way here.

King Rawtorn

That is somewhat good news.

Thorten

As for the rest of Tream, there seems to be less trade from wars breaking out around most places. Adventurers like me and my friends here are finding it harder and harder to find safe places to stay.

Boden

The King stares at Sierra and Roarden for a long time. His eyes yearning.

King Rawtorn

Tream is in turmoil, these are bad times indeed.

Thorten

What plans do you have for the Zombies?

King Rawtorn

We have had several meetings and we still haven't agreed on anything. There just seems to be too much risk if we want to get out from this place.

Sierra

Maybe we can help in the planning.

King Rawtorn

Maybe, we will have to wait and see. For now, the meeting here must commence. Guard, please show them to a suitable room in the guest quarters.

Boden

The Guard salutes and leads them off with the couple they saved. As they leave, the entire room stares at them.

Rowken

I don't think that meeting was about the Zombies. They always seem to bicker, no matter what the meeting.

Boden

They walk through dull passageways till they come to a long corridor with a set of doors in the middle. The Guard opens the room on the near side.

Rowken

In there, you'll find vampire beds.

Boden

They look inside and find beds made for sleeping by hanging upside down. He opens the other room across the hall. Inside are normal beds. Together, the group go into this room and sit around on the beds.

Rowken

The blood root is an unfortunate source of food to be stuck with. Ever so bland and doesn't give the feel of a feed.

Boden

They sit there for the next while, trying to come up with ways to save the town, Sierra and Roarden eating from their packs. Bedtime draws in and they check the chambers and get to sleep. In the middle of the night, when the black sun has long set in the vampire skies, the door to Sierra and Roarden's room opens slowly and silently. Several quiet figures cross the room. They surround the beds, dip their heads, and start to feast.

Einin

That tickles, get off.

Boden

Nairneen lights a lantern in the corner. There, in Sierra's bed, lies Thorten and in Roarden's is Einin.

Thorten

You were right, they really would have attacked them.

Boden

Around the room the group stand. The King steps forward out of the pack.

King Rawtorn

We wouldn't have killed them or enslaved them. We are just hungry for some decent blood.

Einin

They didn't take too much blood, in fairness.

Thorten

Doesn't make it better.

Boden

The King looks to the ceiling.

King Rawtorn

We're sorry. Terribly sorry. It has been very difficult.

Boden

Thorten sits up on the edge of the bed.

Thorten

I will be warning my friends to magic their door during the night.

King Rawtorn

We're sorry again. This shouldn't have happened.

Thorten

No, it shouldn't have.

Boden

Thorten gets up, walks to the hall and knocks on the door to his bedroom. There they find Roarden and Sierra, upside down, with their legs strapped to the beams. Thorten laughs at the sight of Roarden's big red physique and Sierra with her cape hanging from behind her head.

Sierra

We just thought we'd give it a try.

Boden

They unhook themselves from the beam and lower themselves to the floor.

Thorten

I think it advisable for the rest of your stay, that you magic your door.

Sierra

Was there somebody looking for a midnight feast?

King Rawtorn

We're truly, truly sorry.

Roarden

Are you ok?

Einin

Yeah, they didn't take that much blood.

King Rawtorn

I think we should leave now.

Thorten

Good idea.

Boden

The King and his subjects silently vacate the hall.

Thorten

I'm sorry about that.

Sierra

It's not your fault.

Thorten

Well, I did bring you here.

Roarden

Well, if you didn't, we might never have met Einin and Nairneen.

Nairneen

You did save us.

Boden

Thorten smiles.

Thorten

Come on, we need some sleep.

Boden

The next day, they join the Wall Guards stationed along the battlements. From there, they are able to look out on the streets around the castle. In the street below them, they see Zombies wandering around. The crew walk along the wall.

Thorten

Has there been any streets without Zombies on them?

Rowken

No, besides, you can't see the rest of the streets between here and the outside.

Boden

They walk around several more walls and take a junction on the wall tops and walk down a long, thin walkway with battlements, that skirt another wall and looks out over a slightly rising street. As they watch, a large horde of Zombies run together up the street.

Einin

Are they after somebody?

Rowken

No, they tend to do that every so often. We joke that they just need some exercise, so they go for a jog.

Nairneen

Well, that makes leaving here even more treacherous.

Einin

So, you don't have any plans to leave, then?

Rowken

We do, but the risk of becoming them has held us back.

Boden

They return to the dining hall. When they enter, the Vampires all turn and look at them, eyes staring intently.

Roarden

Well, if that isn't creepy.

Thorten

Keep your necks guarded.

Boden

Sierra rolls up her collar and Roarden straps a thick, black neck belt around his neck. They take a seat on a free table. Thorten brings over some blood roots. They look like dark, fibrous, gnarled branches. He, Nairneen and Einin start to chew into them, as the Vampires from the other tables glance over at them.

Nairneen

These aren't so bad.

Einin

No, they're dreadful.

Boden

Nairneen slumps her shoulders.

Nairneen

They are, aren't they?

Thorten

Still, we have to eat up.

Sierra

What are you going to do with the stone?

Thorten

Well, if the King doesn't want it, we will probably have to trade it with
somebody who does.

Boden

That night, Sierra and Roarden magic their door so they won't be disturbed.
They sleep soundly while Thorten swings and sways, trying to think of a way out.
As he does, he hears voices outside in the hall. He goes over to the door and
opens it a crack. There, he sees several Vampires standing around, staring at
Sierra and Roarden's room.

Thorten

May I help you?

Boden

They get a shock and turn to see him.

Man

Ah no, we were just, ah, wandering, yeah, wandering around.

Boden

They smile and quickly disperse.

Thorten

This looks bad.

Nairneen

Will they be able to get through your friend's magic?

Thorten

No, they are very powerful. But I still don't like it.

Boden

Over the next days of them staying there, the stares that the Vampires give Sierra and Roarden become longer and more desperate looking. Thorten eats his vegetables and looks up at his friends with a hunger growing inside him.

Thorten

No, they're my friends, don't ever look at them like that.

Boden

He forces the thought out of his head and looks away from them. His body protesting at his action. All around the room, the Vampires stare at them. Not even trying to mask it as a glance.

Thorten

We are going to have to leave soon.

Boden

Thorten whispers.

Thorten

Or at least you will.

Einin

Yeah, our friends look like they are starting to fall into bloodlust.

Nairneen

I'm starting to feel it myself too.

Boden

Thorten gives her a sharp look.

Nairneen

I would never feed on your friends. I'm just being honest. Self-control is hard, but I can control myself.

Thorten

Good.

Sierra

Are you alright, Thorten?

Thorten

Yes, the sooner we get out of here, the better.

Roarden

What about the stone?

Thorten

We will have a meeting with the King tonight and ask if he will trade. Then, in the morning, we'll leave.

Sierra

We're running low on our food too, so it's a good call.

Boden

Thorten gives them a grim smile. That night, they go into the King's meeting chambers.

Thorten

We would like to know if you would like to trade the stone from the Varren Caves.

King Rawtorn

Now, Thorten.

Boden

The King says, licking his lips as he looks at Sierra and Roarden.

King Rawtorn

You know, I won't be able to tell if it's of any use.

Thorten

Then we will have to trade with somebody else.

Boden's voice turns slimy as he impersonates the King's voice.

King Rawtorn

What's your hurry, Thorten? Maybe I will take your rock, if you allow me something else.

Thorten

I know what you want, but you can't have it.

King Rawtorn

Wait now, I haven't said what I want. Maybe it would be alright if you leave the room Thorten, and I can discuss the matter further with your friends.

Thorten

I'm not leaving them.

King Rawtorn

Don't be so...

Boden

The King runs his tongue over his lips, with a disgusting slithering sound.

King Rawtorn

...hasty.

Boden

The door to their side opens up and a crowd of Vampires come issuing in.

Thorten

As expected.

Boden

Sierra and Roarden raise their shields.

King Rawtorn

Now, now, now, we only want a little blood, that's all. You know, I've never tasted Wizard or Demon before.

Thorten

And you never will.

Boden

The King shoots a volley of jagged yellow energy at them. Thorten drops the stone as he goes to block the King. More energy bolts come from the crowd and Sierra and Roarden's round shields block them. As they do, the stone hits the ground and shatters. A sudden light bursts forward from inside it, igniting the room in a harsh whiteness. The crowd of Vampires hiss as their skin scorches. They surge and scramble to the door, pushing and pulling their way through, bursting out of the room, leaving Sierra and Roarden standing there on their own.

Roarden

So, that's why the stone is valuable.

Boden

As they look at it, the glow from the round gem inside the broken stone gets brighter and brighter. The walls of the chamber begin to smoke as the light burns them. Sierra takes a box out of her backpack and goes over to the glowing gem and puts it inside. The room returns to its grey and inky blacks after she puts it away. Thorten comes in from around the corner of the open door.

Sierra

Are you ok?

Thorten

A little burnt, but fine.

Roarden

What is that gem?

Thorten

They are called Sonus Stones. They hold a light similar to your sun. When shone on us, they cause us to burn and disintegrate.

Roarden

Interesting, I wonder if they work on the Zombies.

Thorten

How did you deal with it?

Sierra

I have it in a box here.

Roarden

It was burning the walls and the floor.

Thorten

Most things from Vampire Worlds will be destroyed by sunlight or be damaged
from the light of that stone.

Roarden

Interesting.

Sierra

Come on, let's check if the Zombies are afraid of it.

Boden

They meet up with Rowken.

Rowken

Is everything alright? A lot of angry people went past as I came here.

Thorten

Yeah, fine. We may have a new weapon to help us with the Zombies.

Boden

As he says that, a large crowd of them run by the bottom of the walls. Thorton,
Sierra and Roarden start shouting over the edge and the Zombies stop in their
tracks and look up.

Thorten

Will they be able to get at us?

No, these battlements are great, they only allow firing out. Near impossible to fire in.

Boden

The Zombies gather round on the street below. Sierra lifts the box and opens it a crack. The bright light streams out, burning the front of the crowd. As they get hit, they start to sizzle and disintegrate, trying to run before falling to dust. The rest of the crowd react in a similar manner, running away, even though they weren't hit.

Rowken

Told you they're smart.

Sierra

Looks like we may have a way out of this mess.

Thorten

Question is, do we want to take the rest of the castle?

Rowken

Why wouldn't you?

Thorten

They tried to have a little nibble on my friends here.

Rowken

They did?!

Boden

The Guard says, shocked.

Thorten

Yeah.

Rowken

What are you going to do?

Sierra

We'll take them with us.

Rowken

Are you sure?

Sierra

Yes, they may find it hard to not eat us, but they are still people.

Roarden

We would help them, regardless.

Rowken

Well, you are good people.

Thorten

They certainly are.

Sierra

Come on, let's get out of here fast, so they can find whatever fruit that will stop their cravings.

Rowken

Ok then, stay here, I'll go talk to them.

Thorten

I'll go with you.

Boden

For the rest of the day, they round up the people of the castle. The King calls them all to his room and apologises to Sierra and Roarden.

King Rawtorn

In truth, we would have never killed or tried to enslave you with our bite. We are truly sorry. Starvation has made us do bad things.

Sierra

It is quite alright, as long as you don't try and bite us as we're leaving.

Boden

With the apologies accepted from the King and his people, Sierra and Roarden take their position at the front of the crowd, ready to leave. The Guards lower the drawbridge and the group head out onto the street. As they go, a massive horde of Zombies comes flooding out into the route in front of them. Sierra raises the lid of her box, and as the Zombies run up towards them, they suddenly start to burn and disintegrate. The group of townspeople behind them also start shooting Vampire Energy at them. The horde, heavily affected by the light, takes off back down the street. Sierra leads the townspeople down the road and through several junctions. They travel down a short thin road, as they go, they can hear hissing form the streets around them. Several Zombies burst forward from a side street. They jump out, grabbing at them and trying to bite them. The Vampires join together and blast them away. More Zombies crowd out and the horde energies start to protect them. They struggle with the Zombies as Sierra runs up close and unleashes the light so it won't hit the people. Roarden protects the others, extending his shield around them. With Sierra blasting away, the Zombies flee the streets around the Vampires.

Sierra

Come on!

Boden

The crowd start to run out of town. As they get to the borders, a massive horde starts chasing from behind.

Rowken

That's the biggest I've seen.

King Rawtorn

It must be nearly the entire town.

Thorten

Come on, we can't stop.

Boden

They chase across the countryside.

Sierra

Ok, I want you to take the box of light and split off from us.

Thorten

But there's too many, you can't fight them.

Roarden

Trust us, we know what we're doing.

Boden

Sierra hands him the light box as they run. Thorten turns around and guides the crowd away from Roarden and Sierra. As they go, the Zombies start towards the crowd, but Thorten uses the light blasts to dissuade them. The Zombies ignore the group as they run off between the trees, and instead go after Sierra and Roarden. Together, the Witch and Demon run across the land through most of the night. The Zombies never tiring in their pursuit. Up ahead on the road, they see a massive portal tree and run through it. They come out under another starlit sky, not stopping for a moment as the Zombies barrel through after them. They continue on running for a long while. The stars heavy in the night sky. After a time, blue streaks start to run through the sky.

Sierra

We did it!

Roarden

We caught them.

Boden

On the edge of the sky, the yellow sun peeks out. Behind them they hear a roaring sizzling sound. They turn as they run, to see the Vampire Zombies start streaming with steam and dark fumes. Cavities opening over their faces, giving off geysers of smoke. The holes expand and the skin in-between starts turning to ooze. As the sun rises further, the rays of light hit the Zombies, and they are immediately evaporated. Roarden and Sierra stop and turn.

Roarden

Well, that was a good long run.

Sierra

Come on, let's get back and see if everybody is alright.

Boden

They go back through the portal tree and walk along the path, to find the Vampires resting in the woods by the monument that they were going to visit before they left. It is of a Vampire, looking coy, with his hands on his hips, fangs protruding and a suit with a triangle shaped cape running down its back. Thorten comes rushing over.

Thorten

Are you ok?

Sierra

Yeah, we made them follow us into the sun.

Thorten

Brilliant.

Nairneen

So, what's the plan?

Thorten

Well, we might be able to reclaim your town.

Einin

That horde looked like the majority of the people from here.

Boden

Together, the group head back into town, using the Sonus Stone to destroy the remaining Zombies. They walk out into a large walled off field, full of blood berry bushes. On seeing the bushes, the Vampires run out and start to gorge on the berries. When they are done, the King comes over to talk to them.

Sierra

Better?

King Rawtorn

Much, that hunger is horrible, but now it is gone. Thank you for saving the town.

Sierra

We are glad we could help.

King Rawtorn

I would like to pay you for the Sonus Stone. It should come in handy if the town needs protecting again.

Thorten

That it should and thank you.

Boden

The King turns to Sierra and Roarden.

King Rawtorn

Sorry again for trying to drink your blood.

Boden

Sierra and Roarden nod and smile to him as he heads off back with Rowken to eat the berries.

Rowken

Maybe we should build a wall around the town.

King Rawtorn

Yes, a good idea.

Nairneen and Einin come over to them.

Nairneen

Thanks for saving us.

Einin

Yeah, we were definitely dead if you hadn't come along.

Boden

With many thanks from the townspeople, Thorten, Sierra and Roarden get a nice pay from the King and a welcome invite to come back and visit Nairneen and Einin. So, that's the story of how Roarden, Sierra and Thorten saved the Vampire Town of Coffer.

Boden smiles at them.

Boden

So, is that a fair trade for your Skulp story?

Salner

I wouldn't go that far.

Boden

But it had Zombie Vampires, not many stories have that.

The Sprite Storyteller smiles.

Salner

It will do as a trade of stories. Thank you.

In the background, Henna, Navek and Bethany come in, looking tired.

Henna

Oh hi, it's the Sprites.

Nairis

Yes Wizards, you look tired.

Henna

Well, we were doing some advanced training yesterday, hard stuff.

Navek

So, you told them a story?

Boden

Yeah, I told them the Sierra and Roarden story with Zombies and Vampires.

Navek

With Thorten?

Boden

Yeah.

Henna

Really? I would have liked to hear that story again.

Boden

Well, you all seemed really tired. I'm sorry.

Henna

It's ok. Sorry about being craggy.

Boden

Ah, no problem.

Tammis

Well, we are to begin dining, if you'd like to join us, you may.

Henna

Sure, that would be nice.

Henna, Bethany and Navek take a seat next to Boden.

Nairis

I have question?

Boden

Sure, fire away.

Nairis

When we visited a human town, we were told a story about witches. They had green skin, long noses and flew on broomsticks. What are those witches?

Bethany

Well, those witches come from an old human story. It is based on Agatha Portance. She was a crazy old Witch that lived amongst humans. The Storyteller embellished her story, giving her green skin and making it up that she could fly around on a broom. Apparently, she would run around in her shop with her broom and pretend to be riding it like a horse, to entertain the kids.

Nairis

I know humans call you witches, they don't mean those sorts of witches, like Agatha, and you call each other "witch" too.

Bethany

Yeah, a witch is a female wizard.

Nairis

Ohhh, I see, and a male wizard is?

Bethany

Well, humans use the term "warlock", but "mage" is the preferred with wizards.

Nairis

Ok, so a mage is a male wizard. Very good.

Salner

I would be interested to hear what other stories you Wizards have come across.

The Adventurers tell them about some of the antics they got up to in the other town.

Tammis

Well, you lot are an interesting bunch. A water fight sounds like a grand idea.

Salner

Yes, definitely something worthy of being in a book.

Henna

You Sprites never had a water fight?

Salner

Well, we are a bit above those sorts of antics, I'm afraid.

Nairis

But this Masquerade sounds interesting.

Tammis

Yes, definitely worth a visit.

Nairis

Have you been to the Vaultgile Library in town? It's quite good.

Bethany

No, but we have planned to go there.

Nairis

Are you looking for anything in particular?

Bethany

Well, we were looking for stories or information on the Legendary
Abominations.

Nairis

What are they?

He says, in piqued interest.

Henna

Legendary Abominations are these terrible creatures. There was a white Orb
that chased us through the Layerden Forests. It was a horrible creature, full of
faces of people screaming in agony. It was an Abomination according to the
materials we found.

Salner

Quite a good name for a creature.

Nairis

Yes, very dramatic.

The Adventurers look at each other and shrug. The group call over the Waiter and order their respective foods. The Adventurers order green couscous salads and fried baskets. The Sprites say, "The usual". The couscous is a light green and has fried noodles, spinach and basil running through it, and sits nicely in the fried baskets. It has a light earthy flavour.

Salner

God, is that what you Wizards are eating? It looks disgusting.

The plates the Sprites have ordered show up. Their meal is made of bright pink, slug shaped food, sticking out of an orange sauce.

Navek

We could say the same about your food.

Salner

Our food is prepared in a traditional style, by this excellent inn.

Navek

Looks like slugs.

Salner

Well, least it doesn't look like a garden. I've never seen so much green in a dish.

Navek

Ha, I'd eat a garden over a plate of slugs any day.

The Sprites grumble at this and eat their food. The Adventurers also eat, and they all forget about the little argument.

Tammis

So, what is the overall purpose of your journey?

The Adventurers look at each other and smile with embarrassment.

Salner

People go on adventures to do something, go somewhere special, save a damsel.

Navek

A damsel?

Salner

You know, a purpose.

Henna

We know.

Salner

So, you're just adventuring for the sake of adventuring?

Boden

We are questing for a quest.

Navek

So far, we have gone on lots of little quests.

Salner

Sounds messy. An adventure always needs a main goal.

Boden

Well, we will try our best.

They finish their meal with good natured jovial chats.

Tammis

So, where are you Wizards off to now?

Boden

I was going to train for the Card Tournament.

Navek

Well then, we'd better train too.

Henna

Yeah.

Bethany

I guess I'll go to the library.

Tammis

We are heading to the Vaultgile Library now, you could accompany us if you like.

Bethany

Yeah, that would be great. I have a Vaultgile badge too.

Tammis

Brilliant.

The group get up and Bethany goes to head off with the Sprites.

Bethany

See ya later.

Henna, Boden, Navek

See ya.

She heads out onto the street, accompanying them as they go, with the rain pouring down around them. The light grey ambience is nice, as Bethany puts up her hood, and the Sprites put up an ornate umbrella with a little scene of Sprites running around a maypole.

Bethany

I love your umbrella.

Salner

Why thank you, it was a gift from our mother.

They walk through the rain-washed streets, going through several junctions until they find the street they are looking for. It has a massive building running along its entire length. The building itself has ginormous, light grey, backward leaning pillars, and the roof is shaped like an open book. The building also has grey walls surrounding green jade panelling. The marble floors along its front are embossed with scenes from books.

This is Trader City's Vaultgile Library.

Wow, it's really big.

The entrance has a wide semi-circular archway over it, with a stone carving of books that has a big title saying "Vaultgile". Bethany goes inside with the Sprites and is greeted with a tall hall, with floors upon floors going up and around the wide-open space surrounding the entrance. Each floor is jam-packed with shoulder high shelves and little yellow lantern lights sitting on the shelf ends. The whole room has a yellow and brown light to it. Between the floors are elaborately carved wooden panels, and between their sides are wooden disks sticking straight out with floral patterns carved through them, and beautiful spikes coming out from their edge. Curved, wooden beams come off the disks, continuing the spikes on their front and leading up to support wooden handrails that have tightly packed balustrades, which run around the upper levels. The entrance floor is long and thin, and made of white marble with black streaks. It has several tall, windowed counters running down its sides and ends, where people are getting their books stamped. There is a hip high table running down the middle of the room, with brass panels dividing up the people sitting at it, as they study.

Well, I hope you find the books you like.

Thank you, hope you do too.

Bethany splits off from the Sprites and decides to go over to the section on the history of wizardry. She leaves the entrance area with its marble floors and walks onto a light brown carpet. She looks through the books for Damned Wizard stuff. Eventually, she pulls out a couple and begins to look through them, going over and sitting in a cosy couch beside the first-floor railings, and placing the books in front of her on a small table. The first book has reference to a battle between a Damned army and a wizard nation. The book shows the battle, which seems to be very unbalanced, as the Damned appear to slaughter their enemy with ease. The next book turns out to be a pop-up book. Bethany looks through the pages and it shows battles between the Damned themselves. Each page shows an army of the Damned facing another army. As she looks at the pictures, the

Wizards move around the battlefield, shooting dark coloured sparks and spells at each other. The pop-ups fold out and move around as she watches, figures jumping out of the page as they attack and interesting scenes tucking into shape before her. She turns to see the next page, and it is another battle, the armies use horrible magic that tears away flesh, causing horrific wounds that flood with black blood. The battles are strange to look at, with bizarre shapes shooting off here and there, and forces creating new and destructive forms of movement and magic that twist and turn around them as they wreck through the battle.

Bethany

These pictures are vile.

Every page contains some kind of battle going on between the Damned, until Bethany comes to a page where she sees a still image. The picture shows a Wizard that has had his clothes ripped from his torso, revealing an odd spiral pyramid mark on his chest. He is holding a Staff high into the air in triumph and his body is surrounded in a black fire. He stands on top of a massive pile of dead Wizards, in the middle of a scene of pure destruction, with bodies covering the ground into the distance like a gruesome carpet.

Bethany

Horrible.

Then Bethany turns to the last page and reveals the image of the spiral pyramid that was on the man's chest. It is a foul, repulsive, repugnant colour that Bethany can't describe, but at the same time is quite persuasive, oily and slimy, it draws the eyes towards it, very enticing, like a horrible act, calling you to watch it. Bethany pulls her eyes away from the image, making her feel sick as she does. She closes the book and sits there, waiting for the illness to leave.

Bethany

Symbol Magic.

She gets up and looks around for more books. She goes over to another wizarding section of the library. The books have diverse titles. There's "Kitchen Magic", "How to Read Magical Runes", "Monsters and Their Use in Magic", "Spell Magic Using Irition Magical Language", "Home Magic", "Fire and Destruction Magic", "Biography of an Enlightened Wizard". Bethany looks through the whole section.

Bethany

<u>Seems there isn't anything on Symbol Magic. I wonder if the other library would have something.</u>

The feeling of frustration washes over her.

Bethany

<u>I think I'll come back later. They don't seem well stocked in wizarding stuff.</u>

As she is walking out, she sees the section on Sprites, which takes up a vast area.

Bethany

<u>No wonder they like this library.</u>

She goes up to the counter with her books on the war with wizards and the pop-up Damned book and has them stamped.

Bethany

You wouldn't have any other sections that are on wizards?

She says to the small man in a black shirt and trousers, with round glasses.

Librarian

Nothing on wizards I am afraid, but there is a general magic and feyora section.

He points to the map on the desk in front of her.

Librarian

If you'd like, you can leave your books here and go look.

Bethany

Oh, thank you, that's very kind.

Bethany goes over to the suggested section of the library. This seems not to have any information on Damned Wizards, but has some interesting books on dragons and other races of creatures that have powers and abilities. Bethany spends most of her time looking at the pictures. Eventually she gets tired and heads to get her books.

Librarian

You find everything you wanted?

Bethany

More or less.

Librarian

Well, if you would like us to look up books, I would be more than happy to check if we have them.

Bethany

I'm doing a project on the Damned. If there were any books you could find, it would be most helpful. Also, anything on Symbol Magic.

Librarian

Of course, I can inquire about that and see what I can find for you.

Bethany

Thank you.

The librarian gets her books and hands her an odd bag.

Librarian

It's raining outside, so you can put them in this, and they won't get wet.

Bethany

Oh, thank you.

Bethany puts the books in her bag, heads out of the library and puts her hood up. On her way back, the rain starts pouring heavier and heavier. The streets are even more jam-packed as people are going about their business. She walks through the crowds, under their net of umbrellas and finally reaches the inn. She goes up to their room and finds Henna on her own, sitting in the corner, with a table in front of her and a large card pile beside her. Some of her Summoning Cards have Monsters reaching out of them and clashing on the table.

Henna

Hey Bethany, found anything interesting?

Bethany

Yeah, I found these books on the Damned.

Henna stops the fight and puts her cards down beside her.

Bethany

Where are the others?

Henna

Oh, they didn't want to give away their secrets, so they went off to train.

Bethany takes the books out of her bag.

Henna

Let's have a gander.

She grabs a seat and puts out the books in front of Henna. They go through them together.

Henna

Interesting, they seem to be their own worst enemy.

She flips a page to a particularly bloody battle.

Henna

These are really gruesome.

Bethany

Yeah, it seems we didn't need to destroy them, the infighting between them was their worst enemy.

Henna flicks on through the pages of the book.

Bethany

The last page of that is weirdly horrible, I warn you.

Henna

Thanks, I'll still look.

Henna turns to the last page.

Henna

Uuuhh, what's that?

Her face turns sour, and she snaps the book closed as if it just let out a horrid stench.

Henna

That colour is horrible.

Bethany

Yeah, it's very sickening, I felt ill after trying to look away from it.

Henna

I don't think I want to open that page again.

Bethany

Yeah, I was wondering if you might know what it is.

Henna

I would say it is Symbol Magic.

Bethany

Yeah, that's what I thought.

Henna gives an awkward expression.

Henna

Pity they never taught it in school.

Bethany

I wonder why.

Henna

I don't know, but I remember Dad telling me that it was an amazingly powerful magic. He said it's very rare, though.

Bethany

Hmm, he didn't tell you anything else?

Henna

Nope, but the boys probably know more.

Bethany

Yeah, Boden might have used it in his inventing.

Henna

Or if it has some power, Navek might have given it a try. Well, I've got to get back to my cards. I am sure you'll find the boys around the inn.

Bethany leaves, as Henna puts her cards back onto the table and creates a small terrain for her to play them in. Bethany walks down the corridor and remembers that Boden likes to sit in lobbies. She goes to the main entrance and takes the door marked "Lobby". Inside, she finds Boden sitting in a corner across from the door. She walks through the seats and sees that he has his cards out and a small castle surrounding them.

Boden

Hey, Bethany.

He puts his cards aside.

Boden

Got anything interesting from the library?

Bethany

Yes, I got these.

Bethany sits in beside him in the chair and takes out the books. Boden looks through the battle scenes.

Boden

Wow, these books are amazing, they have got quite a lot of detail.

Boden watches the skirmishes as they play out in front of him in the book. People grabbing at each other with horrible claw-like hands, lightning gouging holes through Wizards.

Boden

They don't seem to like each other, these Damned Wizards.

Bethany

Yeah, I reckon that's why they weren't much of a threat to the rest of the wizarding community. They still seem very powerful, though.

Boden turns to the page of the victorious wizard standing over the battle.

Boden

Well, that doesn't look good.

Bethany

How so?

Boden

Well, usually when somebody wins in a battle, he has less opposition to deal with. If there was a victor, chances are that he would unite the last of the Damned nations.

Bethany

You reckon there were nations?

Boden

Well, judging from the battles in these books, yes, very lightly.

Bethany

I was interested in this. It's difficult to look at, though.

Boden nods his head and Bethany turns the page and reveals the spiral symbol on the last page.

Boden

Wow, that's powerful.

He looks into it and stares, then turns his head away.

Boden

Well, that has something sinister in it.

He closes the book.

Bethany

Yep, Henna and I reckon it's Symbolic Magic.

Boden

You're probably right.

Bethany

Do you know much about Symbolic Magic?

Boden

Well, I know it can be used as a Binding Magic.

Bethany

A Binding Magic?

Boden

You know the Oath we take as adults. To not kill and to not do bad things. That's a form of Binding Magic. Symbol Magic is similar, it can be used to bind a person's soul.

Bethany

How do you know about it?

Boden

I heard about it from Dad and I was going to use it in making a Staff. Some of the symbols are connected to powerful magics. But I couldn't find any information on how to do it. So, I didn't use it in the end. That's all I know about Symbol Magic.

Henna's dad told her it was very powerful magic.

I reckon it is. I think Navek knows about Symbol Magic too, his dad told him about it.

I'll go and see him then.

We should talk about this later, maybe send some more letters back to Olreon.

Yeah, good idea. Where is Navek?

Oh, he's up on the roof, training.

Thanks.

She leaves Boden, who takes out his deck of cards and starts to summon a red figure into his castle. She walks to the end of the corridor and hits the stairs and heads for the roof. The roof itself is a conservatory of glass walls and ceilings, surrounding her with a white floor and white tables. The rain has stopped, and the sky is blue, with a soft patchwork of clouds up above. In the middle of the room, in the bright light, she finds Navek playing at his cards. She sits down beside him as he summons forth a pair of cards to fight each other. Each Monster comes out of the picture on the surface and starts doing battle. Navek controls them with a streamer from another card.

Do you know what I hate about Spirit Cards?

What?

Navek

You can't use your own magic in the battle.

Bethany

Well, I think that's why people like it above the Spirit Magic battle games.

Navek

Yeah, and that's why I prefer Spirit Magic battle games.

Bethany

Well, you're still unbeaten at Spirit Cards.

Navek

The only way to stay that way is to win the tournament.

Bethany

I have some books from the library, you might want to look at.

Navek looks up from his cards.

Navek

Books?

Bethany

Yeah, they have stuff on the Damned Wizards.

Navek

Oh.

Navek desummons his cards and places them to his side.

Navek

Give us a look.

He takes the books and turns through the pages, looking at the battles.
Ginormous fires spilling out of the Damned hands, incinerating the landscape.

Navek

This magic looks powerful. They are going to cause a lot of trouble for our
Guards.

Navek looks at the page with the man standing on top of the pile of the dead.

Navek

I don't like the look of that black flame.

Bethany

What do you think it is?

Navek

I don't know, but I have never heard of a flame that is black. He must have been
very powerful to create that sort of destruction.

Navek turns to the last page.

Navek

What's this?

Bethany

Me, Henna and Boden think it might be Symbol Magic.

Navek

Symbol Magic, hmm.

He looks into the spiral symbol.

Navek

Feels sly and slick, like you want to follow it, even though it's something horrible.

He closes the book.

Navek

It's insidious, uhh.

Bethany

Yeah, when you look away, it makes you feel ill.

Navek

Hmm, Symbol Magic.

Bethany

Do you know anything about it?

Navek

Yes, Pop said it should be considered an evil magic, though most people don't think of it like that.

Bethany

Did he tell you anything about it?

Navek

Yes, it can be used to enslave and control others.

Bethany

Hmm, that's bad.

Navek

It allows you to transfer horrible things through it. The symbols were used to manipulate nations. Make people think they were doing right when they were doing wrong. Force people's loyalty. They were painted on flags. People would salute them as if they were people.

Bethany

Frightening.

Navek

Yeah.

Bethany and Navek sit there, looking out over the chimney-top views of the city.

Bethany

Well, we should definitely send a letter to the Guard Team.

Navek

They will want to know about this symbol.

Bethany

I'll go straight away.

Navek

Do you need a hand?

Bethany

No, I can write up the letters myself. So, I take it you lot will be working on your cards for the next while?

Navek

I suppose so.

Bethany gets up.

Bethany

Well, I think I'll go training, maybe get some catch up to you on the fireball stuff.

Navek

Good luck.

Navek looks at her, distracted by the idea of training his magic, over training with cards.

Bethany

Well, we can all talk about it tonight.

Bethany leaves Navek there to train with the cards.

Bethany

<u>Ok, I guess I'll send a letter to the Guard Team.</u>

Bethany goes to the front desk and asks where she can send a letter from. The Inn Staff point her to a mailbox beside the booking table. She takes a quill and composes a letter, telling the Guards all about the symbol and the books. She buys an envelope and addresses it to the Olreon Guard, Ganameer. Bethany puts away the quill and ink and heads out for the park. The ground outside is wet and reflects the sun as she goes. The crowds of people passing by are as thick as ever. She makes it to the park, but unfortunately the grass is sodden, so

291

she walks around, looking for a place to practice her magic. Eventually, she finds a wide stone platform with an arbour over it. She begins by creating the magic streamers that Boden used to resist his movement, then begins his training dance. After a while, she tires and moves onto Henna's Dark Lamp spell. So far, she can only shine a soft shadow and not very far. She practices until she tires in this too and takes a break, sitting and looking at the park around her. The arbour she is under has small glass scenes curtaining the edge of its domed, stone top, with tree-like framing from its bottom. Bethany catches her breath, gets up and begins to shoot fireballs and iceballs, causing bursts in the air. After tiring of this, she takes out a small knife and scores a cut along her finger, she uses her magic and heals the cut. As she does this, she notices an aura envelope her, letting off greenish sparks.

Bethany

<u>This must be the Training Aura, which means all the exercise I have done today will continue on in it.</u>

As she trains, she feels the field strengthen her and she feels like she can do another round of training. The exercises feel like they flow into Orio's field and become a part of it. She easily continues training until it starts to get dark. Finally, when she finishes, she notices that the aura is around her as she walks. Eventually, she arrives back to the inn and goes up to her room. She finds Henna again, alone and practicing cards.

Bethany

Are you still training?

Henna

Yeah, got to beat those guys.

Bethany

Have they not come back yet?

Henna

Nope.

Henna looks over at her.

Henna

Hey, you are surrounded by a field of magic.

Yeah, it came on when I was training. It made it a lot easier.

Wow, brilliant. So, Orio's invention is already helping us.

Yah... We need to have dinner I think, I'll round the guys up. You coming?

Yeah, I suppose.

Henna puts her cards away and follows Bethany.

Wow, you're giving of little specs of magic.

It's amazing, I feel like I could go out and train again.

That's incredible.

They go out to lobby and find Boden sending flames across his castle. He turns to see Henna enter.

Hey, no fair.

So, this is your strategy.

Boden takes down his cards and puts them in his backpack.

What's going on, and why are you glowing?

Bethany

Oh, I was training in the park, and it came on me when I got tired. Then I was able to continue training right up till now.

Boden

Woah!

Bethany

Come on, we're gonna get Navek and have some dinner.

Boden

Good idea.

Boden joins the group, and they head for the attic.

Boden

So, you were able to do a lot of training?

Bethany

Yeah, it was incredible. When the field kicked in, I could have exercised all night.

They reach the roof floor, which is a big sunroom.

Henna

Wow, this is nice.

Navek sees them come in and stops his cards immediately.

Navek

Hey, little bit of privacy.

Boden

We're getting dinner, you want to come?

Navek

Yeah, ok. Hey, why are you glowing?

Henna

She was training hard, and she started to emit the Training Aura.

Navek

What were you training in?

Bethany

Well, I was doing your fireball and ice training, also the other training we did at the park. I'll have all the time to catch up to you guys and your magic exercises.

Navek looks disappointed at this.

Navek

Well, maybe I'll come train with you sometimes. What about you guys?

Henna

Well, I think we want to stick to the cards.

Navek

Aww.

Boden

Come on, let's grab some food.

The Adventurers head down to the dining hall and find seats near the counter.

Boden

So, you guys seen the books Bethany got?

Henna

Yeah, they're horrendous.

Navek

I wonder what that spiral symbol is.

Boden

Yeah, and if that Damned Wizard in the forest was related to that or not.

Henna

Maybe he was trying to get in good with the Spiral Damned.

Boden

I wonder how powerful this Spiral Wizard is.

The Waitress comes over and they order another green hedge fried basket.

Henna

I wonder will we run into them again.

Bethany

I hope not, whatever is going on, it's far beyond our power.

Navek

The wall guard will handle it.

Bethany

Do you think they will uncover all that is going on?

Navek

They will work on it and spread the news to the other guards around Tream.

Bethany

This whole Legendary Abomination thing still scares me. What are those creatures capable of? I hope the wall guard handle them with care.

Navek

Well, we will probably see some of the guard from Olreon during the Card Tournament, then they can tell us what is going on.

Bethany

<u>I wonder should I send some letters to my parents.</u>

The meal arrives in front of them, and the Adventurers start doling out the food onto their plates. Today's food is the chewy, crunchy, green fur in the fried basket. They break off bits of the basket and pour salt and vinegar onto it. Over the next while, Bethany trains and the others practice their cards. Some days Navek goes to train with Bethany, but he only trains using the fireball and ice exercise. The days start to get shorter and a din of coldness pierces in the air. On a quiet day, the Adventurers get up early and head to the dining hall in the inn. There they meet the Carriage Builders.

Hector

Oh hi, we were just coming to get you.

Navek

Oh right, the gem cave.

Tarver

We are heading home, so we wanted to get the gem before we went.

Boden

Brilliant.

Hector

We also have good news.

Henna

Yeah?

Hector

Your brother bought our business. He is going to combine our Coach Builders with a group of other builders, to start a land transportation company.

Henna

Wowza!

Tarver

Thanks for putting in a good word for us.

Hector

So, do you know much about gem caves?

Henna

Kind of, we dealt with a small cave in the last town.

Tarver

Then you know how to handle them?

Bethany

Well, they are usually easy stuff.

Hector

Oh good.

Tarver

We don't know much about questing, so we will leave it up to you.

Hector

What will you charge for the quest?

Bethany

Well, we have lots of gold at the moment, am, what do you guys think?

Navek

I wouldn't mind having a go of some of those carriages.

Boden

Yeah, that would be fun.

Tarver

Ok, afterwards, you can each have a go at driving the carriage.

Hector

Also, if there are a lot of gems or we make a lot of gold, you can have a cut of that too.

Bethany

Oh, thank you.

The Adventurers eat their food in a hurry and the group get up to leave.

Hector

Ok, we are set down around the corner.

The Wizards follow the Carriage Builders out of the inn and around the corner. In front of them is a sturdily built, black carriage, with thick walls.

Hector

We have this armoured up a bit, in case we run into any trouble.

Navek

What forest was it in?

Hector

The Hastus Forest.

Boden

That's really tame.

Bethany

Yeah, in the early summer it's usually full of fruit pickers.

Hector

Well, we came through it to test the carriages in forest paths.

Tarver

That's where we saw the gem cave.

Hector

We only ever read about them in books, so it was amazing to see it up close.

They open the carriage with a key, and the Wizards get in with them. Inside, Bethany and Navek sit in the front row with the driver, and Boden and Henna sit in the back row with the horse in-between them, his head sticking out from the rear compartment. Hector pulls a lever, and a protection panel slides down over the front window.

Hector

Ok, let's go.

Hector pushes the pedal at his feet and the horse begins to cycle. Henna pets the horse as it goes. Hector pushes another foot pedal and the carriage lurches forward slowly. Out of the side alley they drive the carriage and go slowly up the street, so as not to hit anybody. As they go, the travelling crowd parts before them, letting them through slowly.

Hector

So, you lot ever travel by carriage before?

Bethany

Well, most of us have travelled by horse-drawn, but never by horse-pedalled, to be honest.

Hector

Well, through the forest roads it doesn't make much difference, but when you are on a clear transportation road, the pedal carriages are a lot faster.

The carriage takes a slow turn at a junction.

Tarver

So, what have you Wizards gotten up to since we last saw you?

Navek

Not much. We've been training mostly.

Hector

For what?

Navek

The Spirit Card Games are coming up and we also need to train ourselves.

Tarver

Oh right, the Spirit Cards. Yeah, we are getting tickets to see it.

Hector

It's a pity only Wizards are able to train cards.

Boden

There are other card games out there.

Hector

Yeah, but they are not the same as Spirit Games.

Boden

True.

The carriage takes a turn onto a wide, tar made road that has a white line down either side.

Hector

This road is for carriages and wagons only.

They get up to speed and travel down a small hill and hit an even wider road, speeding up as they go.

Henna

Wow, this is fast.

Boden

No wonder people moved to horse cycles.

They travel for a while on the long, wide road.

Tarver

You wouldn't want to fall out at this speed.

Hector

I don't know about you Wizards, but we would be stone dead if we hit the road at this pace.

Boden

I'd say.

The jumble of buildings around the road give way to a grass valley as they travel.

Hector

So, do you Wizards not have carriage roads like these in your town?

Boden

Well, our town is self-sufficient, so we don't really need to transport goods too much.

Henna

We do have a few large roads through town, but no carriage-only roads.

Hector

That's odd.

Henna

I'm sure my brother will see to that, though.

Hector

Your brother is a great man, he really knows his trade.

Henna

Well, that's his specialty.

Tarver

We heard about him before, though.

Henna

Really?

Hector

Yeah, he was known as the best employer in the land. Everybody wanted to work for him.

Henna

Wow, really!!?

Hector

Yes, he seems to care about his employees very much.

Henna

Wow, I never knew he had that kind of reputation. Well, he is very kind-hearted.

The scenery before them winds and turns here and there.

Hector

There is a gate into the Hastus Forest, but we have to travel a fair bit to get there.

The sun rises high into the sky as they travel, the group talking about forests and nice places to visit. They finally turn off a side junction and go up a long slope and down a little laneway. They arrive at a small wall on a low brambly hill.

Tarver

It's not used much by travellers, this wall, but it is handy to have.

Hector

It's funny that it was a lot quicker to travel through the forest than via a Road World.

Bethany

Well, that's part of the reason we travel via forests. They are the best means of transport.

Hector

But not the safest.

Bethany

Very true.

The carriage goes up the hill and towards the gate in the grey castle wall. A Guard by the entrance, leaning on a stick, lazily waves to them as they go through the wall. Outside, on the other side, there is a small grass junction. The carriage eases out, sinking lightly into the grass. They take a small, rutted road into the forest among the trees.

Tarver

Now, this path isn't reliable. We had to stop several times to find its direction, so bear with us.

Hector

Tarver, do you have the spy glass?

Tarver takes out a small telescope as they begin up the path. They come to a place where the path is hard to discern, and Hector lets up the pedal and pulls on a break beside his seat. Tarver holds out his spy glass, extends it, and puts it up to his eye. He looks around for the path. Eventually, he points in a direction.

Tarver

Over there.

Hector lets up the break and presses the foot pedal. They take off down the path at a slow speed. The carriage bumps up and down on the jutting road as they travel. They meet another junction and Tarver has to use his spy glass again. Eventually, they make it to a clearing.

Tarver

Here we are. The cave is over there.

Tarver points from the carriage to a path through the trees. The group get out of the carriage and Tarver and Hector lock it off.

Hector

Ok, here we go.

Henna

How did you come across it?

Tarver

Well, we took a break here, as we wandered around, we found it.

They walk together into the woods and come across a small grass area, beside a sheer dark blue and grey rock wall. In it, the entrance of the cave has small sparkling rocks.

Hector

There it is.

Henna

I am not sure if that's a gem cave.

Tarver

How do you mean? Do you see the sparkling rocks around the edge?

Henna

Sparkling rocks doesn't mean gem caves.

Tarver

You sure?

Henna

Yeah, pretty sure.

Hector

I think it's still worth a look.

Tarver

Yeah, we could be right.

Hector

Well, it looks like the entrances to caves we used to see in books.

Tarver and Hector head into the cave.

Navek

Well, I guess we should join them.

The Adventurers follow behind. The group have to duck their heads, as the cave is quite low. Inside, Tarver lights a lamp and the caves black and brown walls brighten up a bit. They travel along a long tunnel through the cave until they hit a junction.

Hector

So, where do you Wizards think we should go?

Boden

All we can do is guess, so that tunnel there.

Boden points.

Hector

Ok then.

The group walk along the tunnel, the rocks glisten with silvery specks and flecks, like somebody threw a light coating of glitter over them. They walk along for a while, eventually Tarver and Hector stop to take a break and sit down.

Hector

Well, hopefully it's not much further.

The Wizards sit by them as they take out a small paper bag of food from a pack that Hector was sitting on.

Hector

Do you guys want some?

Hector holds up a flat sandwich and the Adventurers turn him down. They wait there a while, sitting in the tunnel as the Carriage Builders eat their sandwiches. Eventually, they all get up and continue on up the tunnel. As they go, the covering of silver specs starts to get thicker and thicker. They walk to a part where the cave starts to get wider, coming out into a tall area with a small stream to the side of the path and with stalagmites along the floor beside it. Here the cave is covered in a powdering of little, roundy, glowing gems. They walk along the glimmering, tall cave till they come to the end. Here there is a small hole in the wall, with the thin river running out of it. They squeeze through the hole and into a glowing light blue cavern, that is about the size of a low room. It is covered in a thick crust of the gems, with the blue colours running over everything from the stalagmites and stalactites, to the ground and walls. In the background, the river runs out from a small, round hole in the upper back wall. Lower down, on the wall beside it, behind the sharp teeth of the cave, there is a large, jagged shaped object.

Hector

What's that? Is that the gem?

Navek

No…

They go forward into the cavern and magic some white light. The thing on the wall appears to be a mask that is light purple, with black and white features and a bizarre and twisting shape. When they look at it, the face looks distorted in their vision, and it hurts their eyes. As more light hits it, it starts giving off shadows that crawl along the walls.

306

Hector

What is it?

The shadows turn to an ugly darkness, like that in the museum, morbid feelings wash over the group as Henna's pocket explodes with a horrible sound.

Tarver

Do you think...

Henna

Run!!!

Hector

What?

Henna

RUN!!!

The Coach Builders get a fright as the Adventurers pull them into a run.

Henna

It's not what it seems, it's corrupt, RUN!

They come to a stop near the entrance as there is a man standing there.

Hector

Who are you?

The man's skin is a new dark green that the Wizards have not yet encountered. Its darkness like the shadow on the wall and has a grimy, sickly feeling to look at. His body is emaciated, and his blue clothes are ripped and tattered looking. The man lets out a growl and charges forward. Navek raises his wand and shoots a fireball at the man's chest, blasting him back and disabling him.

Hector

What the h...

Henna

Zombies!

They squeeze through the gap and run as fast as they can along the tunnel, Henna and Bethany providing light from their streamers which are wrapped around their hands. Up ahead, they see another Zombie. He stares at them and doesn't move.

Hector

What do we...

Before he can finish his sentence, the Zombie opens its mouth, stretching till it's down near its chest. An orange flame erupts in its throat, and a fireball comes hurtling out towards them. Navek raises his wand, shooting an iceball into the fireball, causing a loud blast. Then he shoots another iceball that catches the Zombie in its face as it closes its mouth, knocking it over and freezing its jaw shut.

Tarver

Zombies have magic?

Boden

They shouldn't!

They continue cautiously along the path. They see the junction ahead and another Zombie crawling towards them. Boden lifts his wand and lets out a fireball, blasting it. They get to the junction and head along the path towards the entrance. Behind them as they leave, several of the tunnels start flooding out with Zombies.

Henna

Oh no!

The Zombies are fast and start to chase. The group sprints as hard as possible, Boden casting speed spells onto Tarver and Hector to help them keep pace. The Carriage Builders still aren't as fast as the Wizards, so they slow to match their pace to keep them safe. Ahead in the tunnel, a Zombie starts towards them. Bethany blasts it and they trample its body as they run over it. Outside in the grass, there are several Zombies wandering around. The group run out and narrowly dodge being grabbed by them. They get to the carriage and Tarver and Hector begin opening it up.

Hector

We have to turn around.

Boden

We'll keep them at bay.

The Wizards start blasting at each of the Zombies as they come out of the cave or run in from around the forest. Hector and Tarver have the cart open and are turning it around. Suddenly, the horde that was at the junction burst forth.

Henna

Oh GRACK!

The Wizards grab the sides of the cart as it finishes turning, and they head off down the forest.

Hector

Everybody on!?

Boden

Yeah, keep going.

The Wizards continue to blast fireballs as the cart drives off down the forest path. It isn't able to manoeuvre fast enough and has to slow down. Boden stops blasting. A huge glut of Zombies catches up with them. Boden reaches into his robes and takes out the Death Wand. He fires a twisting red and yellow fireball into the middle of the Zombies, a massive explosion bursts from it, blasting lots of limbs off and throwing the horde apart.

Henna

Boden, what the hell?

Boden

We're safe now.

They manage to steal a lead on the Zombies. After a while of travelling, they come to the unclear part of the junction and have to stop.

Hector

Use the tracks to navigate!

Tarver

I can't, they're not there!

Hector

Damn it.

The Wizards get off the carriage and wait behind it.

Henna

Boden, why do you have that wand?

Boden

I thought it might come in handy.

Navek

We could have taken the horde without it.

Tarver

Ok, we got it. Come on.

Tarver shouts, and they grab the side of the carriage as an even larger horde comes chasing towards them, splitting up between the trees as it goes. The carriage rattles as it speeds up and pushes into the woods. The dead are able to catch up to them and a Zombie lurches through the trees for Boden, Boden shoots a glowing fireball at it, blasting it to pieces. Henna, Bethany and Navek start to fire volley after volley of fireballs at the waves of Zombies slipping through the trees and jumping out of the woods. They blast holes in the Zombie's bodies, causing them to fall. As the monsters chase the cart, they avoid Boden. This causes them to bunch up and trip and block each other. The cart manages to make some ground before they hit the next unclear path. In a panic, Tarver looks for the path, shaking as he uses his spy glass. The Zombies get close, and he points.

Tarver

I'm not sure, though.

Hector

I don't think we have a choice.

The cart picks up speed towards the path.

Hector

Hold on!!!

It hits a log and ramps off it, throwing the front wheels up high, then as the back wheels pass over it, they ramp the cart into air and throw it over a large deep puddle. When it lands, it tilts from side to side, going back and forth up on the wheels on either side as it leans and nearly topples, causing the Wizards to have to lean out to stop it from tipping over. As they look back, they see the Zombie horde thinning, as most of them turn back towards the path. A few fast Zombies keep up with them as they drive into the junction with the town wall. They pass through the wall and get off on the inside. Boden screams at the Guard, who gets a shock.

Boden

CLOSE THE GATE!

Guard

What, why?

Boden

JUST DO IT!

The Guard runs up into gatehouse and a large gate starts to close across the tunnel. The Zombies come out of the path and run through the junction towards them.

Hector

Don't let them through.

Pushing along with his back against the carriage side, Boden lifts the skeletal wand and shoots a giant flame through the gap being closed by the gate. The Zombies incinerate in the flame and the gap closes. The Guard comes down from the gatehouse.

Guard

What was that all about?

Boden

There are Zombies outside.

Guard

Zombies, what!? Aren't they mythical?

Henna

Go have a look for yourself.

Guard

I think I will.

The Guard gives her a look and climbs the steps on the wall. The Wizards and Carriage Men follow him up. They look at the clearing through the battlements.

Hector

They can't see us, can they?

Navek

No, Treestone battlements can't be seen into.

Outside the wall, the Zombies wander around aimlessly. Then, as if they had been shocked in unison, they all turn around and begin back along the path together.

Guard

Zombies.

Henna

We told you.

Guard

They seem kinda smart.

Navek

They are a Corrupt Magic Zombie of some kind.

Guard

How can you tell?

Navek

In the cave, a Zombie shot a fireball at us.

Guard

This is bad, we need to alert the city.

Bethany

We'll have to send for the wall guard.

Guard

What do you mean the wall guard? I am the Wall Guard here.

Bethany

No, we mean Olreon's wall guards.

Guard

We have Wizards on our guard, we don't need Olreon's.

Bethany

Ok, but they have to be alerted, they are studying a case of Corrupt Magic.

Hector

Do you think they are related?

Bethany

I am not sure, but they have to know.

Guard

You're not going anywhere till I contact the town guard first.

Hector

Why!?

Guard

I want to make sure we don't have any other Zombies attacking our borders.
Now, how can I send for help?

Hector

Come with us.

Guard

That will mean I have to leave the wall.

Navek

Well then, let us go.

Guard

Ok, but some of you stay, I don't want you running off on me.

Bethany

I'll stay behind.

Henna

Bethany, you can't.

Bethany

Look, we don't have time to argue.

Guard

I need you to go to the Guard Captain. He's stationed in the main Guard House on Felgin Road. Do you know where that is?

Hector

Yes, we do.

Guard

Tell him what happened.

Hector

Ok, let's go.

Navek, Boden, Henna and the Carriage Men get into the carriage and set off back for town. The sun goes down as they travel, and Tarver lights the carriage front lamps, casting long thin lights on the dark road ahead.

Hector

Why were there Zombies there?

Boden

We don't know.

Tarver

Do you think it was the mask that sent them?

Navek

Not sure, but we will find out.

Henna

Do you think this carriage is ok? Is it safe to go at this speed?

Hector

Oh yeah, this thing is as tough as an old boot.

The night outside turns pitch black as they go, the ends of the lamplights shining down the middle of the road and on the sides of the valley. After a while, the buildings in the city at the side of the road come into view.

Hector

Ok, we are nearly there.

Henna

Could you drop us at a post office or the inn?

Boden

Yeah, anywhere we could send a message from.

Hector

Why?

Henna

We have to inform Olreon.

Hector

Ok, I'll let you out near the inn, but we head to the Guard House together.

Henna

Ok.

They hit the traffic outside the inn and run in. Boden quickly writes down what they have just seen, and Henna buys a stamp. Together, they put it in the post box beside the counter, being informed by the Steward that the night mail will receive it. They run back out to the carriage, which is slowly making its way up the crowded streets.

Navek

Hhh, you'd be better off leaving it here, it's hard to get through the crowds with the carriage.

They park up on the corner and lock the carriage, then run on through the streets as fast as the crowds will allow.

Navek

Where is it?

Hector

We are nearly there.

The carriage owners run on ahead. They slow into a jog after a while.

Boden

What's wrong?

Hector

We're tired.

Boden shoots magic at them to speed them up.

Boden

That should do.

They run on until they come to the Guard Station on the large wide Felgin Street Road. The building is an old grey castle with battlements on top and made of square cut stone. They run inside to find a room with armoured windows for people to report to the Guard. They walk up and Navek takes the lead.

Navek

Hello, we would like to report an incident at your walls. It's an emergency.

Assistant

Ok, what's the emergency?

A roundy faced man replies.

Navek

We were in the Hastus Woods and we were attacked by Zombies.

Assistant

Zombies?

The man looks at them, perplexed.

Navek

Yes, Zombies, the wall has been closed and they were in those woods.

Assistant

Really? Zombies, like in the stories?

Navek

Yes, real Zombies.

Assistant

Ok... and you say the wall is closed?

Navek

Yes.

Assistant

Hhhmmm, let me talk to the Commander.

The man shuffles off from behind his desk and goes into a room behind him. The group stand there, waiting impatiently for the man to return. After a long while, he comes back with an old, plump man, who leans back as he walks, wearing semicircle glasses, a dark denim uniform with a badge that says, "Commander" and looking down his nose because of his posture.

Commander

So, these are the Wizards with the Zombies?

Navek

Yes, we are. Could you contact your Guards, so they will be on the lookout for Zombies.

Commander

Why would I do that? It would cause a panic.

Navek

Well, if you're attacked by Zombies, don't you want the walls closed?

Commander

Personally, I think it would be a financial disaster if we closed the walls, or spread rumours of Zombies.

Navek

What the hell are you saying?

Commander

Look, take me to the wall where the Zombies were, and I will decide what to do from there.

The Commander points in a direction.

Commander

Meet me by the side gate.

The group go out and around to the side alley beside the Guard House. There they look in through a window beside a door. Through it, they see the Guard come through a big heavy armoured door. It closes behind him and he comes across the small hall between and opens the door onto the street to let himself out.

318

Commander

Sorry, this place has been made to be impenetrable. Now, which wall is it your Zombies were attacking?

Navek

It's the Hastus Wall.

Commander

The Hastus Wall...

The Commander looks into the air.

Commander

Ah yes... Oh wait!

His face is horror-struck.

Commander

You mean we have to travel to the Hastus Wall? That's quite a journey.

The Commander says, with a wheeze in his voice.

Navek

We have a carriage.

The old man smiles with relief on hearing this.

Commander

Ok, bring it around and we will go to the wall.

Navek

It would be quicker if you just came with us. It's outside the Round Duke Inn.

Commander

The Round Duke Inn. Hhh, I am sure the problem will sort itself out.

Hector

We can get the carriage, wait here.

Commander

Good, good.

The Commander sits down on the step for the door, and the Wizards wait in the alley while the Carriage Men run off.

Commander

So, you're Wizards, are you?

Navek

Yes.

Commander

You lot are having a Card Tournament?

Navek

Yes.

Commander

Will you watch it?

Navek

We'll be in it.

Commander

Oh brilliant, yes, it's quite entertaining, the Spirit Games. I used to watch them as a child growing up here.

Navek

Ok.

Commander

You don't seem like a lively bunch.

Navek

Our friend is still at the wall and the Zombies are Corrupt Magical Zombies. Sorry if we don't want to talk about the Spirit Games.

The plump Commander gulps.

Commander

Corrupt Magic?

Navek

Yes, very dark.

Commander

Hmmm, reminds me of that time we had to close a wall off because somebody pretended to be a monster in the woods.

Navek

Well, did this monster shoot fireballs.

The Commander's eyes go wide.

Commander

Fireballs?

Navek

Yes.

Commander

No.

The Commander looks at Navek with fear.

Commander

Hmmm, so these Zombies, why were they chasing you?

Henna

We were in a cave in the woods, and they came after us.

Commander

Why were you in a cave?

Henna

Because we were after gems.

Commander

Gem caves and Zombies, oh my.

The carriage comes round beside the alley and the Wizards and Commander go to get in. Boden has to get down to help the old Guard up as the others shuffle to their seats. Nobody talks as they journey back to the wall. The Commander sits back and wheezes between his teeth as they head down the carriage road. They arrive to find Bethany and the Guard leaning against the wall. The group get out of the carriage and head over to the Guard.

Commander

Well, what's all the commotion?

Guard

The wall was attacked by Zombies. I had to close the gate, Sir.

Commander

So, there were Zombies?

Guard

Yes Sir, very much so.

Commander

What an incredible incident.

Guard

What do you think we should do?

Commander

Do you have a seat in the Guard House up there?

Guard

Yes, why?

Commander

Well, I am going to sit down, that cart ride took it out of me. You are going to go back with the Wizards and get a platoon to watch this wall, and send another platoon around to warn the other Guards on the other walls.

He looks at the Guard's expectant face.

Commander

That's all I can offer for now, please go.

The old Commander wheezes as he heads up into the wall's hut and leaves them there.

Guard

Ok, I guess you guys can take me back.

Hector

Yeah, sure.

Bethany and the Guard join them in the carriage, and they head back onto the road.

Navek

Anything happen while we were away?

Bethany

Some of the Zombies re-emerged from the woods.

Boden

Oh yeah?

Bethany

They shot fireballs at the wall, then went back.

Navek

Well, that's not going to break the wall.

Hector

You guys sure of that?

Navek

Yes, definitely.

Guard

So, you guys were lucky you didn't get bitten.

Boden

It might not have done anything if we did.

Guard

How do you mean?

Boden

Well, it was an animated corpse, it might not have had anything to spread to us. They used them for wars in bygone eras.

Guard

Wars? You think they might use them against Trader City?

Boden

We don't know, but hopefully not.

They drive their way back through the carriage roads and in through the city.

Guard

Take me to the Guard Station.

The carriage gets them near, and they hop out and run to the building together. The Guard asks to be let in. They go around the side and are let through by the attending officer, who is watching the side entrance. Inside, they find the Guards lounging around a room full of low chairs, with hip high walls running around the area they are in. The Guards eat and chat nonchalantly.

Guard

I need a platoon.

The Guard shouts on the top of his voice.

Guard

We need guards for the wall.

A Witch comes over.

324

Witch Guard

Is there any way I can help?

Guard

Yes Mam, I need a platoon to guard the Hastus Wall and another to help me put the other walls on alert.

The Witch begins shouting to the room.

Witch Guard

Ok, Trod Squad and Stomp Squad, get your teams together!

She turns to the Adventurers and Carriage Men.

Witch Guard

Who are these Wizards and those lot?

Guard

They were chased by Zombies in the Hastus Woods. That's why the Commander ordered this.

Witch Guard

Ok, send them out. We don't need our tactics being seen by another town.

Bethany

You sure we can't help?

Witch Guard

Why did the Zombies attack?

Guard

They were following this lot back to the wall from a gem cave.

Witch Guard

Ok, I don't want them in here, get them out.

The Guard turns around to them.

Guard

I'm sorry, but could you please leave.

The group, with shocked expressions, are quickly ushered out by another Guard, out the door again and back onto the street.

Navek

Well, that wasn't very nice.

Boden

Ok, I guess we call it a night.

Hector

What? Really? After what just happened?

Navek

Well, they don't want us interfering. We'd probably cause more anger than good if we try to help.

Hector

But still.

Bethany

Hhhh, we know, but least they are guarding the walls.

Tarver

You lot sure?

Navek

Yeah.

Hector

Oh yeah, we can still pay you if you'd like, before we leave. I know we didn't get a gem, but you saved our lives.

Navek

Don't worry about it.

Hector

Well, least let us drop you to the inn.

Navek

Ok then.

The group head back and get into the carriage. As they head down the road, it starts to rain again. The sound of the raindrops splatter on the cabin roof.

Hector

So, what do you make of all that?

Boden

It's hard to tell, but I reckon it's to do with Wizards.

Tarver

You think? What about Demons?

Boden

Could be, but not very likely. They don't live near us.

Tarver

I wonder what that mask was.

Hector

It was horrible.

Tarver

Yeah, that shadow that was coming off it made me want to throw up.

Hector

Is that why you said "Run"?

Henna

Yes, it appeared to be very dark energies coming off it. I have seen a darkness like it before and I could detect it with my orb.

Hector

Is that what the sound was from you?

Henna holds out her orb.

Henna

Yes, it can detect things that cause great damage.

They arrive outside the inn.

Hector

Here we are.

Tarver

I'll be glad to go back to the Road Worlds.

Hector

Yeah, me too. Is there anything else we can do for you Wizards?

Bethany

No, but thanks for offering.

Hector

Are you sure? We are leaving in the morning.

Navek

No, just keep safe.

The Wizards get out of the carriage into the inky dark, raining night.

Hector

I'm sorry we were a burden.

Bethany

You weren't at all.

Navek

Besides, it was kind of fun.

The Wizards wave them off and go into the inn and up to their room.

Boden

Well, that was astonishing.

Bethany

Yeah, I know, Zombies!

Henna

We keep running into trouble wherever we go.

Boden sits on his bed.

Henna

Why were you carrying that wand?

Bethany

Yeah Boden, why?

Boden

I thought it may come in handy.

Henna

I don't like that you carry that thing around.

Bethany

It doesn't have a hold on you?

He looks at them and frowns.

Boden

A hold?

Henna

Well, I didn't feel any kind of hold when I used it.

Bethany

Hhh, I think we should get rid of it.

Henna

I know you know a lot about wands, but you never came across anything like this before, Boden.

Boden

Ok, if you're that concerned, I'll get rid of it. I just thought if we did run into a Damned Wizard, it would be good to have the upper hand.

Navek

He has a point.

Henna

What?!

Navek

No, I don't like it, but if we do ever come across a Damned Wizard or a Legendary Abomination again, we should use everything we have at hand to survive.

Bethany

No, Navek, we need to avoid confrontation.

Navek

The forest we just went to was considered safe. The forest with the Orb was considered safe. My father let us have it, maybe that is the reason.

Bethany

Hmm, do you think we should take a road on our next journey?

Boden

No, but maybe we should skip the forest also.

Bethany

What do you suggest?

Boden

Well, there are some Countryside Worlds between us and the next town.

Bethany

Hmm, very tame, and we would still be adventuring. Well, we'll see, we will have to decide when we go to travel to the next town.

Navek

Can I have a look at the wand?

Boden

Yeah, sure.

Boden takes the wand from his robes and throws it to Navek. Navek makes a streamer with it, and it turns an ugly dark colour.

Navek

Its power! You can feel it surge through your arm.

Henna

Yeah, it's not nice, is it?

Navek

I can't say that I enjoy it, but it does feel exhilarating.

He puts the wand onto the desk beside him.

Boden

Yep, so are we settled about keeping it?

Navek

I'm ok if you guys are.

Bethany

I don't know, I think we should still get rid of it.

Boden

Well, when the Guards show up, we might consider it.

Navek

If they'll take it.

Boden gets up and stares out the window.

Boden

Amazing... Zombies.

Henna

Yeah, and fireballs.

Bethany

It would be handy to read up more on them.

Navek

Who knows, maybe it's a magical disease this time.

Boden

You mean most likely a disease made by wizards?

Navek

Yeah.

Bethany

A scary thought.

Boden

Well, whatever they were, I think it's time we get some sleep. We can ask for news in the morning.

Boden shuts the curtains, and the Wizards go to sleep. In the morning, they get up and head to the front desk.

Clerk

A message has arrived for you.

The Clerk hands them a letter with a wax seal on it.

Navek

Who is it from?

Bethany

The Olreon Guards, probably from when I wrote to them about the symbol and the books.

Bethany takes the envelope and opens the letter.

Bethany

"Dear Adventurers"

"We received your letter about the book discovered in the library of Trader City. We will send a small troop out to meet you. As we are quite busy at the moment, a group heading for the Card Tournament will be in town and will make contact with you. Keep the book out from the library and let us know how you are getting on."

"Yours sincerely,"

"Ganameer."

Boden

They will probably get my letter in the next while, make them want to hurry.

Bethany

What letter?

Boden

I sent a letter before we went to the Guards, telling Olreon about the Zombies.

The Wizards head down to lunch.

Boden

So, what are you lot going to get up to today?

Bethany

I don't know, I was thinking of training, but I might hit the library and see if they have anything on Zombies.

Henna

Sounds like a good idea, let us know how it turns out.

333

Bethany

You don't feel like coming?

Boden, Henna, and Navek look at each other.

Henna

We have to train our cards.

Bethany

Oh, for goodness sake, you lot and your silly game.

Boden

The Card Tournament is soon and there will be top players from the other
Wizarding Worlds.

Bethany

Well, I will be looking into this Zombie thing.

The Waitress comes over and they order some breakfast cereal.

Boden

Ok, we'll help you look.

Navek

What?!

Boden

Come on, we can give a bit of time over to this.

Navek

Oh ok.

Navek says, with a small shake of his head and a smile.

Their Waitress comes back and serves them golden flakes and some cold milk
and sugar. The Wizards eat the crunchy chewy breakfast and head out for the
library. Inside, they find books on Zombies, most of them stories, but Bethany
manages to find a Zombie guide. The group gather round a table to look at the
book. Bethany opens it and reads through the introduction.

Bethany

"Throughout the world, there have been many types of Zombies. Most stem from some sort of disease, but there are cases of Zombies being created and used as weapons. Throughout this book, we will explore the many types of Zombies and look through their features."

Bethany turns the page and there is the first type of Zombie. A big title sits below. Bethany reads:

Bethany

"Cave Zombie"

"The Zombie's appearance is grey, with dark or ashen hair. It stands at the edge of caves. A benign Zombie type, known to live off of sucking minerals and lichen from rocks. They come about from the reanimation of corpses of travellers or long dead cavemen.

Features include:

Very slow.

Non-infectious.

Non-violent.

Light sensitive.

Slow healing."

Bethany flicks the page over and another Zombie appears.

Bethany

"Gaunts"

This Zombie has green skin and glowing red, sunken eyes.

Bethany

"Coming from the Gaunt disease.

Origin unknown.

They have been known to infect a multitude of races, including humans, goblins, and dogs. Their plague has ravaged human and goblin kind. Several incidents of entire towns being wiped out from ancient times has been observed.

Features include:

Violent nature.

Very infectious.

Disease transfer through bite.

Light sensitive.

Slow healing.

Medium speed."

The next page they stop at has a picture of a Vampire Zombie.

Boden

That's the Zombies I told the Sprites about in the story.

Henna

Oh yeah!

Boden

"Alveric Zombies"

"Coming from the spore based Zamway mushroom, an almost extinct species of mushroom, destroyed for obvious reasons. The Alveric disease is known as the worst Vampire Zombie disease. It has wiped out entire cities of vampires and it survives harsh conditions. The disease is caused when vampires ingest the Zamway spores, which are sprayed in small droplets of liquid onto areas surrounding the mushrooms. The Zombies have been seen hocking up phlegm, and the mushrooms have been witnessed growing from this foul substance. The disease is only known to effect vampires, but if an Alveric Vampire Zombie bites a non-vampire, its modified bite causes brain necrosis and slow death. Mushrooms will then grow from the dead body.

Features:

Extremely violent nature.

Fast.

Horde energies.

Quick healing.

Collective intelligence.

Extreme Light aversion.

Disease transfer through bite.

Transfer through mushroom spores.

Unageing Zombies.”

Bethany

Wow, horrible!

Navek

A very nasty strain.

Bethany skips through till she comes to a page about magical Zombies.

Bethany

“Magic Zombies.”

“There have been a range of magical diseases throughout history. Wizards have been the most notable practitioners of Zombie creation. The majority, if not all forms of this magic, came from the time of the Damned. Armies of the dead made powerful weapons and tipped the balance in major battles. Magical Zombies were also used as slaves. A Slave Zombie was an excellent servant, obedient to a fault and could be ordered to do jobs that would cause normal slaves to feel pain. They were bought and sold in their droves and their use caused many wars. Eventually, after the fall of the Damned, they were wiped out and their families were able to bury their beloved kin. Some of the key uses of Slave Zombies include testing medicine, testing weapons, manual labour, carrying goods between towns, setting off traps and many more. It is not known how the Damned worked their craft. Some of the diseases are pure magical creations, while others are modifications to already existing diseases, or a creation from the combination of both. The craft has been long lost since the extinction of the Damned. Naturally occurring magical diseases are very rare, but some very virulent strains still exist."

They turn the next page and there is a Zombie with a wizard's robes on.

Navek

"Cawcul Zombies"

"A rare Zombie disease.

Origin: The Festering Swamp.

This disease has all but been wiped out and its place of origin has been destroyed. The disease was known to especially infect wizards and elves. They, being of stronger constitution than races like humans, made the disease curable. A person could return to a normal life when properly treated. Some wizards were known to have defeated the infection without need of a cure.

Features:

Fast.

Heal fast.

Sunlight gives nourishment.

Transfer through spitting.

Violent."

Henna

Glad that has been wiped out.

The next page, they see a horrendous looking Zombie. It has a body made of deep green skin, with round bulging folds squeezed over and around each other, and lots of loose hanging skin. There are holes all over its body, with putrid green liquids spewing out of them.

Henna

"Blab Zombie"

"These horrendous creatures were known for spraying many types of foul substances, which could cause extreme damage. These Zombies were not created from a disease, but rather some form of reproduction, where each Zombie body was created from the bite's constituents consuming the creature that was bitten. They have been shown to reproduce through many, many races.

Features:

Extremely Violent.

Fast.

Fast healing.

Sprays corrosives.

Sprays to infect.

Bites to infect.

Shoots sharp needles.

Fully eats creatures.

Horde powers. "

Bethany

This stuff is going to give me nightmares.

Boden

Yeah, let's call it day.

Henna

Ok then, back to training.

Bethany gets the book out and they leave the library. Over the next days, Bethany goes back to training in the park, with Boden, Henna and Navek joining her here and there. The days start to wane, and nights get colder. Eventually, the time for the tournament comes close. The Adventurers are sitting out on their balcony, when they see a very long, white carriage coming up the street.

Henna

That looks like a very large wizard carriage!

Bethany

Yeah.

The Adventurers look down through the carriage windows and see lots of Wizards inside looking out at them and at the street around them. A few of the Wizards have cards on their laps in front of them.

Boden

Well, I guess the tournament is close.

As the Adventurers look down the street, they see a convoy of long wizard carriages coming up the street.

Henna

I wonder where they all will stay.

Navek

I hope they don't stay here, I want to get some more practice before the sign-up day.

Bethany

I don't think they will.

Henna

Come on, let's go have breakfast.

The Adventurers order a crunchy nugget cereal and take it with them to sit on the inn steps by the entrance door, watching the carriages.

Navek

Hopefully there will be tough opponents in the battles ahead.

Henna

Yeah, Jared and Cece[see see] will be there.

Navek

Should be fun, whatever happens.

Henna

Yeah.

The Adventurers finish their breakfast and go out and follow the carriages up the street.

Navek

We should check out if the Olreoners are here.

Henna

Yeah, good idea.

They head up a side street and go looking for the wall that connects Olreon's world.

Henna

Do you know where it is?

Bethany

I had a look on the map the other day, while you lot were playing Cards.

Navek

Oh good.

They follow Bethany as she takes them across town. Eventually, they come to a large wall with a big wide gate. Through it comes several long coaches, side by side.

Henna

There they are!

Henna says, excitedly.

Bethany

Oh look, there's your parents with your brother, Henna.

Henna

And there's your parents, Boden.

The Adventurers see Boden's, Navek's, Bethany's and Henna's parents in the coach. They wave to them, and their parents wave back excitedly.

Navek

I don't see my pop.

Henna

He's probably in back.

Navek

Probably too busy.

Navek says, in a huff. They follow the carriages along their path and end up in a big palace grounds.

Henna

Wow, this place is enormous.

The palace has a big upward curving scroll-shaped top, with a glass sphere in the middle. The walls are a pale fantasy pink colour, with a yellowish tint. The sides have large, white, flat rectangular stones, stacked to frame the building. The front has large stone carvings running across tall, stone beams from side to side. The windows are long and made of rectangular frames, surrounded by beautifully carved lintels and have ivy trailing down from their bases. The features of the palace are in a slightly darker pink, and the whole place seem overwhelmingly large.

Henna

It's so amazing.

Bethany

The famous Allacation Manor Halls of Trader City.

Henna

They look so splendid.

The Wizards start to thread out of the carriages and form a giant circle in the palace courtyard. The Adventurers go up to join their families.

Boden's Mom : Mara

Hey you guys.

Their parents come over and hug them.

Navek

Where's Pop?

Navek's Mother : Larna

Sorry Honey, he's busy with wall duties, but he wishes you well in the tournament. He really wanted to be here.

Navek

Hmm, ok.

Bethany's Father : Tideus

Thank Chandrin for this.

Chandrin

Oh really, it was nothing.

Bethany's Mother : Mediena

He arranged the trip and everything, said you guys would like us around.

Chandrin

Yeah, it will be great for them to have you here. Unfortunately, I won't be able to stay to the finals.

Henna

Why?

Chandrin

Work stuff.

Henna

It doesn't matter anyway, we probably won't make the finals.

Henna says, with a humorous smile.

Chandrin

I wouldn't put yourselves down.

Henna's Father : Falcoy

So, when are you going to sign up?

Henna

That's later.

Roary

So, how's Stonker Face?

Navek turns to see Roary behind him.

Navek

You came?

Roary

Yeah, I came to see you lose.

Navek

What makes you think I'll lose?

Roary

Cece is in the tournament.

Navek

So.

Roary

She is trained in wall guard training.

Navek

Doesn't mean she'll win.

Navek gives his brother a dig on the arm.

Navek

So, you won't be supporting me then?

Roary

Ha, I suppose I'll have to.

Navek and Roary smile.

Boden's Father : Trin

So, how's the training coming?

Boden

Oh, well, we learned a new technique to train with. This Witch Orio showed us.

Gallya

What is it?

Boden

It's a Training Aura, it prevents us from falling behind if we stop exercising and enhances our training.

Gallya

Interesting, a Training Aura, wow!

Henna's Mother : Cade

So, have you lot also learned any new magic?

Henna

Here, look.

Henna lets out a streamer and changes its colour to the colour she created in Orio's class. The crowd of parents and siblings turn to see it change.

Cade

Wow!

They clap when she stops, and Henna blushes.

Falcoy

So, you guys have learned a lot of new magic.

Henna

Yeah, we learned a lot of Colour Magic and some adventurey stuff.

Gallya

Did you invent any new spells?

Boden

Funny, we haven't really gotten round to creating magic. Apart from the colour stuff.

Boden shrugs.

Boden

So, how's school faring?

Gallya

Oh brilliant, we learned a lot of new magic, and I finally got the hang of sparks.

Boden

Excellent, give us a look.

Gallya lets out a spark from her hand and knocks Boden's hat off.

Boden

Ha, ha, ha, very good!

Gallya smiles and Boden picks his hat up.

Roary

Yeah, and I learned to do streamers.

Roary comes over and shoots a streamer, which punches Navek in the face.

Navek

Damn you!

Navek chases his little brother.

Roary

Sorry Navek, I was aiming for your hat.

Gallya

He's in my class.

Boden

Do you get on?

Gallya

Yeah, he's great. He's so into his wall guards.

Boden

Navek said he was like that when he was younger, too.

Gallya

It's fun though, the walls are really interesting. Hm, so who are you guys watching for in the fights, apart from each other?

Boden

Well, I might fight Jared again.

Gallya

Jared, wasn't he the guy that you fought and got the game banned?

Boden

Yeahhh, everybody blamed me for that, though.

Mara

It wasn't your fault, they were looking for any excuse to ban it.

Gallya

All Spirit Games are banned in school now. We are helping with some of the other students in the higher classes. They are starting a petition to have them brought back.

Bethany

Sounds interesting.

Gallya

Well, they are sending letters, and we collected signatures from our class for them, but we haven't been successful.

Bethany

Aww, well, don't give up.

Bethany pats Gallya on the shoulder.

Gallya

We won't!

Gallya smiles up at her.

Trin

Have you seen any of your opposition?

Boden

Not yet.

Chandrin

Well, Cece and Jared are coming later. There is a team coming on a special carriage from Olreon, they'll probably be on it and will head up first thing to sign up.

Gallya

You guys worried about facing friends?

Henna and Boden look at each other.

Henna

A little.

Boden

Should be interesting.

Gallya

Are you guys gonna hold back?

Henna

No way.

Boden

Good friends never hold back.

They both smile, Navek finally sprints and catches his little brother, giving him a thick dig in the arm and coming back to the group.

Navek

I don't know about these guys, but I am definitely bringing my A game.

Larna

We got the newspaper from Sunlin.

Gallya

Oh yeah!

Roary

That water fight sounds amazing.

Gallya

I can't believe you guys did that!

Boden

Well, it was Bethany's idea.

Roary

We should throw a water fight when we get home.

Larna

No, you won't.

Navek's mom says, with a smile.

Henna

You guys should see the colour museum while you're here.

Navek

It's amazing.

Chandrin

I have already arranged for them to see it.

Henna

Trust you to have everything organized.

Chandrin smiles at this.

Chandrin

Ok, I think it's time we sign in to the palace. We will see you at the tournament. I presume you will want to train until then.

Henna

Yeah, pretty much.

Chandrin

What about you, Bethany?

Bethany

I should probably help them.

Chandrin

Ok then, we will see you then.

They hug goodbye with their families and head back to their inn. The World of Cards heavy on their minds as they get ready for its adventure.

Join our Adventurers in part C, as they take on the Card Tournament
and meet old enemies and new friends.